I0526670

# Alien Innkeeper

## by

## Roxanne Barbour

*Out of This World Series*

**Alien Innkeeper**

Cover Art by *Debbie Taylor*

The Wild Rose Press, Inc.
PO Box 708
Adams Basin, NY 14410-0708
Visit us at www.thewildrosepress.com

Publishing History
First Fantasy Rose Edition, 2017
Print ISBN 978-1-5092-1378-8
Digital ISBN 978-1-5092-1379-5

*Out of This World Series*
Published in the United States of America

**The light made my head hurt so I closed my** eyes. Wait a minute, where am I? My mushy brain had no information.

"I know you are awake. Respond," said a deep voice.

My heart stuttered after hearing those words, so I opened my eyes again only to recognize Master Tyre leering over me. Then Simon and Tareera grabbed my arms and pulled me to a sitting position. Thankfully the dizziness quickly cleared, but my heart continued to beat irregularly. The trio walked away and conferred, so I studied my surroundings. I kept an eye on them while doing so. The room included rough gray stone walls, black shuttered windows, a single bed, and not much else.

"Why am I here? Why did you abduct me?" I asked, but no one responded.

I needed information. "Why are you here, Tareera? Why did you poison me at the hotel?" Not particularly appropriate, but the words spilled out. My brain had yet to catch up with my surroundings.

"No questions. You will remain," said the Skuttem.

"Where is Sain? Did you hurt him?" I started to shake thinking about what they could have done to him and Branson.

"Master Tyre said no questions. If necessary, we'll tie you up and cover your mouth," said Simon. The Skuttem and Tareera walked to the door—Simon did so backward, keeping an eye on me.

Should I jump up and attack? Then I got a grip on reality—three to one weren't great odds.

## Dedication

To my husband, Norm,
who never fails to be amused
when he discovers me
staring off into space—plotting

Chapter One

For some reason, my com always rings when I try to relax. After spending ten hours running the Mars Best-Tycho Basin hotel today, unwinding had been my first priority tonight.

"Syl, you need to get back," squeaked James, one of my front desk staff. His face appeared on the small screen of my com, a sheen of sweat on his dark face.

"Why?" James tended to be an alarmist, and his slumped posture confirmed his distress.

"Something… There's a situation I can't handle." He took a big gulp of air. "We've got aliens!"

The recent discovery of more than one alien species, and the lack of information regarding them, meant the Mars Best hotel chain's human resources had yet to develop appropriate customer service training modules for its employees.

"An excellent reason to call, James. Where are you?" I actually knew where he was from his surrounding background, but talking would ease his anxiety.

A small smile graced his face. His shoulders relaxed a trifle. My encouragement had hit its mark.

"I'm in your office. I asked Sue to take check-in information from the two new guests."

I reminded myself to ask Sue later if she'd discovered any glitches in our registration software.

"Are you sure they're aliens?"

"Oh, yes." Although his face flushed, his voice carried no doubt. "From what I've seen on the news, they're Irions."

"By the way, how did you communicate with them?"

"Who? Yes, yes. Sorry. I don't know how I understood them, and I never thought about them understanding me." His gaze darted about.

Not a bright question, I admonished myself. "What do our visitors require?" I asked, to get both of us back on track.

"A two bedroom suite and Earth furnishings are fine." A normal request helped James relax a bit more, and relief flooded my mind. Hotel management had yet to provide alien furniture, and I hadn't even thought to ask. Some hotel manager I was. I knew aliens would eventually want to stay in our hotel, and I'd done nothing to anticipate providing for their comfort. Even though the few alien species discovered so far breathed oxygen, and the gravity on Mars would suit Irions, although a trifle heavy, I'd been neglectful in my managerial preparations.

I thought for a moment. "Here's what you need to do. Suggest to the Irions they relax in the lounge. Tell them their suite is being cleaned and will be ready momentarily. Get housekeeping up to the Houston Suite to do a fast and perfect cleaning. Actually, ask Sue to settle our guests in the lounge and arrange for free refreshments." Sue's poise would handle the situation, and gain me a bit of time.

Bouncy had become James' middle name today.

"James," I said, in a voice loud enough to get his

attention, "do you require instruction regarding your next actions?"

"No, no. I'll get right on it. I'm so glad I called. I didn't know what to do. My mind emptied of any ideas on how to handle this situation." On the com, James took a deep breath and briefly closed his eyes.

The Irions had discovered our solar system last year, but so far the Martian public had only received vague images from our news networks.

I knew my good friend Hart Adair, a scientist, had struggled to find out everything he could about the Irions, but the information he'd been able to access had been minimal.

On our last get-together, he'd offered a few tidbits. The gravity on the Irion's home planet was a bit lighter than Mars, but the oxygen in their atmosphere compared to Earth—thank goodness. Hart had found out Irion was going through a bit of a dry cycle, but they still had adequate water for plant and population sustenance. And, apparently, the governments of Mars and Irion were in contact.

Now added to my to-do list would be finding out what other alien species might be popping in for a visit.

Although humans had only had a permanent presence on Mars for seventy-five years, we'd adjusted to the lower gravity and made a comfortable life. And we'd become independent from Earth. Although we could manufacture all necessities, we still imported goods to maintain a balance of trade with the home planet and, of course, the necessary tourist industry.

Grabbing a fresh blouse, pants, and jacket from my closet, I dressed, retied my hair, and took the elevator upstairs. The manager of a Mars Best hotel always lived onsite, and it hadn't taken me long to understand why. Being available twenty-four / seven, or the Martian equivalent, meant quick access. My recent promotion to manager had doubled my need for being nearby.

After entering the lobby, I found James at the spotted gray, marbled front desk. A few human guests lingered in the spacious brown and golden hued lobby. A quiet time of day.

"Is the Houston suite ready?" I asked, after he'd ended his call.

"Yes, that was housekeeping." James' hands flapped toward the com.

"Well done." Not a bad worker, but inexperienced. I decided to ramp up his training, particularly in difficult situations.

I turned and strode into the Lovell Lounge. The lounge's recent renovations had created a sparkly blue ambiance reminiscent of standing on an observation deck staring out into the depths of space. Most of the time, the colors and the impression of openness soothed, but now the appearance of aliens had tightened my stomach.

The predominantly humanoid Irions wore two piece costumes. The top garment included short sleeves or, more accurately, short flared fabric covering their glistening blue-tinged skin to the elbows, with the rest of the top clinging to their well-toned upper bodies. The looser bottom piece simulated baggy pants, and stopped a couple of inches above their bare three-toed feet.

The colors of their wardrobe complemented their skin, and the copper-colored pendants draped around their stubby necks. Their faces were of normal proportions, and their skin set off their brown eyes.

Was brown the only color for Irion eyes?

Their six-fingered hands intrigued me. Did they have more dexterity than human hands? And their three-toed feet exuded stability. Would any of our floorings bother unadorned feet?

The older human male, who accompanied the Irions, sported cropped silver hair and a formal human suit. He stood after I reached their table. Glancing at my name tag, he said, "Ms. Amera, I'm Charles Clarke from the diplomatic corps. My assignment is to assist the Irions during their stay on Mars. May I introduce businessman Dedare Sath and his assistant Coline Tare?" He gestured to each as he made introductions. While he spoke, the aliens stood and their pendants flashed in various colors and patterns.

"Gentlemen, this is Ms. Sylvestine Amera, the manager of the Mars Best-Tycho Basin hotel."

I bowed. Should I greet them as I would normally receive a guest? I glanced at the ambassador for enlightenment.

Interpreting my questioning look, the diplomat said, "You may shake hands. Dedare and Coline understand the concept."

Touching their skin, I received the impression of fine sandpaper—dry but not unpleasant. Curious, but not sure who to ask, I said, "What type of greeting do Irions employ?"

"Touch heads," responded Dedare. Barely two seconds passed before he asked, "May I?"

I took a deep breath. Then I nodded an uncomfortable acceptance and tried to relax my shoulders. I hoped bashing heads together wouldn't hurt too much, I thought, as I bent my body slightly.

"Ms. Amera's head motion means agreement," clarified Charles Clarke. I noticed he sported a slight smile.

After Dedare's six-fingered hand touched my head, I straightened. As I took a step closer to Dedare, I perceived a faint aroma. The scent reminded me of a spice or two—perhaps pepper and allspice. Only a little taller than my own five-foot-eight inches, my hand encountered no difficulty in touching his warm and smooth hairless head. A pleasant experience, after all, especially since I thought Dedare meant we would touch our foreheads together.

Coline made no such greeting motion, so I decided the time had arrived to do my job. "Gentlemen, your suite is now ready. I'm sorry for the delay—the previous occupants checked out a bit late. Please follow me." A fabrication, but no harm done.

The four of us accessed one of the hotel's elevators and, at the entrance to their suite, I stopped and motioned the Irions inside.

"Ambassador, why are the Irions here?" I whispered. I wanted to gain control of the situation, and I needed information to formulate my decisions.

"I'm a lowly diplomat, just call me Charles."

His politician's smile didn't surprise me.

"After months of negotiations, including investigations by our scientists regarding contamination and other issues, Mars has received a party of four Irions. The two diplomatic staff are staying in our official accommodations, but Dedare Sath wanted a tourist facility. Dedare's quite innovative and curious. Of course, since this world is new to him, he's looking for opportunities as a businessman. Hopefully, their visit will prove beneficial for Martians and Irions alike."

I started to mentally fuss, but gave myself a lecture: Do your best and life will proceed as it should.

Easy for my conscience to say.

"Why did I not receive a heads-up?" I asked. A suite ready for the Irions, knowledge of their requirements… I needed to be prepared and in control.

"I did leave a message for the general manager, ah, Simon Worth, some days ago, but he never returned my call."

Charles' answer surprised me. My boss, Simon, loved to micro-manage. And receiving advance notice would have given me time for the appropriate preparations.

"Don't worry, Ms. Amera. The Mars Best chain's excellent reputation put your hotel first on the list of accommodations given to the Irions."

Nice to know, but my mind still swirled with questions. The important one being, "How do we understand each other? Did the Irions learn English?"

"Those flashing chains around their necks are translators," said the ambassador, "but don't ask me how they work."

A topic to discuss with Hart, I decided. I motioned inside, and we entered the suite to find the Irions conferring.

"Manager Amera, accommodation is lovely," said Dedare Sath, turning to face us. "I understand why the Mars Best chain was suggested. Questions?"

"Of course, but call me Syl—my nickname." He had questions? Is that what he meant?

I interpreted his expression as confusion, so I

explained, "A nickname is a shortened name—friendlier."

"Like the concept. Please call me Dedare."

Not much shorter, but I didn't have the heart to tell him so.

While Dedare and I walked through the suite, I answered his queries. How different were Irion accommodations? I vowed to ask for details at a suitable time.

"Manager Amera—Syl." Dedare paused for a moment. "I chose the Mars Best-Tycho Basin hotel because of your slogan *Mars Best supplies your needs, or your stay is free*. Innovative."

An interesting comment from an alien, I thought. How did Irions handle customer service? "I'll certainly endeavor to live up to the Mars Best motto. But you do understand this excludes any illegal activities and anything impossible—like time travel?"

After glancing at Coline, Dedare said, "Yes."

"Any requirements?" I hoped not. My to-do list now included a rapid study of Irions.

"*Zyre*," said Dedare.

I glanced at Charles and then at the Irions. "What's *Zyre*?"

"Let me find out," replied the ambassador. "Apparently, the translator has a missing word."

Charles tapped into his com while the three of us waited in silence—I had no idea how to make idle conversation with an Irion, but I'd be learning fast.

"Got it," said the diplomat. "*Zyre* means a pool of water." He smiled, pleased with his success.

Although I found his answer less than useful, I summoned up a smidgen of tact. "What kind of pool of water? Big? Small? What's it used for?" Images flashed through my mind—buckets of water, Olympic-sized swimming pools, rivers…

"Meditation." Dedare interrupted my thoughts. "Large enough for sitting. Shallow."

Interesting. "How soon do you need *Zyre*? Will a day or so be appropriate?"

"Yes," said Dedare.

Although I had no idea how to accomplish this task, I'd received a day's respite. "Any other requirements?" Why did my job require asking these loaded questions?

"No. Accommodations are excellent. I would like to talk about Mars, but tomorrow. Coline and I need rest."

Dedare smiled. Or did his expression mean something entirely different?

After taking our leave of the Irions, Charles and I stopped at the front desk.

"Any recommendations?" I asked.

"Mars needs tourism, and having aliens on our planet will increase the excitement. Don't worry, Dedare is comfortable with you already. So relax and enjoy their stay."

How naïve. How was I supposed to enjoy their visit with the pressure of the world, the universe, upon me?

"Here's my contact information," said Charles, handing me a card. "The Irions are now in your hands. If you have any questions, or problems, give me a call."

After Charles left, I checked with my staff. Satisfied the hotel ran smoothly, I returned to my suite. Of course, everyone had sworn to call me the moment the Irions made any kind of appearance.

Before I'd finished a glass of wine and started my computer research, Simon called.

"Why haven't you updated me on our alien guests?" he sputtered.

Chapter Two

The question from the general manager of the Mars Best hotel chain angered me. "Why didn't *you* tell me the Irions would be arriving?" I asked. "I had to improvise on the spot!"

Not that tactful—considering my probationary status. Then a thought popped into my mind—who told him the Irions were here?

Simon Worth blew out a breath. "My assistant forgot to give me Ambassador Charles' message. I had no idea they'd be staying at my hotel."

A big dollop of relief settled on my psyche, but I stared at him, on my com, anyway. I hoped my displeasure showed. His short stature, gray crew cut, and unpleasant nature were not enhanced by his perpetual frown. I really didn't like him, but I needed to suck it up and pretend otherwise.

"However, you should've called me after you settled them in their room. They're happy, right?" Simon ran his right hand through his hair, what there was left anyway.

"Yes, they're very happy—they complimented our facility. I'll be working closely with the Irions."

"Good. Keep me updated. Your future with Mars Best is riding on the Irions' well-being."

"Of course," I replied. What a jerk! If he wanted to micro-manage, I'd let him, but I wouldn't spill the news about my first challenge—a pool of water. If I did, he'd only interfere.

After a couple of glasses of wine, and unsatisfactory Irion research, I attempted to sleep.

**** 

Since I predicted a challenging day, I arrived to work early the next morning. "Any inquiries from our special guests?" I asked James, who sat behind the front desk.

"Not a peep. I would've called you right away." In a good mood, a smile threatened to emerge on his face.

"By the way, why are you here? Aren't you currently scheduled for afternoons?" Scheduling took up a goodly amount of my time.

"I changed shifts with Ariana. I want to be available when the Irions might appear."

James had become a convert. Would his interest become fanaticism? "Okay, but be classy. We need our new friends to encounter us at our best," I emphasized, although I had to smile at his enthusiasm.

"The Irions are so fascinating," James responded. "Did you know—"

I interrupted his bouncing. "We'll talk about your research later. Don't overdo your shifts. I need you alert and able to analyze any situation that might occur. I know you can do this."

James preened, sat up straighter, and tried to repress a grin.

Such a young one, I thought. However my office beckoned so I started walking. On my way, one of the elevator doors opened, and out stepped Dedare and Coline. With a gait resembling humans, they caught up to me.

"Syl, talk." Dedare approached and put his hand on my head. I reciprocated. Today I noticed the skin on his bald head seemed toned and not wrinkled. And the flecks of gold and silver in his brown eyes intrigued me. Certainly more than I'd noticed in my dazed first encounter yesterday.

"Locations chosen," said Dedare, after we'd completed our greeting.

What did he mean? "What kind of locations? Where do you want to go?"

"Visual understanding." Dedare clasped his hands, and then glanced at Coline.

I took a stab at deciphering his last statement. "Sightseeing, or seeing sites and locations, is a good way to understand our culture." The translators draped around their necks tried to cope.

"Found while studying materials." One of his six-fingered hands pointed to the rack of pamphlets adorning a wall in the lobby. The tourist industry had tried to do away with physical brochures in favor of electronic versions, but the concept had proven unsuccessful. Travelers wanted a tactile memento.

"*Sightseeing.* Interesting word," responded Dedare.

"Perhaps *location-seeing* would be better understood." After a moment of no response from the Irions, I continued, "How did you manage to understand our written language?"

"Machine scans words and translates them." Dedare pulled a small black object out of an opening in the subdued brown two-piece garment he wore today. Although I would've liked to give the machine a try, he put it away before I had an opportunity.

"Useful." Humans would need a similar device

when we travelled to Irion.

Dedare rubbed one of his hands around the top of his head. "In two days, Syl, recommend other locations to help us understand Mars and humans. Meanwhile, enough activities are scheduled." His body language seemed to imply confusion. Perhaps my physical movements had sent strange signals to the Irions. I attempted to remember how I'd moved, but with no luck.

"What means of transport will you be using during your sightseeing?" I asked.

"Vehicle and Mars driver arranged for within your enclosed city. Not presume to operate a vehicle on an alien world." He paused for a moment, and then added, "A request."

"Of course." How outlandish could it be?

"We will return this evening for our main meal. We would like a food item like *grake*. *Grake* is a favorite," said Dedare.

"I'm sure we can find something similar. I'll do my best." After the Irions joined their driver, patiently waiting by Reception, I kicked myself for not at least asking what type of food I needed to procure.

My mind swirled, what kind of day would they have? I hope they wouldn't run into any misunderstandings with the locals. What they really needed was a guide. Hopefully, their driver had sufficient knowledge to be useful.

Enough daydreaming—I had puzzles to unravel.

My first step involved talking to our hotel chef. However, he wasn't much use as he didn't even know Irions existed. This surprised me—employee gossip, and the news media, should've given him a bit of knowledge.

My next move, regarding *grake*, I decided involved Charles. I returned to my office and called him.

"I didn't expect contact so soon," the ambassador commented.

"I've had requests from Dedare. I need to understand Irion nutrition. What can they eat? Dedare asked for a dinner item similar to *grake*."

"I have no knowledge of *grake*, but I did leave a list of human foods the Irions *cannot* tolerate with one of the lounge personnel last night."

"Please send me a copy." I needed to look into this lapse. Why hadn't I received his memo from my staff?

"Of course," said Charles, tapping away. "Check your com—you should have the list now. I'll talk to the Irions here at the embassy. They should know what *grake* is."

"Thanks, Charles. Your help is appreciated." I thought for a moment. "Now all I need to do is find some *grake* when I know what it is."

"I'll look into that. And say hello to your mother," he said, before he rang off.

Another one of her friends, I supposed. She had acquaintances everywhere.

Next stop on my quest for knowledge, my scientist buddy, Hart Adair. "Oh *expert on everything*, I need your help." Hart loved flattery.

"With what?" he asked, brushing his long red hair off his shoulders.

A scientist at MarsU—our one and only university on Mars—he played the geeky academic well, and I loved him dearly. We'd met at a science fiction convention—I had my own secret collection of graphic novels—and somehow he'd figured out my passion. After that con we'd become the best of friends.

"We have a couple of Irions staying here at the hotel." *What a strange sentence to utter.*

"I know. It's all over the news. So far I've resisted asking for an introduction. Maybe I can buy them dinner, or something." Hart's face turned a tiny bit red, and he glanced away.

Not surprised a planetary scientist would drool over aliens, I hid my smile.

"Sorry, I would've called you sooner to chat, but I'm trying to stay on top of things. So my question is, have you heard any mention of *grake*? Some kind of food item. Dedare, one of the Irions staying here, asked for a similar foodstuff for dinner tonight. And if we actually found the real *grake*, I'm sure he'd be appreciative."

"No clue. Let me make some calls." Hart's grin returned—he would get to deal with aliens, more or less.

If anyone could dig out this information, Hart would be the one.

I settled back in my chair feeling a bit pleased with myself, and then realized I'd forgotten an important detail. I called Engineering to talk to our chief master-of-all-things-technical, Miles Smith.

"Miles, Miles, I need a big favor." He'd always been able to help me out in the past, and my request today shouldn't be totally outlandish, I hoped.

"Well, you haven't called me in a long while, so I might accommodate you," he replied. He grinned and rubbed his hand through his short brown hair. Stocky and short, his sparkly brown eyes always seemed to spew enthusiasm which made him appear taller. We'd gone out for a short time, but never clicked well enough to have a long term relationship.

Such a comedian. "Accommodate me. We have Irions staying here at the hotel. I'm sure you've heard all about them."

"I'm up-to-date on all the news—even topics you don't want to know about."

I had no idea what he referred to, and I decided I probably didn't want to be enlightened.

"Okay. Anyway, Dedare, one of the Irions, would like a pool of water in his suite so he can meditate. I told him we'd have it done by tomorrow." I held my breath while I waited for his objections.

"We're pretty busy in Engineering. For some reason, a bunch of machinery has decided to fall apart, all at the same time. How about the day after?"

"Miles, I promised—"

"I'm just teasing, Syl. You know all engineers like to say something's impossible and then show you they're a miracle worker." Miles started laughing like a crazy man.

"Are you trying to turn my hair gray?"

"No, not at all. I love your hair the way it is—all blond and frizzy." He continued to laugh so hard his face reddened.

Humph. Apparently, Miles didn't find my hair attractive. "So, can you do it? Can you install something like a hot tub?"

"Of course. We'll invade their suite first thing in the morning. Don't worry, leave your request in my hands."

"I owe you one." One project off my plate.

"No problem. Now I need to find the appropriate parts—go away."

Why did so many technical people lack people skills? A question I'd never been able to answer.

While waiting for someone, *anyone*, to find the answer regarding *grake*, I checked with the hotel staff. The restaurant manager had noticed an upswing in reservations, and I'd spotted numerous non-guests milling around the hotel lobby, so I decided to arrange extra security. Then I returned to my office to research *grake* myself but got nowhere. So I puttered about and irritated any staff I found for the next three hours.

Eventually, my patience evaporated, although some would've said I had none today. "Hart, I need answers!"

"I'm getting close. I've found a person in our consulate who's had contact with someone who's actually spoken with an Irion."

"Awfully vague." I wasn't even quite sure what he'd said.

"Not as vague as you think. This Irion is the chef on their spaceship."

"Now we're cooking. How did they meet?"

A disgusted look appeared on Hart's face after my attempt at humor. "They met in the marketplace by the spaceport." He grinned. "Relax, hope is nearby."

"I need answers sooner than later. The Irions, well Dedare, want this dish for dinner, and time's flying." I tried not to sound cranky—not sure I succeeded. Wisely, I said nothing further.

"Got it. I'll call you back in an hour, or less."

I needed to keep occupied, so I went to our hotel kitchen where the Chef and I had a long chat. We studied Charles' list of items intolerable to Irions and planned tonight's menu, to the best of our abilities.

While in the kitchen, my com rang.

"I've got your answer," said Hart. "*Grake* is a kind of fish. The Irions like *grake* delicately sautéed with a spice garnish."

"What kind of fish? What kind of spices?" My shoulders slumped.

"The only information I received described *a fish with white flesh*." Hart made a clucking sound, and his dissatisfaction showed.

"You're the best. Don't worry; I'll get you an introduction to the Irions. Right now I need to get on top of this. Thanks a bunch."

After I relayed the information to Chef, he said, "No problem. I have fresh Basa from the market and, from the list provided, I know which spices to use. Pepper is the key. Leave this with me."

I basked in relief, for about two minutes. Then I remembered Charles was still on the case searching for *grake*, so I gave him a call.

My fatigue made me remember my day had started a few hours earlier than usual. So I went home, took a power nap and then, refreshed, returned to the front desk.

While I checked in a guest, Dedare and Coline entered the lobby from outside the hotel and headed to the elevators. In a few moments they returned and walked to the restaurant.

Should I be concerned they hadn't spoken to me as they passed the front desk? Perhaps I needed to follow them into the restaurant? With great willpower, I talked myself out of hovering. The dining room staff understood tonight's menu, and I'd only be in the way. And as hotel manager I reminded myself I needed to be discreet. However, I hungered to listen to their conversations—I could learn so much.

I puttered at reception until I received a call from the general manager.

"What's our status with the Irions?" asked Simon. "I expected updates."

"I apologize. I've been busy anticipating and supplying their needs. Out all day, Dedare and Coline are now enjoying dinner in our restaurant. Appearances indicate they're pleased with the services we've provided so far. I'm waiting to receive word on how they enjoyed their dinner this evening, since they requested a special item." I hoped the GM recognized my point.

Simon frowned. "This is a crucial time for Mars Best, Sylvestine. Stay on top of everything and keep me updated."

After I closed my com, I tried to suppress my anger. I'd screwed up by not keeping him in the loop, but Simon's lack of management skills more than irked me.

Another sixty Mars minutes passed. I twitched and then couldn't stop myself from checking on the dining room. As I approached, the Irions exited.

"How did your day go?" I asked.

"Fine," said Dedare. Without another word they walked to the elevator.

During the evening, my thoughts continued to swirl with worry. I even called Hart to discuss my encounter, but we came to no conclusions about the lack of conversation from the Irions.

In order to get some rest, I tried to convince myself I'd handled everything in a thoroughly competent manner.

After a few hours of restless sleep I gave up and paced about my apartment. Early morning had never seemed so bleak. Eventually, I dressed and took the elevator upstairs. If nothing else, I'd work.

Later in the morning, Dedare appeared while I conversed on the com.

At his first opportunity, he asked, "Unhappy last evening?"

What should I say? "I thought perhaps your dinner was unacceptable, or perhaps your day hadn't been pleasing."

"No." Dedare clasped his hands and became still.

What did his actions, or lack of, mean? How should I respond?

Finally he spoke again. "Apologize. Sightseeing tiring. No excuse for being rude when you helped."

"No problem," I said, adding a smile of relief to my face.

Dedare took a moment to process my short statement. "Such a wealth of information in only two words. Compliment your food preparer—excellent meal. Your version of *grake* was delicious."

A crisis had been averted. My day had improved immeasurably.

"May I touch your nose?" asked Dedare.

Any thoughts starting to form in my mind were immediately erased. What a strange request. "Of course," I said. What else could I say, and what else would he want to touch?

Dedare placed two fingers on the top of my nose

for a few seconds, then moved them down the sides.

Everyone in the lobby stared, and I couldn't blame them.

"Cool," he commented, after removing his fingers. Dedare continued to contemplate my nose, and I became uneasy.

"Sometimes my nose is cool, but other times warm. May I touch yours?" A brave request, on my part.

"Yes." Dedare came closer—he'd recognized I had a shorter reach.

I reached out with my right hand and gently touched his nose. "Yours is quite warm and a little gritty." Oops, perhaps not as tactful as I could've been.

"Higher body temperature. The gritty feeling is a residue allowing perspiration. Necessary on worlds unlike our own."

Interesting, but I wasn't exactly sure what his comment implied. I'd pass the information along to Hart for enlightenment.

Dedare continued, "Today, a tour of your solar farms. I will try to pace myself, so I am not tired. Another request."

What unusual challenge would he present?

"Will you join me for my evening meal?"

His suggestion delighted me, and a sigh of relief escaped. "I'd love to. Our restaurant?"

"Yes. Most adequate."

His response brought another smile to my face. Chef would be pleased. "What would you like Chef to prepare?" I crossed my fingers and hoped he wouldn't ask for anything new.

"Chef is what you call the food preparer?"

I nodded, amazed how words could create gulfs

between cultures.

"Tell him—is *him* correct?" asked Dedare.

I nodded again. "Yes."

"Tell him to surprise me. I am sure his creativity will shine. So far, wonderful selections."

We agreed upon a time. I surprised myself when my thoughts turned to apparel. However, I needed to get back to business. "Dedare, your meditation water pool will be installed in your suite today. To minimize your inconvenience, when will your suite be empty?"

"Leaving shortly and returning late afternoon."

"The work will be done while you're away," I said. A quick call to Miles was in order, since he'd said he'd install it in the morning.

"Excellent. Please bring a guest to dinner. You know someone who would like to talk to aliens?" A flicker of a smile crossed his face—amusement, I supposed.

"Oh, yes. I have a friend who's dying to meet you."

Oh, oh! From the look on Dedare's face, the word *dying* surprised him. "My friend is a planetary scientist, so meeting Irions would please him considerably."

"Understandable. I will join the two of you this evening," said Dedare.

Oh my, what would Hart say?

Chef needed calming and compliments after I told him about the next dinner he needed to prepare. I contacted Miles to give him his window of opportunity for the installation of the hot tub, and then I called Hart.

"So what do you think?" I asked, after I explained Dedare's offer. "Can you find time this evening to join us for dinner?" I thought my humor appropriate.

Hart hesitated, and then said, "Of course I can,

although I didn't expect the opportunity so soon. I'll need to cancel some plans, but I don't anticipate any problem. I'm quite speechless." And then he grinned.

"Enjoy yourself tonight," I added.

"Right. More research deemed necessary." Hart grinned again. I knew he'd find appropriate conversational topics which would help our understanding of Irions.

Anxiety and excitement mutually filled my thoughts as my work day progressed. Then, after a long day of solving major and minor hotel problems, I retired for a short rest. I fell asleep reminiscing on how much I loved my career.

After waking, I changed into a relaxed, yet formal, garment.

For our evening encounter, Hart, of course, arrived early. So the two of us chatted at Reception while we waited for Dedare and Coline. After introducing Dedare to Hart, I led the way into the dining room. I'd arranged for a secluded table, away from prying eyes. Although curious why Coline hadn't joined us, I decided not to ask.

We ordered our meals, and then began our cultural explorations.

His recent research allowed Hart to introduce a wide variety of topics. To no one's surprise, the Irions' technology exceeded ours, especially in the areas of space travel and production. A detailed discussion on food production explained their love of fish. A water world, the Irions cultivated many species of fish and water-based vegetation.

"This *almost grake* is delicious," said Dedare. "Try?" he asked, offering me a piece on his spoon.

Hart and I exchanged glances.

"Of course," I said, opening my lips so Dedare could place the morsel in my mouth.

After chewing and swallowing, I spoke, "This is delightful. I'll tell Chef." I'd previously eaten Basa but not with this particular combination of spices.

Dedare studied Hart and me. "Why did you look at each other? What did you convey?"

I decided to be forthright. "In our culture, offering food to someone may convey intimacy."

"Also on Irion," said Dedare.

No one spoke. This situation confounded me. I should've asked Dedare about his home life. I had so little information.

Hart broke the silence. "Dedare, would you recite some Irion history? Little is available on Mars."

Dedare discussed Irion's recent cultural and political activities. Their world seemed unusually benign. Perhaps Irion was benign, but time would tell.

"What're your plans for tomorrow?" I asked, as our meal grew to a close.

"Tomorrow is the eighth day of my cycle. This day is dedicated to rest and reflection."

Resting for only one day out of eight caught my attention—given the exhaustion Dedare had radiated after one day of sightseeing.

"Does every Irion practice this eight day cycle?" asked Hart.

"Yes, but different rotations," said Dedare.

A race with eight different cycles, what a concept. Hart shook his head. "Wow, I imagine that must complicate your business and social lives."

"Correct—our lives are conflicted," Dedare made a

motion similar to a shrug. "Syl, requests."

I nodded. "Certainly."

Of course you have requests, I added silently. I loved working for the Mars Best chain, but our slogan threatened my sanity.

"A list of opportunities to learn human history. Also tour food production plants."

"History is an immense subject. What kinds of opportunities?" His request befuddled me. What did he mean by opportunities?

"Museums, libraries, sights—whatever appropriate. Send a short summary of your history tonight. I will pick out areas of interest and then you match facilities, while I rest tomorrow. Do not forget Martian food processing."

On that note, our evening ended.

"Give Chef my compliments. Excellent meal pairings," added Dedare.

We walked Dedare to the elevator, and then Hart and I settled in my suite.

"Do you think Dedare meant Earth, along with Mars, regarding his history request?" asked Hart.

"Yes. Oh, yes. I'm sure he implied our solar system—the history of the human race. Where am I going to find a summary like that?" I ran my hands through my loosened hair.

"Let's both get into cyberspace. Two searches are better than one," suggested Hart.

Hart's attempt to cheer me up, although only marginally successful, gave me a task to occupy my mind.

After a couple of hours of finding nothing but long-winded history texts, I opened a bottle of wine. Hart and I sat back from our coms and took a break.

"Expansive meanderings is all I can find. That's not what Dedare's looking for," I said.

"I'm having the same result. Dedare needs something like one of your larger brochures."

"You're right. The brochures we have are only for individual museums and interesting sites. We need one that combines those and adds…"

A beep from Hart's com interrupted me. I gave him a questioning look.

"I set my com to do a wide-ranging search while we took our break. The algorithm found a likely candidate. Let me check." Hart pecked away. "Okay, I sent you the link. The computer found a missive called *Human History in Five Minutes.*"

The report he forwarded astounded me. After studying the document for ten minutes, not five, I blurted, "Earth and Mars have a pretty war-like past."

"Agreed. This excerpt seems to be perfect for Dedare, though. Do you think we should revise it? After all, Dedare's summary of Irion history exuded stability."

"Tempting, Hart, but I don't imagine we have the authority to rewrite history," I commented.

He laughed. "You're right. We might regret our actions."

Exhausted, I said, "Enough for today. I may need help tomorrow finding suitable locations. It will depend on what Dedare chooses to study."

After I sent Dedare the summary, Hart and I had a another glass of wine, and then he left. I then attempted to settle down for the night, with minimal success.

\*\*\*\*

The next morning, I checked my com and noticed I'd received Dedare's requests.

After a quick read, I called Hart. "Dedare picked out all sorts of items regarding our past wars, and our race to space. What's he up to?"

"Probably nothing. He'd want to understand how we've gotten to this point in spacefaring. Perhaps they consider our young race a threat," Hart said. "As for the wars, I did warn you. Although what else would he focus on—the history of agriculture, perhaps?" Hart shook his head. "No, I think his choices are natural."

Hart and I spent a couple of hours working on an itinerary. Mars had a space museum focusing on both Martian and Earth history, and also a general museum. For most of our war history, though, Dedare would need to do online research—physical libraries didn't exist on Mars.

After he received the itinerary, Dedare thanked me.

My next challenge involved finding a food production plant allowing tours. After numerous calls to Charles and the major farms, I came to the realization no one on Mars wanted Dedare anywhere near their sites.

Chapter Three

I stood and straightened my spine before I called Dedare. "I have further information," I announced. I knew I'd interrupted his rest day, but my conclusion needed to be delivered.

"The itinerary I received does not need change," said the Irion.

"No, no. What I meant was I cannot find any Martian food company who'll allow you to tour their facilities."

Dedare stared at me over the com—interpreting his expression didn't prove difficult.

"I tried everything. I talked to Ambassador Clarke numerous times, and to all the owners, but no one's cooperating. I'm sorry. I can't arrange a visit." Normally not a babbler, none-the-less my words spewed out.

"Disappointing," said Dedare. "I believe your people fear competition."

I couldn't argue, that'd been my own conclusion. He didn't bring up the subject of the Mars Best slogan, but failure consumed my thoughts.

"Thank you for your information," concluded Dedare. "Tomorrow, Coline, and I will follow your provided itinerary."

Not unexpectedly, our discussion impacted my mood for the remainder of my day.

\*\*\*\*

"I'm going to spend today at the hotel, even though it's my day off," I told Hart the next morning. "I'm behind in my paperwork."

"Is that your real reason?"

I sighed, I hadn't fooled my best buddy. "No. I want to be around in case Dedare has requests."

"I know, I know. Silly question. You can tell me all about your day when I buy you dinner," said Hart.

"I will. I'm sure I'll need to unload by then." Such a good friend.

Dedare spoke little after he returned in the early evening.

Perhaps he was tired again.

\*\*\*\*

The next morning, Dedare called with three requests: information on the psychology of human relationships, *myrl* for dinner, and to meet with a lawyer specializing in intergalactic law.

Finding a psychologist who'd talk with aliens proved difficult, much to my surprise. Chef came to the rescue with the *myrl*, and Charles, the diplomat, found a knowledgeable lawyer. Of course, the ambassador berated me for causing the situation. Athough he didn't enlighten me on what he thought the situation was.

That night Charles and his lawyer joined Dedare for dinner.

After a long day, I left the front desk and retired to my rooms, immersed in a sense of disquiet.

\*\*\*\*

Early the next day, Dedare sent me a message asking for lodging for two nights at the Mars Best-Olympus Mons.

Visiting another city on Mars was a reasonable request, so why did I worry? At least, he wanted to see more of Mars and stay in one of our hotels.

Later the same day I received a call from Simon Worth. The GM fumed because the Irions left without speaking to him. I *had* personally told him they'd moved to our other hotel, so I really didn't understand his crankiness.

Dedare and Coline returned from Olympus Mons in the late afternoon, a couple of days later. In my office doing administrative work, I received word Dedare would like to speak with me.

After settling him in my office, I asked, "How may I help?" Although I hated such loaded questions.

"One final request before we return to Irion," said Dedare.

"Of course." An impossible request?

Dedare hesitated. I thought I read discomfort on his face. In fact, I swore the color of his skin changed.

"Tour your spaceship facilities."

"Which ones?" Would the Martian government allow this?

"All. Part of your spaceport was revealed when we arrived, but I desire a more detailed view. Also your spaceship manufacturing and other related areas." Dedare ran his hand around his scalp.

"Your request is a toughy," I said, while I mentally ran through my options.

"*Toughy*?" Dedare fiddled with his universal translator to make it behave.

I had to laugh. "I meant *tough to arrange*. I'm sure our government will have all sorts of security issues to throw in my face." With my mind in a whirl, I attempted to relax my shoulders.

"Please arrange for tomorrow," said Dedare. "Not much time left. I must return to Irion."

Without another word, Dedare stood and then strode out the door.

I can't remember how many people I spoke with during the remainder of that fateful day.

****

Early the next morning, I reported to Dedare. "I have good news and bad news."

"Oh?"

Dedare kept his body perfectly still so his response was hard to decipher. I decided I needed to watch my human expressions—more than ever.

"What I'm trying to say is the managers of our government ship facilities are happy to give you access," I paused, "There is a prerequisite, however—they wish to tour your ship."

"No problem," said Dedare, sounding like a Martian.

Really? No problem? I worried all night for nothing? Was Dedare being humorous?

"Excellent. Please call this number." I rattled off an access code. "Our Minister of Space Development is waiting for your contact." What a load off my mind!

We stared at each other until Dedare said, "Well done, Syl. I will speak with you when I return from my tour."

For the first time, in a long time, I relaxed.

I was manning the front desk when the Irions returned late that afternoon. Dedare stopped to talk to me, but Coline continued to the elevator.

"Syl, would you join me for main meal this

evening? Items to discuss."

"Certainly. I'll speak with Chef and inform him you're dining here."

"Seven," Dedare said before turning away.

What did he want to discuss? Thoughts rattled through my mind while I dressed in casual clothes—something loose-fitting to ease my tight stomach. Joining Dedare at Reception, the two of us found a secluded table.

Again, Chef outdid himself. "This *coutuk* is so fresh, and the *tartar* is superbly spiced," commented Dedare.

Evidently Chef had found new recipes. The *coutuk* reminded me of a heap of mushy beets, but I kept my opinion under wraps.

"I do not know what Charles revealed, but I own many businesses on Irion." Dedare paused to take a bite or two.

"What types?" Some I'd heard about, but I suspected he owned many more.

"Manufacturing facilities. We create space travelling ships, manufacture foodstuffs, build water-refining facilities, and such. I also have a chain of hotels. I wish to discuss the hotels." Dedare waited for my response.

Did my hotel not live up to his expectations? "Was your stay on Mars enjoyable?"

"Beyond my imagination." He smiled. "After consultation with Charles and his lawyer, I have a proposal. I would like you to join me on Irion and manage my flagship hotel."

My fork clattered on the table.

"You accommodated every reasonable request I

made, and with flair and class. I love the motto of the Mars Best chain, and I want you to implement the same for the Sath-Satre Golden Hotel. I wish to create a chain of hotels for off-worlders. Their future comfort would be in your hands."

My brain froze, but at the same time, I fought an urge to bounce in my chair.

Chapter Four

Managing an Irion hotel? Managing a hotel on another planet? Supervising aliens? Running a hotel in a society with radically different belief systems? My mind had difficulty grasping the concepts—my pulse hammered and sweat began to form on my forehead. I hoped the symptoms were caused by excitement.

"Why do you want an alien to run your hotel?" I smiled after describing myself that way, but that's what I'd be on Irion—much more than just a foreigner.

"I want to create a hotel catering to all kinds of beings. Earth and Mars have only recently been introduced to the galactic stage, so you do not realize the extent of other worlds holding life. My hotels must be able to accommodate all civilizations, and soon, as Irion has decided to open its doors to space tourism. You coped well with my demands, as an alien, so I know you would also do well with all manner of new visitors. The numerous races are starting to make their way to my planet, so you and I would need to anticipate their needs. Quite a challenge."

What an understatement—the situation sounded impossible. And what a wordy speech from Dedare!

"I have concerns about any Irion being able to manage a hotel with such requirements. If you are typical, humans appear flexible and able to adapt, so I am offering you the position—you caught my attention."

What should I say? I took a moment to settle my thoughts, at least a trifle. "I'm honored by your offer. However, there're many things to consider. May I have time to evaluate my options?"

"Yes, but only a short time. I must leave for Irion within three days to capture optimum travel time. You would need to accompany me. Space travel is complicated, and it may be some time before I return to Mars."

Three days? Decision time. Did I have the guts to do this? I took a deep breath. "Okay. Let's meet for dinner tomorrow. I should have a decision by then."

Dedare clasped his hands, then rubbed one of his hands about his hairless head. "To help you decide I would like to offer your friend, Hart, a position within my operation. His title would be scientific consultant, and he would be perfect for the job. You would have another human for companionship, and I remember Hart saying he was also a medical doctor. That should alleviate concerns about your physical well-being." Dedare laughed. "Our doctors will love to study humans up close. And the Sath-Satre Golden Hotel will need medical staff, or at least knowledge, to cover all species that visit."

So many things to consider. Where would I start? "I must tell you, Dedare, I'm already leaning toward saying yes, but I have much to consider."

I tried to analyze my emotions. Much to my surprise, the thought of spending more time with this alien flooded my mind.

Before I had a chance to consider that thought, Dedare said, "Much to analyze. I want to assure you I investigated the most important questions. You can breathe the air on Irion, if I can here. I have taken care of finding out if you will have appropriate food for your health—the food you will be able to eat on Irion will be adequate for your needs, but not too variable. So I am looking into taking supplies from Mars on our journey to Irion—until I get a trade route operational. And we have the equivalent of wine." He smiled. "The beverage is called *taugh* and is tolerable by humans."

Yea! I want to try some now.

"As for remuneration for your work, the diplomats are refining exchange rates and other tangibles. Do not worry. You will be more than adequately compensated, but I cannot yet tell you how much."

I stifled my urge to jump up and run around.

We stared at each other for a time until Dedare broke the silence. "If you come to Irion, you can meet my darling daughter."

Daughter? Was there a spouse or two in the picture? And why did I care? Again my thoughts were interrupted before I blurted out any personal questions.

"You have much to consider, Syl. Call me whenever you wish before we meet for dinner tomorrow. Hart must join us, so I know his decision too. Contact Hart soon."

Dedare stood. "I will reiterate an expression I have encountered numerous times on Mars—have a pleasant evening."

I swore he had a smile on his face, but I had no words. I didn't even say goodbye.

Remaining in the restaurant while my mind swirled, I eventually roused. I needed to make decisions, and I wasn't being fair to my best friend.

"Meet me at my suite. I have big news, and you're involved." I tried to keep a grin off my face, but I wasn't entirely successful.

"What're you talking about?" Hart growled.

"Get over here, and bring lots of wine. We're both going to need copious amounts."

Without a word, Hart hung up. He knew me well enough to understand I wouldn't give orders unless a good reason or two existed.

I left the restaurant, stopped at Reception, and then sat in the lobby and thought about my life.

"Hey, Mars to Syl, who're you communicating with?" asked Hart, appearing in front of me.

"Oh, aliens, of course," I said with a sigh. "Let's go. We've a lot to discuss."

We trundled down to my suite, and Hart poured wine while I changed. I settled in my favorite chair and took a sip. Hart, on the other hand, made me think of a caged squirrel rattling around my living room.

"I don't know how to start, so I guess I'll have to be blunt. Dedare wants me to go to Irion and manage his flagship hotel. He wants to create a new chain of accommodations for intergalactic travelers."

Hart responded by being speechless—quite unusual but he managed to sit down—after he understood my words. I gave him a moment to untangle his brain.

"That's great! Though I can't quite comprehend what you're telling me. Are you going to Irion? Have you accepted Dedare's offer?"

I took another sip of wine before I said, "I've made no final decision, but I do have information you need to hear. Dedare wants you to come along as, what did he call it? Oh yes, scientific consultant. Since you're also a medical doctor, he decided I'd be more comfortable on Irion with medical backup. What do you think?"

Hart once again lost his ability to respond while his face turned a shiny pink. He jumped up and started pacing again. This time at a pretty frantic rate. "I can't believe what I'm hearing. This is the opportunity of a lifetime." He glanced at me. "Sorry, I should be thrilled for you. Think of your CV—intergalactic hotel manager."

Hart always made me laugh. "I don't think my work experience is my first priority, but I do understand where you're coming from."

He plunked himself down again, and we each pursued our own chaotic thoughts. Then I glanced over, and his grin said it all.

"What else did Dedare say? Has he looked into all the problems we could encounter?" Hart took out his com and started poking at it—a list had started.

"He mentioned our nourishment requirements, and he's working with the diplomats on monetary compensation. We'll have to bring some of our own food along, or we'd die of boredom with the limited available Irion options. Dedare says that's under control—after all, producing and transporting foodstuffs is one of his main businesses. He also mentioned Irion has *taugh*, the equivalent of wine and human compatible."

"I wonder what *taugh*'s made from," babbled Hart. "I can only imagine the issues with money, but Dedare strikes me as someone who'd be more than fair regarding salary."

"Agreed. I'm not worried about compensation."

"Well, what are you worried about then?" asked

Hart.

"I don't know. I'm quite confused. I've never contemplated making such a momentous decision. What do you think should concern me?" Perhaps, like Hart, I needed to start a list. Before he had a chance to reply, I asked, "Is space travel dangerous? Maybe the Irions aren't very good at it, and we should be worried. After all, we'd be going on an Irion ship, I think?"

Hart shook his head. "Certainly, we'd be going on Dedare's ship. Mars only has spaceships that travel within our solar system."

I wouldn't argue with a planetary scientist. "But won't this be dangerous?"

He sighed. "All space travel is dangerous. However, since Dedare has his own spaceship and travels a lot, I think you can be reassured the danger has been minimized."

"Okay, but what about all the things I haven't even asked about. I don't even know my job description. And, and, what would I wear? And…"

Hart interrupted me. "Syl, your decision is quite simple."

Simple was not the word I would've used for our situation.

"Do you have any reason to stay on Mars? And do you want to go to Irion, and I mean *want*?"

"This must be the scientist in you, but you've nailed the bottom line." My breath came a little faster. "As much as I love managing the Mars Best-Tycho Basin, I now realize the opportunity to run a hotel on another planet is much better—an order of magnitude better! But…"

"But what?" asked Hart, frowning after I stopped

talking.

"My mother." I poured more wine for the both of us.

We thought about her during the silence following my statement.

My only relative on Mars, I'd miss her greatly. Actually, I didn't know if I had other relatives because my father's identity was unknown to me, and Mom was an only child. Regardless, how could I leave her—the wisest person I knew?

"She does complicate your decision," agreed Hart.

I shook my head, and my headache worsened. I depended on Mom for so much.

"Syl, breathe. By the way, *order of magnitude* should be my expression, not yours." He started to laugh. "Something to use when I talk to my department head at Mars University. However, I'm sure I can find something better than *order of magnitude*." Hart picked up his com.

"You sound like you're already on board." I studied Hart, after I uttered the words. His shoulders had relaxed, and he also had a slight smile.

"Of course, I am. Why do you even ask?" He gave me a look I couldn't fathom. "I have no family on Mars, and you're my closest friend. Do you think I'd let you go traipsing around the galaxy on your own—without my expert advice?"

The thought of someone I knew along for the ride brought a smile to my face.

"So you'll have no problem getting a leave from the university?"

"If they don't let me go, I'll quit. This is an adventure I wouldn't miss, but I don't foresee a problem. MarsU will not want to antagonize the first aliens who've landed on our planet."

Hart had an excellent point.

"So how much time before we leave? A couple of months?" He continued to tap into his com.

I cringed and grimaced, at the same time. "No. Dedare needs to leave in three days—something about planetary orbits and providing optimal travel time. At least, I think that's what he said. Your department, not mine."

Hart's mouth opened and stayed open, for a moment. "Okay...I need to go home and think, and continue my lists. But I want to talk to Dedare and clarify what he means by scientific consultant. You and I need to consider all sorts of things—much will pop up into our dreams tonight, trust me." Overwhelmed, he rested his head in his hands. After a moment, he peeked up at me. "Syl, have you decided to emigrate?"

Emigrate? Such a big word. "Talking to you has helped. I'm almost at the point of saying yes, but I need to sleep on the decision."

"Of course you do. We both do. And you need to talk to your mother. I'll make lists. When shall we meet?"

"First, let me send you Dedare's number. He said to call any time. By the way, we're meeting him for dinner tomorrow—he needs our decisions then." I sighed. "How about you and I have lunch at the hotel, and we can discuss any concerns that've popped up. We have this evening and tomorrow morning to talk to people and..." My head hurt. "Hart, this isn't an easy decision."

"This's your life we're talking about, and you're

choosing a path. Why should it be easy?" Hart smiled. "You're expanding into a bigger and better life experience."

"When did you become so philosophical?" Cranky, even to my own ears, a big sigh escaped from my mouth.

He smiled. "I'll see you at lunch. Have another glass of wine. You aren't relaxed enough to sleep, let alone consider positives and negatives."

Hart left, and I recognized the astuteness of my friend. And I wouldn't call Mom tonight—I needed further consideration of my situation before doing so.

Later in the evening I received a call from Simon, the general manager, I threw my com on the couch and didn't answer. I had yet to make a decision about my future.

Chapter Five

After a half-eaten breakfast, I went upstairs to Reception.

"Good morning, Syl. How're you?" asked James.

"Not bad, but not quite awake yet." James' cheerfulness contrasted with my decision-making gloominess of the previous evening. I took my usual practiced glance around the lobby, checking for anomalies.

"How was your dinner with Dedare?" His question appeared innocent.

"Pleasant. Dedare told me about his experiences on Mars, and what else he wanted to do during the remainder of his stay. He also spoke about Irion life. By the way, he and Coline won't be here much longer."

James smiled. "Too bad. The hotel's business has increased during their stay."

"No doubt," I replied, but I needed to get on with my eventful day. "Do you need help on Reception?"

He shook his head. Mornings were often quiet. He gestured at my office. "I made a pot of tea for you."

"Thanks. I definitely need caffeine." I'd miss James. His skills had definitely improved during the time we'd been together.

In my office, I decided the first item on my agenda involved calling the general manager. "You left a message," I said.

"I need an update on the Irions." Simon glowered.

"Last night, I joined Dedare for dinner. We discussed what he'd seen during his visit. He also updated me on his trip to Olympus Mons."

"Does he have any requests?" Simon asked while he rustled papers on his desk.

How should I answer Simon without giving away the *biggest* question of my life?

"No requests. The Irions will be leaving in three days, so they're going to spend the rest of their time here in Tycho Basin."

"Leaving so soon? Are they unhappy?" Simon turned a focused gaze on me.

*Little did he know.* "Not that I'm aware of. Time to leave, Dedare said. He talked about optimal transit times and orbits and such. I didn't totally understand his explanation."

"Makes sense. Please tell him I'd like to speak with him before he leaves Mars," said Simon.

"Of course. We're having dinner again tonight, so I'll give him your message."

"I'm glad you're spending time with the Irions. Good for business."

I made no response, and then I hung up. At the moment, I could deal with a clueless Simon. I took a deep breath, and then called Charles. "What's new on the diplomatic front?"

The ambassador laughed. "You're funny. The biggest news is you! Have you made your decision?"

"Not a final one, but I will today. I need to speak to a few people, and I have topics to still think about. Who knows about Dedare's offer?"

"A few diplomats. Mars and Irion need to sort

some things out before we can start transporting people, manufacturing items, and such, on a large scale. Thank goodness, Mars is independent from Earth, or we'd never get anything accomplished."

Those implications hadn't crossed my mind, but then I wasn't a diplomat. "Do you have any advice to help me with my deliberations?"

"Sylvestine, you're smart enough to examine all the necessary angles and ramifications. Remember, Dedare thinks the world of you and your abilities."

I basked in his compliment. I suspected he'd helped with my decision.

"By the way, my assistant and I are also going to Irion. We'll be setting up the first Martian embassy on a non-human world. I'm looking forward to the challenge."

However, Charles looked like he'd been struck with lightning. I wisely just said, "So you have the same decisions to make as I do before you leave?"

"Oh yes. Although, the situation might be a little easier for me, being a diplomat, since travel is part of my job description. If you need any more help, please call."

Although not quite sure what help Charles had given, at least he'd confirmed I had lots to think about.

My next step involved my mother, Sylvia Amera. "Do you have time to come over to the hotel for coffee? Something important has come up and I need to talk to you."

"Of course, dear. Let me cancel an appointment, and I'll be around in a second."

I studied her face, while still visible. Although I had the same blond hair, Mom kept hers cut short. I noticed some gray had crept in—perfectly natural at sixty-five, especially with her youthful looking skin. I hoped to look so great, at her age.

Such a supportive person, how could I leave her?

After Mom arrived, we went into the Lovell Lounge and found a quiet corner. The deserted area was the perfect venue for a serious discussion.

I said nothing for a long time, while I searched for words.

"Darling daughter, what's on your mind? Something to do with those Irions you told me about? I'd like to meet them." Mom's eyes sparkled. A voracious reader, she'd introduced me to science fiction in my youth.

Because of her prod, I blurted out my story. "Dedare wants me to run one of his hotels on Irion. I'd have to leave Mars, and I don't know when I'd be able to return. I'd be back sometime, since Dedare is setting up trade routes. He's probably going to start manufacturing on Mars. He's also into…"

Mom interrupted. "An excellent opportunity. When would you leave?"

I had a hard time grasping her words. She'd always supported whatever I wanted to do, but this was a big step, even for her. And an even bigger step for me.

"You're okay with this? You're really okay with me leaving Mars?"

"I'll miss you, of course, but this is a once-in-a-lifetime opportunity. How can you turn it down? Think of all the letters—well, communications of some sort I guess—I'll receive from you detailing your exploits. Too bad I wasn't younger, or I'd stow away on your spaceship. The Irions do use spaceships, don't they?"

Mom always made me laugh. "Yes, they use spaceships. You're such a sweetheart. I really do think I want to go, but I didn't want to leave you behind."

"How can I hold you back?" She grinned. "Running a hotel on another planet? Think of all the novels you could produce!" Mom squirmed in her chair.

After retiring, she'd put her hand to writing, and was having a great time—although more success had come with her renditions of Martian history than with her fiction. But, from the look in her eyes, I knew a new plot had started to take form, probably with me at the center.

"When will you leave? A few weeks? We have a lot to do." She pulled out her com.

Should I laugh or cry? "No, a much shorter time. Dedare needs to leave in three days. It has to do with planetary orbits, or some such technical concept. We need to go when Dedare does."

"We? Who else are you talking about? Someone I know?" She tilted her head as she questioned me.

"Oh, sorry. Dedare also offered Hart a job as a scientific consultant. We're both weighing our decisions. I'm meeting Hart for lunch, then we're joining Dedare for dinner—quite a busy day, with a momentous decision for both of us."

"Agreed. However, it sounds to me like you've already made up your mind." Mom watched for my reaction to her statement.

"Sort of, but you were my stumbling block. I don't want to leave you alone." Although, what I really meant was I'd miss her terribly.

"I'm not alone. Don't you realize how busy I am?

In fact, I'm trying to decide which activities I should reduce. I always get way too involved, and I need to concentrate on my writing." Mom's face lit up. "By the way, I sold a book on Martian history to a small press!"

"Wonderful! I need a copy," I said. Although happy for her success, my mind continued to swirl, and I needed to discuss my thoughts with Mom. Before I had a chance to start, we were interrupted.

"Hey, Mama A, what's happening?" asked Hart.

Mom gave Hart a hug. "I've been hearing all about your new adventure. Tell me you're going! You've made your decision?"

"Pretty much, but I need to discuss a few things with Syl. There's much to consider."

She gave each of us a shrewd glance. "I can only imagine. I must go. I have a lunch meeting—some committee or other. I expect both of you to check in after your dinner with Mr. Sath. I won't tell anyone anything until I hear from you, but don't be tardy." Mom gave us both a hug, and then strode out of the Lovell Lounge.

Hart stared at me. "Your mother's something else, isn't she?"

"You have no idea. I need to check in with Reception, and then we'll go to lunch. I'm starving."

****

Hart and I stared at the food before us. Due to our chaotic thoughts, our brains had malfunctioned when ordering.

"We better make a dent, or Chef will think we don't like his cooking." We both picked up our utensils, and ate for a few moments. "Hart, you start. Tell me what you've decided."

49

"I've decided I love your mother, and I'm going to adopt her—or maybe she can adopt me." A lop-sided grin graced his face. Since his parents' tragic accident, he'd been lonely.

"Go for it, a brother would be nice." I grinned. "However, what I meant was are you going to Irion?"

He stared at his plate like he didn't know why it was there. "Yes, yes. Last night I made more lists, then this morning Dedare and I chatted. His offer is more fantastic than you'd led me to believe. I'll get to delve into all of his enterprises and give advice on how to improve operations, manufacturing, and who knows what else. I'll be learning about Irion life and science and much more. What else could I ask for? I have an alien world to uncover!"

He grinned, and then began eating again, so I commented. "You're right. Dedare created the perfect job for you. What else do we need to consider?"

His fork waved around. "We'll want to contact Mars from Irion, so we need to talk to Dedare about communication. And we don't know how to read Irion literature, so we'll need to fill up our electronic pads, and perhaps get one or two extra. With no idea how long we'll be gone from Mars, we'll need a supply of electronic books because we both love to read."

"I might have a solution regarding reading Irion literature. Remind me to bring the topic up with Dedare," I said. "Did you ask him about accommodations? Foolishly, I assumed I'd be staying at the hotel, like I do here."

Hart shook his head. "Don't kick yourself. This is an adventure we never dreamed of having, so we have no clue what to consider. However, I do exaggerate.

We're smart, so we do have clues, just not enough. For example, am I going to need to learn how to cook?"

I laughed—Hart never cooked. Prepackaged meals were his forte.

He continued, "The questions to ask Dedare are numerous, and we'll think of more as the days progress. It's just that the short time frame boggles my mind."

Wordless, we ate for a few moments.

"I need to stop worrying about the little details," I said. "Okay, maybe some aren't so little, but Dedare must've considered the majority. By the way, Charles Clarke, the diplomat, and his assistant are also going to Irion to open an embassy. I'm sure Charles knows exactly what to consider. I'll call him this afternoon to pick his brains."

This time Hart waved a spoon. "You've decided, I can tell."

"Yes. I believe we've been offered a wonderful opportunity. I'll miss my mother, of course, but since you've told me you're going along, there's no one else I need worry about."

"With you beside me, I wouldn't miss this! What I'm going to learn is bound to be astronomical."

I ignored his choice of words, but something I'd said niggled at the back of my mind.

Great friends could not be underestimated—Hart and I understood each other. I sighed. "This afternoon I'm going to sit in my office and do a detailed, careful consideration of the situation, which includes calling Charles. Dinner may be a long meal as I anticipate a long list of questions. What're you going to do before dinner?"

"I think I'll clean out my office. The next couple of

days are going to be busy and I need to get started."

"Don't let out what's going on until after our dinner with Dedare—just in case everything falls apart." I had to laugh. Now who's being paranoid?

"Okay, my office will not be touched. I'll make lists and figure out what I should bring to Irion. Maybe even start packing my apartment." Hart smiled and promised to meet me at seven for dinner.

I retired to my office. Before I had a chance to call Charles, numerous hotel disasters popped up, so I spent the next few hours tying the required threads back together.

Finally I had a moment to breathe but not much time remained before dinner to talk to Charles.

"What can I do for you?" he asked. His hair, although short, sprang in various directions like he'd been pulling at clumps.

"Hart and I've been looking into all sorts of issues about our offers. We wondered if you had any ideas about what to focus on?"

"Don't worry. The two of you have probably thought of all sorts of things I haven't even considered. Think of this as a golden opportunity. Call me tomorrow and tell me about your dinner with Dedare. I must run. I have further meetings."

Not particularly helpful—actually, not helpful at all—but what had I expected?

Hart showed up at my office door. Startled, I glanced at my timepiece and noticed it was already six thirty. My pulse quickened. "I haven't changed!"

"I figured you'd get lost in some project or other, so here I am to get you moving. Let's go to your apartment, and you can tell me all about your afternoon, while you get ready."

Eventually, Hart and I returned to the lobby, with time to spare, so we chatted with James until Dedare appeared. In the afternoon, I'd squeezed out a moment to give Chef a heads-up about dinner, and to reserve a table.

Dedare opened the discussion, after we'd received our drinks. "Decisions made?"

"Yes. We're both on board to join Sath Enterprises," I said.

Hart nodded and grinned. "In fact, I'm having trouble not telling the world."

"Tomorrow. In the meantime, I imagine many questions about the logistics of your move will need to be discussed. Let me give details, and then we can examine what I may have missed."

Dedare took a sip of his drink. "Communication with Mars will be minimal, at first. I hope to introduce a trade route between our worlds, and then contact will proceed in a regular manner. Who are you leaving behind you wish to communicate with, Hart?"

"No family on Mars, but I have friends. My closest friend is Syl, so I'll be around to keep her in line when we're on Irion."

I glared at Hart. I hoped he got my message this wasn't the time to be funny—Dedare didn't yet understand our humor.

"Syl? With whom would you like to remain in contact?" asked Dedare.

"I'm going to miss my mother. We have no other Martian relatives so we're very close." The thought of not being in contact with my mother continued to hit me hard.

"What does she work at?" asked Dedare.

"Oh, she's retired, but she keeps herself busy writing and participating in various activities." Such a whirlwind, I had no idea where she found her energy, at her age.

"What kind of writing?" asked Dedare.

"I believe she secretly wants to be a novelist but, in the meantime, she's having success writing books on Martian history—human Martian history, I mean." The rest had yet to be determined.

"Is your mother available? I would like to meet her. She could join us for dinner," said Dedare.

"Let me find out." I stood and walked a few steps away and gave her a call. After I returned, I said, "She's absolutely delighted, and will be here shortly."

"Have you talked to her about your Irion opportunity?" asked Dedare.

Embarrassed to have let out our secret, I said, "Yes, we talked this morning, and she's quite taken with our situation. In fact, she suggested she would've stowed away on your ship, if she'd been a little younger."

Hart and I laughed, and I believe Dedare was also amused—if rubbing his arms indicated anything. At least, he didn't appear concerned that I'd already spilled the news.

"How do you feel about Syl's mother, Hart?"

"Only today, I suggested to Syl her mother should adopt me. I love Sylvia dearly, and then Syl would become my sister. We were only joking around, but I'm very fond of Mama A."

Confusion appeared on Dedare's face, and I knew why. "Mama A is Hart's nickname for my mother.

While we wait for her, would you tell us about our living arrangements?"

"Good topic. Normally, Irion employees reside off-site in their own homes. However, in your case, the top floor of the hotel you are going to manage has one large suite, and three smaller ones. The largest suite is home to my daughter, my brother, and myself. I thought two of the smaller accommodations would be perfect for you and Hart." Dedare waved his hand. "Syl, this would give you instant access to the hotel, in case of any problems, and since I will need frequent consultations with both of you, the nearness would be convenient. I think the suites I have in mind will work out well for everyone." He studied us. "If not, we can make other arrangements."

Hart and I caught each other's eyes—we didn't need words. "I believe Hart and I agree you've found the perfect solution for our housing needs. Wonderful, actually." I took a deep breath and tried to contain my excitement.

"By the way, we wondered about your literature, fiction I mean, since we both love to read. Will we be able to comprehend any? Maybe we need something like that gadget letting you read our writing," I said.

"I believe my equipment would be able to be reverse-engineered." Dedare smiled. "I think you found my scientific consultant's first project." Dedare put his hand in an opening in his garment, and then handed an item to Hart.

Dedare and I gazed at Hart. He hadn't taken long to get a faraway gleam in his eyes.

"Mars to Hart," I said, trying not to laugh.

"Sorry, this's fascinating. I need to make a study of

the innards. May I borrow this, Dedare?" Hart licked his lips.

"Report to me when you have completed your research. Any other questions?" asked Dedare.

Before we had a chance to pour them out, my mother appeared. After introductions, we ordered her some food, and returned to eating ours.

"Ms. Amera, may I ask a question?" asked Dedare.

Mom and I both looked at him, but Mom spoke first. "Of course, but call me Sylvia. What would you like to know?"

"I have been told you would like to visit Irion. Why?" Curiosity infused Dedare's voice, or at least I thought so.

"Primarily to be close to my daughter, of course, but I think I'd get lots of great ideas for my fiction. Studying another culture, and an alien one, will make me think outside the box." Not recognizing Dedare's facial expression, my mother made an intuitive leap. "Outside the box means thinking outside my normal parameters, my normal world."

"I understand. What other types of writing do you practice?"

"History books. I've written one on a portion of Martian history, and I've found a print publisher." She rummaged in her hand bag, and handed a copy to Dedare. "A present for you."

"Thank you." Dedare held out his hand to Hart. "May I?"

Hart took a moment to understand Dedare's question, but then he reluctantly relinquished the print translator.

"Please chat for a few moments. I would like to

read a small portion of this manuscript," said Dedare.

Mom glowed. To keep her mind occupied, we discussed what we thought we should pack for our trip. Items would be able to be acquired on Irion, but we needed to figure out what we'd not be able to replace.

Dedare spoke. "This is well-written, Sylvia. I like your style. Of course, a few descriptions and phrases confused me. I did pick up the flavor of your story telling—adventures in history."

Mom clapped her hands. "Great! Not everyone figures out what I'm trying to portray." She sat back and beamed.

Amused, I thought, *Mom's going to be insufferable.*

"Before we continue our discussions about what to pack—I *was* listening—I have a proposal to make," said Dedare.

An unexpected turn of events; Hart and I glanced at each other in surprise.

"Sylvia, would you like to join Syl and Hart on Irion and become the historian for Sath Enterprises?"

Chapter Six

My mother lost her ability to speak, and I wasn't far behind. Dedare's offer certainly relieved my anxiety at leaving her behind but was she really as adventurous as she'd indicated?

I leaned over and gave my mom a hug. "What do you say? Want to come on an adventure with Hart and me?"

She dabbed at her eyes for a moment—Hart and I had a pretty good inkling of what tumbled around her mind—and then she kissed my cheek. "Dedare, this's a wonderful opportunity you've offered, and I'm happy to accept. I get to be with my favorite people including you, of course, and my time will be occupied with a worthwhile endeavor."

Mom took a short break to gather her thoughts and emotions. And since we understood what she was going through, we gave her some quiet time as we finished our food.

"I gather, from Syl, time is of the essence," said my mother, after she'd regained her composure.

"Yes. The next two full days are available to pack and finalize necessary arrangements. I cannot help you with Martian formalities as I do not understand what is required."

Dedare continued, "We leave on the morning of the third day. Bring your two hundred pounds of belongings, and we will leave directly after all items are stowed. I will send final instructions tomorrow."

Dedare studied his com. "Sylvia, I am confused with the names Syl and Sylvia. They are similar. May I call you Mama A, like Hart does?"

"I'd be honored." Mom smiled. "Now, I realize you had discussions with Syl and Hart before I arrived. Is there anything I should know before I pick their brains?"

I expected Dedare to jump on *pick their brains* but, for some reason, the translator had correctly interpreted the expression.

"We should discuss your new historian position. Syl and Hart could retire to Syl's suite and start packing. Call if you have any questions. Then, Mama A, you can join them after we have finished our meeting."

"Excellent ideas. Syl, Hart, I have ideas on how to streamline our last two days on Mars. I'll join you shortly."

I had to laugh. We'd been dismissed.

"Of course, Mom. Dedare, Simon would like you to call. He wants to discuss your stay on Mars."

"I am sure I will be conversing with the general manager when you give him your news tomorrow," said Dedare.

Okay, that put a damper on my enthusiasm. I hated to give notice, and I had a pretty good idea how Simon would react to the news I'd be leaving in a couple of days.

Hart and I returned to my suite, and we sat down with drinks—we sorely needed them. "I'm a little overcome with my decision, I must say. Do I really know what I'm doing, Hart?"

"Yes, you do. We're the first Martians invited to live and work on Irion. Imagine what we'll experience—actually, I don't think I can imagine more than the tip of the iceberg. Feeling overwhelmed?" Hart grinned.

"Definitely. But perhaps the feeling has started to change into excitement."

"Not to worry. Your mother will soon arrive and whip us into shape. A good thing, I'm sure. Now let's work on the lists we've started since we have little time."

"Less time than I expect I'll need. I do believe we've made the right decision." I grinned. "Mom didn't take long to accept."

"Such a character, offering to stow away. Now, what do I really, really need on Irion?" Hart mumbled and tapped into his com.

Hart's pointed question made me ask myself— what did I really, really, need in life?

Before I had a chance to contemplate my own question, Mom arrived.

"Don't you two look busy and confused, any wine around here?"

When I motioned toward the bottle, she grabbed a glass, settled into a chair, and took a sip. "I learned a few new things from Dedare. For example, I'd hoped we'd have time on the trip to Irion to learn about their culture and history. However, they don't have sufficient accommodations or eating facilities on his spaceship so we'll be experiencing cryostasis. Hart, I believe I understood from Dedare that means we'll be *frozen* for the duration of the trip. Does that make any sense?"

"Absolutely. All sorts of space needed for sleeping, eating, leisure, and such would be saved. What a great idea!" Hart jumped out of his chair and paced around my living area. "But, they've never tested cryostasis on humans—or maybe they have? I'd better talk to Dedare, after all I *am* his scientific consultant. I'll go into the kitchen and give him a call."

Mom smiled after Hart left the room. "He never changes, does he? Anyway, I'm happy with the thought we'll all be living close to each other. Our adjustment should be easier."

"What do you mean?" I asked.

"I have a suite on the same floor as yours and Hart's. Isn't that great!"

"Right. Dedare did say there were three empty suites." Perhaps a little too close to my parent, but I'd cope.

Mom continued. "My historian position sounds fascinating. Dedare has so many enterprises, and I shall learn a lot. Now what burning questions do you have, darling daughter?"

"The most important is what to pack? I don't own any of the furniture in here. My possessions are limited to a few dishes and, of course, my books and clothes. Even so, more than two hundred pounds."

"Your excess will not be a problem. I have lots of room, so you can store your leftovers at my place. My apartment is paid for, and any fees automatically come out of my adequately-supplied bank account. And I'll have a friend periodically check on my rooms, while we're gone."

Hart came back into my living room. "Guess what? Dedare's been reassured the cryostasis will be safe for humans but, just to confirm, I'm going to give it a try tomorrow."

"Are you sure? Sounds a little risky," I said. Hart might love being a scientist and conducting experiments but this particular one could prove disastrous.

"I'll take along people from the university when I go over to Dedare's ship—a few medical types. They can monitor my physical reactions."

"Hart, do you have a lot of packing?" asked Mom. She wanted to break up our staring match.

"A bit, but the weight limit isn't much. My lot will be mostly clothes and necessities. Of course, books will be added to the pile, but most'll be electronic, and there'll be some other stuff I can't live without. What I need to figure out is what to do with the furniture and belongings I'm not going to take along and don't want to get rid of, and then I need to cancel stuff like getting out of my lease. And I need to talk to a few people before I go, most particularly my boss at MarsU." Hart shook his head—his brain mentally revised his lists, as we spoke.

"Do you have a large amount to leave behind?" asked my mother.

"Not really. I don't have much furniture so I can probably find a storage facility for that and everything else."

Mom laughed. "We'll squeeze your stuff into my place. I have a ton of room, well, maybe not by the time we're finished, but we'll make it work."

Hart grinned. "You're the best. By the way, Dedare was so cute wanting to call you Mama A. I think he likes you."

"Hart, you're being an idiot. Now, both of you get lots of packing done tonight. We have no idea what interruptions we'll face before we leave. Don't call anyone until tomorrow. Just sort your belongings. You're going to have difficult decisions to make—trust me."

So we did what we were told to do, because you should never underestimate a mother's wisdom, and Hart and I understood how all-knowing Mama A was.

****

Last evening I devised a plan, and also started on my packing. The first item on my to-do list this morning, though, taxed me even before I was fully awake. I needed to call Simon and give my employment notice.

Thankfully, he answered. I didn't know how my nerves would've reacted if I'd needed to wait for his return call.

I took the plunge. "Simon, Dedare's offered me a position in his hotel on Irion, and I've accepted." With trepidation, I waited for his response. He didn't speak for a moment, and I couldn't read his expression.

"Really? How much time will you have to train your replacement?"

Replacement? He'd never seemed happy with my work—why would he want me to train someone? "I'm leaving with Dedare when he returns to Irion in two days' time."

I may have surprised him, but I noticed Simon didn't jump to make a counter-offer or ask me to stay. Humph! Perhaps I was being unfair—I had dropped my announcement in his lap with no warning.

"Your behavior is unprofessional. I'm most

disappointed with you, Sylvestine. I hope Mr. Sath understands your shortcomings."

Shortcomings? Of a mind to disappear at once, nevertheless, I held my words.

"Are you in your office?" Simon continued.

Speaking seemed out of the question, so I nodded.

"I must call our embassy and speak with Charles. Stay put until I speak with you again."

Somewhat rattled, I tried to work on my to-do lists. Then I noticed a darkening of my doorway. Sam blocked the outside light.

"What have you done, Syl? The general manager called and asked me to keep an eye on you." A friend of mine, Sam worked security in my hotel.

"I quit my job. I'm going to Irion to manage one of Dedare's hotels. We're leaving in two days. Simon's not pleased. Actually, he's being a jerk." Why was I surprised?

"Yes, he can be unreasonable, but what a great opportunity for you. Want to take me along?" The smile on Sam's face relieved a portion of my tension.

"Should I station myself outside, or wait in your office?" Sam asked.

I just shook my head.

"The GM said he'd call pretty soon."

"You can keep me company in here. If Simon says he'll call, he will. In the meantime, I'll start piling up my personal belongings." I rummaged through my desk. Sam took the items I handed him and piled them on my work table. After about fifteen minutes, my com rang.

"Sylvestine, I've made some decisions. First, I want to say how disappointed I am with your behavior and your actions regarding Irion. You should be loyal to Mars."

We glared at each other. I looked away first and noticed Sam stifling a smirk.

Simon continued, "The manager from Olympus Mons will be taking over your duties. However, he cannot start until the morning you leave. Will you remain on duty for the next two days, as a favor?"

Not as a favor, I would not. However... "I'll divide the remainder of my time on Mars between running this hotel and packing up my suite. I have many things to organize before I leave." Would he catch my sarcasm?

"That's satisfactory," said Simon.

Good thing or I would've been out of here immediately. "Do you still wish to have Sam follow me around?"

"Sam? Oh, the security guard. Company policy, so yes he needs to stay."

"So he's going to sleep in my suite with me?" Simon needed a jab or two, and my mood was up to the task.

"No, no, of course not." Simon's face flushed dark red. "He'll just be with you during working hours. He should check your packing, though, to make sure you don't take anything belonging to the hotel."

Sam rolled his eyes. He'd tease me about this conversation, *forever*.

"Fine. Anything else?" My irritation threshold had almost been reached.

Simon hung up, without another word. Apparently, he'd recognized my limits were about to be breached.

I had so many things to do, where should I start?

The list I'd made last night, and updated this

morning, caught my eye. I glanced up. "Sam, no comments from you." We smiled at each other. "What I first need to do is talk to James and Chef, and a few other people from the hotel. If a second person is on the front desk, would you send James in, then find Chef— he should be on duty by now. I promise not to leave my office until you're back."

"Of course, and I'll bring a pot of tea. You need caffeine and a breather," commented my buddy.

Such a sweetheart!

After a moment, I heard a quiet tap on my door. "Syl, you wanted to see me?" asked James, peeking into my office.

"Yes, I do. Please, take a seat." I gestured in the direction of my visitor's chair. My words apparently made him uneasy. "What's wrong?" I asked.

"Are you unhappy with my work?" His hands and jaw were clenched.

Ah, my body language had confused him. "Not at all. You've learned a great deal in the time you've been here, and you've helped me immensely."

"Thank you, Syl. I know I have much more to learn. I love working with you," said James.

My announcement had just been made more difficult. "James, you know the Irions that've been staying here?"

"Of course. They're quite fascinating. Did you know…"

"James." I needed to be firm, or our conversation would never end.

"Sorry. I find their culture interesting."

"Yes, we all do. Now, listen carefully. I've accepted a position to manage one of Dedare's hotels, and I'll be leaving for Irion in two days. I wanted to let you know personally. I've been extremely happy with your work at Tycho Basin. You'll have a new manager the morning I leave, and you'll be fine."

Actually, I wasn't all that sure. The new guy had a reputation for over-management.

"But, Syl…" James took a deep breath, and then tried again. "Who's my new manager?"

"Brad, from Olympus Mons."

"Oh, man. I've heard bad things about him." James stared at me.

"Brad was Simon's decision. I've promised to spend today and tomorrow helping out here. Brad starts the day I leave, so you and I need to run this hotel for two days. I'll tell him all sorts of good things about you, never fear. Will you help me until I leave?" Guilt riddled my brain.

I swear, James' eyes filled with tears, and mine threatened the same.

"Of course I will. You're the best. I don't suppose I could go along with you to Irion?"

"If any opportunities develop, I'll get word to you," I said.

Desperation showed on his face, and then James stood and ran for the door. I predicted my emotional challenges would continue throughout the days following. How could I handle the situations better?

Needing to settle my mind, I checked my list for the next task, but before I had a chance to choose, a knock sounded at my door.

"Syl, I waited for a few moments after James left, but Chef is here. Will you talk to him now?" asked Sam.

I nodded. "Certainly. Bring him in." I did a little deep breathing.

After Chef settled into my guest chair, I asked, "Heard any rumors?"

He put his hands on his ample front, and said, "Yes, but I won't tell you my source."

Such a comedian. Sam hadn't contained his excitement, and that would help spread the word of my departure.

I laughed. "Perhaps the news has already reached Earth." Although I didn't know why it would. I really didn't know anyone there and had spent my entire life on Mars.

Then Chef surprised me with a high-five. "This is a golden opportunity for you, Syl. A new planet, new recipes, new problems." He laughed.

But I sighed. "I'm having second thoughts about leaving all my friends at Mars Best. And I think we've worked well together."

"Our relationship is special—you understand the difficulties of running a kitchen, not many do. Don't be misled by my statement—a couple of your requests were downright impossible—but we'll blame the Irions for those."

I decided laughter beat crying. "I'll miss you, Chef. You've made my life so much easier during my employment with Mars Best." He'd gone out of his way to help me satisfy our motto.

"Syl, you always brought me interesting challenges. I wish you the best on your new adventure. Be sure and drop me a line. I'd like to hear about your culinary challenges." Much to my surprise, Chef stood and moved around my desk and gave me a hug and a kiss on my cheek. "Now, I must get back to work. Apparently, we have new guests with unusual dietary requests."

"I'll give the general manager a big thumbs-up about all your help." Chef had been more than accommodating—especially during our experiences with the Irions.

Chef waved as he left my office.

Already frazzled, I knew the rest of my calls and meetings would be a challenge.

Sam came to my door. "Can I help with anything?"

"Get me a new life?" I rubbed my forehead. "Sorry, I'm a little overwhelmed. How's James?"

"Spending a lot of time spreading the word," said Sam. "I think he likes to gossip."

I laughed. "James is a social person and perfect for Reception."

Gazing around my office, I decided I was pretty much done with gathering up my personal belongings. "Sam, I have one more call to make, and then we can go down to my suite and start packing. Simon wants you to keep an eye on me, and that's fine. So how about getting some packing boxes from storage while I make my call? I'll stay in my office and not steal anything. You can always ask James to keep an eye on me."

"Syl, you're being ridiculous. No one expects you to steal anything—well, perhaps Simon, but he doesn't count."

I got up from my desk and gave Sam a hug. Everyone was making me feel better about my decision.

Besides Hart, another of my best friends was Sweety Finn, and I should've called her yesterday and asked for advice regarding my decision. The shock to my system had pushed her out of my mind and now guilt surfaced. "Sweety, I have news," I said, after she answered her com.

"Syl, you must learn how to make conversation. Leading delicately into difficult topics is a social responsibility." Her bouncing red ringlets indicated disapproval.

If Mars had socialites, Sweety would be part of the group. She came from money and I wasn't sure how she spent her time, but she was always busy. We'd met at a hotel function, and somehow became good friends.

"Yes, and I will take lessons from you—someday. In the meantime, I have big news; I'm leaving Mars."

"Earth really isn't terribly attractive," replied Sweety, giving me a puzzled look.

I laughed—I couldn't argue with her logic. "No, I'm going to Irion. You know, that recently discovered alien world."

Sweety shook her head, then shook it again—her long red locks floated about her face. "I don't know what to say. This is beyond my comprehension!"

Far smarter than she liked the world to grasp, she didn't fool me. "You've heard of the Irions?"

"Oh, those aliens on the news. Aren't some of them staying at your hotel?"

I knew she implied I hadn't been very social lately. "Yes. I've been invited to go to Irion and manage one of Dedare's hotels."

"Well, that's great! A wonderful travel experience and an unbelievable advancement for you."

Such a friend! "Out-of-this world, literally. I'll miss you, sister, really. I don't know when I'll be back." Reality took another slice of my soul, and I wanted to curl up and hide.

"Stop worrying, this relocation will be good for you, but I'll miss you too. However, ideas are floating around my brain, so don't think I'm not far behind."

I had no idea what she babbled about. I often used the word scatterbrained for Sweety, but she'd surprised me many times with her acumen.

"Darling, have a great trip! Must run, have things to plan!" A smooch landed my way over the com.

Sweety had always been a drama queen, but this outdid her usual performance. Oh well, I really would miss her. I called a few other friends while I waited for Sam to return.

James tapped on the door and broke my concentration. "Syl, the hotel is running smoothly, but we have a lot of people asking questions about your departure. What do you want me to tell them?"

"The truth—I'm going to Irion to manage one of Dedare's hotels."

"I tried but they ask a thousand different questions," said James. "And I don't know the answers."

Obviously, I hadn't thought this through. "If they have further questions, they can call me, of course, but there's not much more to know." Was that because I hadn't asked enough questions of Dedare?

"Thanks, I'll tell them to call you. By the way, Simon's not returning my messages," said James. "I want to talk to him about my future."

Not surprised by Simon's lack of response, I said, "Hang in there, James. Your new manager will be here soon. You should see how that goes before you make any decisions." I pointed at the box of personal items

I'd gathered up from my office, and said, "Shortly, I'm going down to my suite to pack. If you have any hotel problems, call."

Sam soon returned with more packing boxes and we spent a few hours figuring out which belongings to store at Mom's. I had way too much stuff—accumulation killed mobility.

Eventually I lost my enthusiasm. "Sam, that's enough. Thanks for your help, but I don't think you need to stick around this evening. Simon probably only wants you to keep me company when I'm up in the hotel—although I certainly appreciate your offer to help pack. How about I meet you tomorrow morning at my usual start time?"

With our plans agreed upon, Sam took off. I needed to meet Mom and Hart for dinner in the hotel restaurant. Dirty and dusty from packing, I showered and changed. Sitting beside Hart and sipping wine, I let out a sigh of relief. For the first time today, I relaxed.

Mom arrived and sat across from us, "So how was everyone's day?" she asked.

"Busy. As predicted, my department head was not pleased with me asking for a leave of absence. However, we both knew he couldn't deny my request without causing an intergalactic incident," said Hart.

"Are we going between galaxies?" I wondered. "Or are we all in the same one?"

Hart's astonished expression revealed he'd not considered my question. "Goodness, Syl, something to ponder." He rubbed his earlobe. "My department head did demand a favor. He wants me to send him regular science reports."

"Shouldn't be difficult," I remarked. "Dedare

managed to get here, and he wants to set up a trade route."

"You're right. I just need to look into how we're going to send information to Mars." Hart waved both hands in the air. "On a bright note, I finished my packing—one small pile to take along and one large pile to store."

"My goodness, you're efficient. What about the cryostasis experiment?" asked Mom. "From my side of the table you look healthy."

"No problems. I felt nothing, other than the initial needle prick. The test was a success," said Hart.

"Good, one less thing to worry about." I'd had concerns about Hart being a guinea pig. "My day was less exciting," I continued. "The general manager was really annoyed with my announcement, as we all imagined he'd be. So annoyed he assigned me a guard so I wouldn't steal anything from the hotel."

"What a nasty person. I should give him a piece of my mind," said Mama A.

"No, Mom. It won't help—Simon's set in his ways. Anyway, the hotel security guy is a friend of mine, and he helped me pack. Unfortunately, I'm not nearly as far along as Hart—I have much still to do."

"I'd offer my assistance," said Mom, "but numerous issues remain to be tidied up, and they're time-consuming. On the plus side, I've almost packed my trip allotment."

I sighed. "Finishing my packing's going to be a major challenge since I agreed to help out at the hotel until I leave. Today wasn't busy, and I'm hoping tomorrow won't be either so I have enough time to finish."

"My publisher wants more history books!" said my mother, after waiting for me to finish talking.

"Martian history?" asked Hart.

"Martian, Irion, whatever I want to write. I made him promise to consider any novels I produce, and if you guys write anything, he'll look at those too. Isn't this exciting?"

Mom's enthusiasm erupted regularly. "Your publisher must really like your work. This publishing house sounds like a good fit."

Grinning at my remark, Mom asked, "Did you pack your paints?"

"I did. I hope I find some opportunities to be creative on Irion—I haven't had much time lately. I just packed my paints, though. I'll need to find something like a canvas on Irion. They take up quite a bit of room so I'm leaving them behind."

"No room for what?" Dedare had sneaked up on us. We greeted him the Irion way, and he sat beside Mom.

"Oh, I like to paint and I can't find room for any canvas boards in my luggage."

A few moments passed before Dedare understood the concept of artistic painting. I don't think our explanations were very clear. Then he said, "I think we can find room for a few canvases since you say they are light weight. On Irion, I imagine Hart will research your needs."

I laughed—of course, he would. "Thank you, Dedare, for supplying the room. Did you have a busy day?"

"Coline and I were occupied with business planning—we did not leave the hotel. I spoke with a

74

few people on Mars."

The curiosity on Hart's and Mom's faces blasted at him, but Dedare didn't elaborate. "Mama A, how are your activities progressing?" asked Dedare.

Before she had a chance to respond, my intuition made me turn around. "Simon?"

"Ms. Amera, would you please introduce me to the people I haven't met?"

How would I know whom he hadn't met?

Shocked at his presence and his request, I stood, and took my best guess. "Of course. Dedare, may I introduce Simon Worth, the general manager of the Mars Best chain. Simon, this is Mr. Dedare Sath, from Irion."

Dedare stood and they shook hands, and then Dedare returned to his seat. He didn't offer Simon an Irion greeting.

"Simon, this is my mother, Sylvia Amera. Mom, this is Simon Worth." They also touched hands, but neither said a word. Then I introduced Hart.

Why had Simon interrupted our meal?

"Mr. Sath, you're gaining a fine employee with Ms. Amera. She has proven to be an exceptional manager. Mars Best is going to miss her expertise."

Silence gripped us as we tried to grasp Simon's words. His contrary comments confused me—he'd called me unprofessional earlier today.

Simon interrupted our thoughts. "Mr. Sath, may I have a moment to speak with you? I have a business arrangement I'd like to discuss."

Dedare stood and gestured to a nearby table—far enough away for a private conversation.

"Okay, what's going on? Simon never said

anything nice about me before." I rubbed my forehead—my hand came away sticky with sweat.

"He's up to something. I know him, I mean his type. Now, let's finish our desert while they have their conversation," said my mother, picking up her fork.

The pie did taste delicious. What food items would I miss during my stay on Irion?

Shortly Dedare rejoined our table, and Simon left the restaurant without speaking to us.

"Would you like some dinner or desert?" my mother asked.

"No, thank you. I have already dined." Dedare studied the three of us. "Perhaps you would like to know the subject of our conversation?"

I swear he smiled. "Yes, we're curious," I said. "I certainly am." And especially after Simon's compliments.

"Mr. Worth would like to take a business trip to Irion, on behalf of the Mars Best chain. He would like to go immediately."

"Do you have room for another passenger?" Hart asked.

"More than one. I agreed to his request," said Dedare.

Did Mars Best want to expand? The thought of Simon on Irion made me squirm.

"Have you had other requests?" asked Hart.

"Yes." Dedare put his hands on the table.

With that one action, our intuition told us to leave the subject. So Mom popped into the breach. "Hart, my adopted son, has done all his packing. He's such a good boy!"

Hart flushed.

"Sorry, Hart, I didn't mean to embarrass you. Is it possible to send his trip luggage over tonight? The rest of his possessions will be going to my apartment, and we'll be making those arrangements after we leave here."

"A good idea, Mama A, better than having everything arrive at my spaceship at the same time. I will send staff to pick up Hart's baggage. Syl?"

"I'm still packing, and Mom hasn't finished either. So tomorrow night would be best for both of us."

"Well planned. Now let me tell you about my personal life and my precious daughter," said Dedare.

Chapter Seven

"Yes, you mentioned your daughter," said Mom. "How old is she? Do you have other children? How about the mother of your child, does she live on Irion?"

Dedare stopped my mother's spew of words by putting both hands on the back of his head. His alien gesture proved effective.

"Good questions and I will attempt to answer." Dedare gestured to the hovering waiter, and asked for a glass of *muth*.

*Muth?* I wanted to quiz him about the drink but I didn't want to interrupt his narrative. I'd ask at a later time.

"My daughter, Reena Sath, is at home on Irion. She lives with me and my brother. Reena's mother is dead, so although I am away a lot, Sain, my brother, who works for Sath Enterprises, is around to guide her."

I didn't know what to say or ask but, of course, Mom jumped in.

"How old is Reena?" asked Mom.

"Since human and Irion years are roughly equivalent, she has sixteen cycles."

"Ah, a teenager. Those are the most difficult times when raising a child," said Mom. "You must miss your wife. How did she die?"

"She caught an incurable disease in her biology lab. Now Reena wants to follow the same career path."

Dedare stopped talking. Even we humans saw the grief on his face, and the unhappiness regarding his daughter's decision.

"She doesn't want to be a businesswoman and follow her father around?" I asked.

"Last cycle. Next cycle, I do not know?" Dedare pulled at his earlobe.

Then I understood. His action was equivalent to a laugh! I surprised myself when I wondered about the texture of his earlobes.

The other humans also laughed—after they caught on. "One of the many things young adults go through, and why their parents get gray hairs," said my mother. Mom glanced at a bald Dedare and elaborated, "Well, at least for humans."

Dedare smiled. "Was Syl difficult at that age?"

"Oh my, yes. But I managed and look where she is now!" Mom beamed. "And where we're all going!"

"Your father, Syl, what does he say about your new adventure?" asked Dedare.

I shook my head, and put my hand on his arm. Yes, this might be the perfect opportunity to find out more about my father, but Mom's look negated any discussion. "Dedare, how much traveling do you do? How often are you home?" I asked.

He didn't pursue his question about my father. He'd gotten my message. "Half the time. Many businesses on Irion, and I hope to expand to other worlds. Many inhabited planets discovered during the last few cycles."

"I look forward to hearing about these new races," said Mom. "I will have much to write about. However, the day has grown long, and we must get Hart organized for our trip."

"I will send over ship staff to gather Hart's allotment." Hart and Dedare organized the pickup location and time. "I will speak with everyone tomorrow," said Dedare.

After he left, I said, "I'd like to meet Dedare's daughter, Reena."

"I imagine we will," said Mom. "Most likely across the hall from our apartments."

I mentally smacked myself. I don't know how I'd forgotten about our Irion living arrangements, but I suspected an overloaded mind. A situation that might continue for some time.

"Let's go," said my mother. "We need to make sure Hart packed everything he needs."

"Yes, Mom," said a smiling Hart.

In the end, we added a couple of things to Hart's trip boxes but, mostly, he'd done very well.

After his allotment disappeared to Dedare's ship, we concentrated on the remainder of Hart's belongings. Since he had everything labelled and arranged, we taped the boxes closed and waited for Mom's movers.

After they left, I remarked, "They waited for your call. How did you manage an after-hours pickup?"

"Oh, the owner of the company is a good friend of mine," she said. Mom knew everyone.

"Amazingly, everything's coming together," I said. "Now you two better hurry over to meet your movers, Mom. I'm going home to pack for a while. Dinner tomorrow?"

\*\*\*\*

Too optimistic about the next day's activities, my day turned out to be full of hotel challenges not leaving me much time to pack.

"James, the cleaning staff understand the room schedules—nothing's changed. Why do they need to talk to me?" Exasperation crept into my voice.

He shrugged. "Rosa wants you to come down to the supply room, just for a moment, she said. She suggested now would be a good time as they'd need to start cleaning pretty soon."

"Good point. Okay, okay, I'll go." My time continued to be eaten up.

I marched down to our lowest level. A large room occupied one end of the bottom floor, holding supplies for the whole hotel.

I encountered no one while I walked from the elevator to the far end of the corridor.

"Surprise!" flowed over my consciousness after I opened the double doors. Dozens and dozens of hotel staff filled the room.

Chef stepped up and enveloped me.

"But, but...who's running the hotel?"

"Don't worry," said Chef, "Ariana and James are taking turns on Reception and answering the com. If they need help, they'll let us know. Now, relax and enjoy your party! We're all going to miss you—really miss you—and that's all the speech you're going to get." Putting his arm around me, he turned my body and said, "So step up to the punch bowl and start drinking. You have lots of people to talk to. And we have a lovely cake I made."

Tears streamed down my face. I couldn't get my breath. Ariana stepped up and gave me a hug and a cloth to wipe my eyes, and then walked me over to Rosa.

"Over to the punch bowl we go," said Rosa, grabbing my arm.

"But why is everyone here?" My brain wouldn't function.

"Simply, we'll all miss you. You were more than fair in your dealings, and you treated us equally," said Rosa, "even when a reprimand was due."

My tears streamed again, so Rosa took the cloth from my hand and wiped my face. "No more crying. Everyone wants to say goodbye, so grab some punch and start talking. Some of us need to get back to work, so I'll herd as best I can." I gave her a hug, and let her drag me along.

A couple of hours passed, and then the party was deemed over. "What's going on, Ms. Amera?" asked Simon, after he entered the supply room.

I didn't know how to respond, so Rosa jumped in. "This is Syl's last day, so we wanted to honor our excellent manager—we'll really miss her." Rosa gave me a big smile. "However, I agree the time to return to our duties has arrived so we'll wrap this up. You may return to your office, general manager."

Rosa handled the situation so well Simon didn't know how to respond. Finally, he said, "Of course. Let me know if you encounter any problems."

After he left the room, Rosa announced, "Our going-away party is over." She sighed. "Syl has promised to send me regular updates on her life, so let's all give her a hug and let her go."

After a lifetime of goodbyes, I said, "How clever, Rosa! Of course I'll send updates. I'm just not sure how or when."

"I understand. But you need to realize how much

your abilities have made this hotel flourish. Ignore Simon and come back to us."

I had no words but Rosa understood. I gave her a last hug and departed the supply room—a momentous day I'd remember forever.

Back at reception, I calmed down enough to say, "Sneaky, James. I wouldn't have believed you could lie so well."

"This is your last day, and everyone wanted to talk to you before you left. What else were we going to do? Of course, I had help from Ariana. And she arranged the cake with Chef."

"I appreciate your efforts, more than you know, and I'll miss you. Stay with the Mars Best, it's an excellent training field." I tried to hold my tears back. I'd done enough crying today.

"My new manager may be an issue." He didn't radiate happiness, but he had a good point.

However, I needed to divert his attention. "James, anything else you need me for? If not, I really need to finish packing." I started to panic about my remaining commitments.

"Don't worry. I'll call you if anything untoward happens."

I moved behind the Reception desk and put my arm around him. "I'll be in contact, somehow." Then I backed up and gave a goodbye wave. Downstairs, I stared at my suite. I'd miss my home and that thought surprised me. Today's going-away party had given me much to think about.

Thankfully, my packing didn't take long, and the time arrived for our last dinner on Mars. Upstairs, I discovered Mom and Hart had beaten me to the restaurant.

"We wondered about your absence. Everything finished?" asked Mom. They were consuming appetizers.

"All done. I got back to my suite a little late because the hotel staff threw me a party! Simon crashed it, by the way. Apparently I'm a better manager than I realized. I'm exhausted, both emotionally and physically. How about you guys?"

"I managed to tie up all my loose ends, so I'm quite relaxed, and I also finished my packing. The last things on my list are to get our journey shipments over to Dedare's ship, and move your other stuff to my suite. A snap." Mom turned to her menu. "Now, what shall I order? Something I may not taste for a couple of years would be most appropriate."

Hart and I looked at each other while Mom's profound statement echoed around our table. As always, she'd nailed the point. What would I miss? So I ordered a couple of favorites and wine, and tried not to think about my future. "Hart, how did your day go?"

"Quite well. Since I'd finished my packing, I decided to wander about MarsU, and were my eyes opened!"

"What do you mean?" I had no idea where he was going with his comment.

"Everyone I talked to suggested research topics. I felt like a very important person." His grin was contagious. "I've never had so much attention, and they all want me to stay in contact!"

"You are an important person," said Dedare, joining us. "What kinds of topics?"

"Oh, everything from physics to anthropology to

anatomy." Hart couldn't stop grinning.

Dedare said, "Hart, these are viable topics for you, as my science advisor. I predict Syl and Mama A will also be interested in the information you uncover, as we all have much to learn. I am pleased I have chosen the three of you as some of the first humans on Irion."

Some of the first humans? "Are there other Martians, besides Simon, traveling with us?"

"Yes. Charles and his assistant will be opening an embassy."

I'd forgotten about the ambassador. "Dedare, have you started trade between Mars and Irion?" The look on his face made me say, "What I meant was, have you purchased items on Mars to take home?"

"An excellent question. I acquired small quantities of various products to introduce on Irion. Most of them I will try out in my hotel, so you will be involved in a substantive way. A few of my purchases are for other businesses. Researching trade goods was a major reason for coming to Mars."

"You have a lot of things to juggle, as a businessman," said Mom. "Will you be glad to get home?"

"Yes. I miss my daughter, but you must realize business fascinates me. I see the world—all worlds and activities—as one big puzzle. It is time to go home and interpret and integrate what I have learned on this trip. I have you three to be thankful for—many ideas and paths to explore."

Mom, Hart, and I were three grinning idiots—if the two of them were any indication.

Dedare stood. "I have a few things to accomplish this evening, so I must leave. Syl and Mama A, are your boxes ready?"

"Yes, that's why we're relaxing a bit," said my mother.

"I will send my staff to the appropriate locations," said Dedare. He recorded our addresses. "Have a pleasant evening. A great journey awaits us."

Dedare left the table and silence descended.

"You know I haven't even asked Dedare what my job description is," I blurted out. "This is crazy, running off to an unknown world. Whatever was I thinking?"

Mom and Hart exchanged glances, then Mom said, "You're thinking about an adventure. With Hart and me along for the ride, you really don't have much holding you to Mars."

"You're right. I have no significant other and my best buddies are coming along. Don't worry. I'll cheer up." Why could I never sustain a personal relationship for very long? At thirty-eight, I should've expected one or two.

Before I had a chance to wallow, Mom said, "Well, I guess that's dinner. I'm starting to bounce a bit anyway. Hart, please go with Syl and wait for Dedare's staff. I expect they'll arrive pretty soon. I'll go home, in case he sends others to me, at the same time. And I'll call my movers for Syl's other stuff."

So that's what we did. Everything happened quickly. Eventually, Hart and I went to Mom's. After a couple of glasses of wine, we retired fairly early—we looked forward to a fresh start in the morning—I knew I did.

\*\*\*\*

"Okay, everyone, up, up, up. Have your showers and let's get going! I talked to Dedare last night, and his driver will be here in thirty minutes."

Hart and I groaned. Mom was organizing her children, so we obeyed.

"A bit of caffeine would've been nice," I complained, after I was ready.

"You won't need any. We'll be going to sleep very soon," said Mom.

A good point, and Dedare's driver arrived promptly. Numerous vehicles converged on Dedare's spaceship at the same time as ours. Shocked, I said, "Sweety, what're you doing here? I'm leaving for Irion right now."

"I know, and I'm going with you! I have a berth on the ship—I talked Dedare into taking me along as a paying customer. I've arranged a two month stay at his hotel. So I'm going to be by your side!" Sweety bounced more than usual.

"That's great. That's really great! Whatever gave you this idea?" Delighted, I grinned.

Before she had a chance to respond, we were herded into the ship—time was of the essence, we were told.

After being led to the stasis chamber, Martians were settled, one by one, on individual slabs poking out from tubes, and were injected with the stasis drug. I watched each subject lose consciousness, and then be inserted into the wall for their silent journey.

I noticed Hart standing by my side. "Why aren't you already frozen or whatever we're doing?"

"I'm a medical doctor; I'm waiting for last in case any problems occur with the Martians."

His statement made sense. I watched Mom and Charles being stored in the wall after successful freezing.

Then a few Irions met the same fate. I looked around—only Hart, Dedare, a technician, and I remained standing.

"Your turn," said Hart, gesturing to me.

After I climbed onto the bed, I said, "See you soon," as I drifted under.

Chapter Eight

I slowly became conscious of my surroundings. We'd all received a short tour of the spaceship before starting cryostasis and thus I recognized Dedare's stateroom.

Grunting as I tried to sit up, Hart and Dedare burst into the room.

"Syl, stop! Let us help," said Hart. "You may be weak."

For some reason, Hart's order irritated me, but I stifled my response. The two of them lifted me into a sitting position. "What happened? Are we there yet?"

Hart shook his head. "Unfortunately, you had an allergic reaction to the stasis drugs, and fell into a coma—although a strange one as you thrashed about and almost fell off your slab. Thankfully, MarsU had prepared an antidote before I took my original test of the procedure, and I'd kept the bottle."

"So we haven't left Mars?" Inside Dedare's spaceship, I couldn't tell.

"No. How do you feel?" asked Dedare.

I assessed my body, but nothing caught my attention. "Help me stand," I said to the two of them, before admitting anything.

Hart gave Dedare the *don't argue* glance. Without a word, they helped me off the table.

With my hovering bodyguards, I took a couple of

steps. "Okay, normal. Your antidote seems to work, Hart."

"Excellent. The techs promised no side effects, but they also said the stasis drugs would be fine for everyone. I'm upset you were affected."

"Not your fault." But my words didn't cheer Hart.

"Let us sit in the eating area. Discussion," said Dedare.

Dedare held my arm during our short stroll. In my previous tour of his spaceship, I'd discovered the ship had two cabins, a combined kitchen/lounge area, the flight deck, and the stasis area and cargo hold. The captain had one cabin and Dedare the other, when required. If Dedare stayed awake for the trip, the first officer slept on the bridge. Apparently, two experienced officers were needed to cover the shifts necessary to run the ship. Dedare had the skills to fill in as first officer, if need be.

Hart brought me a glass of water, after I'd settled at the small four seat table.

"Syl, after your unfortunate reaction, we have a number of options," said Dedare. "You could stay behind and wait for the next Irion spaceship. The university may have developed a Martian stasis drug during that time."

Hart waved me quiet—he saw the protest on my face.

Dedare continued, "Or you can stay awake for the next ten days or so and reside in my cabin. The only two scenarios possible, I believe. What do you want to do?"

An easy decision. "I'll stay awake. I have e-books and my painting, so I should have enough to keep occupied. Will I be able to access any computer databases for research?"

"You will be able to contact the ship's computer from my stateroom. The system contains enormous amounts of data I need for my own research."

"Perfect," I said, with some relief. I needed to keep busy.

"I'll stay with you," said Hart. "I need research time, too."

Dedare made a motion with his head. "I have already spoken with the crew. The first officer and captain will remain awake, and Syl will have my cabin."

In other words, no room for Hart. The three of us went silent.

Would this work? "I like your plan, Dedare. Ten days should be no problem. Hart, let's put you away," I said.

We all laughed at my remark—although Hart and I weren't sure Dedare understood our humor.

After Hart began his sleeping journey, Dedare asked, "Would you like me to stay awake?"

I studied him and tried to decipher his alien thoughts. His suggestion tempted me—I really wanted to know him a lot better. "I'd certainly enjoy your company and conversation, but the situation wouldn't be fair. I understand your need for stasis to prolong your life because of your many travels and, of course, your daughter. So let's get this done. I'll be fine."

The captain put his employer in stasis, then I settled into Dedare's cabin.

My decision, to travel to Irion alone, turned out to be a mistake.

Chapter Nine

*Disaster* is what I decided to call my life, while I stomped around the stateroom. I hadn't recognized how much I'd become used to being surrounded by people—hotel guests and staff during working hours, friends and family at other times. For the next ten days, I'd require a major adjustment.

And after a day and a half, I'd realized the ship's crew didn't want any unnecessary interaction with me. Not nasty—after all, they answered my questions—but the captain and first officer spent their available time on the bridge and appeared to go out of their way to avoid contact. After being alone and antsy for far too long, I asked the captain to retrieve a portion of my belongings from the hold.

My boxes were deeply buried, but we eventually found what I wanted. I settled in Dedare's stateroom and began to paint.

After a couple of hours I stepped back and contemplated my canvas. Being an abstract artist, I always let my mind wander while I stroked on the paint, and then I kicked my brain back into action to determine the message. Today, the subject of my painting eluded me. The mix of colors and shapes was surprising. Perhaps the thought of Irion had triggered my new canvas—a topic to consider.

Not in the mood for more painting, I puttered about

the galley, ate, and began to read one of Mom's books. Her prose, and obvious enthusiasm, made me consider doing some writing of my own. What should it be— fiction or non-fiction?

Writing a novel piqued my curiosity, so I started researching.

The rest of my lonely journey involved plotting and painting. Time now quickly and pleasantly passed, thank goodness.

****

The captain interrupted my breakfast. "Arrive soon. Pack."

Relief invaded my mind. "Do you have a view screen on the bridge? May I watch our arrival?"

Captain Syre studied me, for the longest time. "Gather up, first," he said, before leaving the galley.

I ran to my room, and packed like a maniac. Mom wouldn't have approved of my chaos, but I didn't care. Quivering, I knocked on the bridge door. The first officer let me in and led me to the only available chair. He walked over and stood behind the captain.

"Thank you, Captain Syre, for allowing me on the bridge. How soon will we arrive at Irion?"

He pointed at the view screen, and said, "Now."

I peered closer and noticed a dot. Then the image zoomed in and an amazing planet burst into view. Irion had more land mass than Earth, as I'd expected, and more visible water than Mars. Although Mars had started terraforming, we had a long way to go to reach Earth-like conditions. The shapes of the continents appeared to flow from left—my left—to right. And the screen visuals appeared blurry, for some reason. The planet's colors tended to blend into a warm spectrum.

Predominately light and dark brown tones caught my eye. The bridge officers remained silent, so I enjoyed the viewing of our arrival.

Captain Syre interrupted my thoughts. "Land soon. Wake Dedare. Join?"

"You want me to help you wake Dedare?" I asked.

"Yes. Dedare at landing."

Ah, so Dedare, my favorite Irion, liked to watch his spaceship land—such a romantic. I followed Captain Syre into the stasis chamber. The captain turned up the lights, and I took a closer look at the interior. A rough count suggested the spaceship would hold around thirty passengers in cryostasis.

Captain Syre carefully pulled Dedare's *casket*, for want of a better word, out of his slot. He hooked up a drip to the catheter in his boss' hand. As he scrutinized Dedare's life signs, I detected no concern.

After a short time, Dedare twitched, and then opened his eyes. "Syl, how are you?"

"I should be asking how you are," I replied. "How do you feel? I'm sure Captain Syre would like to know."

Dedare laughed. "A moment, then I will sit. I wish to view Irion." His color appeared normal, but we let him rest.

After a short time, the captain and I helped Dedare out of his bed and onto the bridge.

"Syl, beautiful?" Dedare asked, after he settled into the seat I'd previously occupied.

"Yes. Irion is a wonderful looking planet." I laughed to myself. I had no illusions he referred to my beauty. "The colors are quite different from Mars."

"Nice to be home," said Dedare, rubbing his head.

In the coming months, how would I feel about being away from Mars? I'd been too busy, in the days before we left, to spend time thinking about the future, but during my sojourn on the ship my mind had drifted to those subjects and more.

After a short rest, Dedare stood, letting the first officer sit in his rightful place and help the captain with our landing.

Descending through the atmosphere gave an amazing opportunity to view the countryside. A vast uninhabited area surrounded the space port. An elevated line ran from the port's landing field and adjacent buildings to the distant city. Perhaps a trick of lighting, but the city seemed to glow with a golden hue. Difficult to check many details at this height, I resolved to dig out every last bit of information during my stay on Irion.

Dedare interrupted. "Wait in the galley. The captain will make arrangements to allow disembarkation."

I kept a close eye on him during our short walk. Dedare made himself a light meal. After stasis, a stomach needed a gentle reminder of its purpose. We chatted for a few moments about Dedare's holdings until Captain Syre came to the entrance of the common room. He motioned Dedare outside. At least I think that's what happened—Irion body movements still confounded me.

Dedare re-entered the galley and gave me a long stare. Two Irions stood behind him. "Mars people not allowed on Irion," he said.

"Why not?" I asked. Should I be really upset or simply annoyed?

Dedare studied the floor. "Diplomatic arrangements not made."

"What do you mean? You visited Mars. We can't be on Irion?" I foresaw throwing a fit might be in my future.

"Confusion." Dedare started to pace in the small room.

"I guess." I really couldn't believe his words. "What're you going to do? You've, you've…" I took a deep breath. "You've brought tons of Martians to Irion." My voice rose as I stuttered. Had this been a wasted trip? A major disaster?

"Clear up." Dedare gave me a look I couldn't interpret. "Go with officers."

I swore Dedare cringed, after uttering his order. "Me? Why do I need to go? I thought Martians weren't allowed to leave your ship? Shouldn't you go?"

"I fix. You go." He grasped one of my hands in both of his, obvious concern on his face. He left me no choice. We both knew he'd hear about this later—if there was a later.

Reluctantly letting go of my hand, Dedare rubbed my cheek.

The two immigration officers—I didn't know what else to call them—gently grabbed my arms. After glancing at Dedare, I let them shepherd me outside.

Generously, they let me stop for a moment to ogle my surroundings. Not quite sure of the Irion time of day, I thought perhaps I experienced sunset. The spaceport buildings had the golden glow I'd seen from above—perhaps from a reflective coating, as the surrounding area had more of a blue tinge. My eyes followed the elevated line noting the collection of buildings I assumed was a major Irion city.

The city skyline bothered me until I realized few tall buildings were visible. Some, to be sure, but not as many as I would've expected.

Sneaking out to my right, from the city, I noticed another elevated line. However, a nearby roadway made me decide the tall structure had a different, unknown, function. The roadway led toward low mountains and a lake.

In the opposite direction from the elevated line, a paved strip wandered off into the distance. If I ever got the chance, I had many areas to explore.

Then my tourist time evaporated. The officials bundled me into their compact three-wheeled vehicle. We drove a short distance to what I suspected was their main administrative area. Finding an immigration office, at a landing port, didn't surprise me.

The Irions stuck me in a locked room and left me with a couple of bottles of water. I took a short time to regain my equilibrium, and then I noticed the equipment-filled shelving ringing the walls. Not much of a scientist, I decided to investigate anyway. Where was Hart when I needed him?

Before any deductions about the equipment came to my non-scientific brain, the door opened and two Irions entered. Without a word, they motioned me to a chair situated in front of one of the ranks of shelving.

Much to my surprise, they strapped me down. Shocked, I yelled, "What're you doing?" I received no response. Their touch was gentle, but my nerves sizzled. Why wouldn't they talk? Were they afraid of aliens?

After being hooked up to various gadgets, my brain

kicked into gear. They had no clue what I said—they didn't have translators!

So I sat there—and beeped.

Time passed at a slow rate as various instruments were attached, recordings made, and other equipment rotated in. Offered more water but no food, my growling stomach interested the scientists. What other kinds of sounds would they like to hear, I grumbled to myself?

Eventually, I closed my eyes. Their antics became beyond my caring; I must've dozed off because the next thing I heard was the Martian ambassador, Charles.

"Ms. Amera, please wake up."

I opened my eyes. Not a dream—Charles loomed. "What're you doing?" I asked. I decided Charles wasn't the first Martian I wanted to encounter.

"Retrieving you. All diplomatic problems have been solved. Let's go back to the ship."

I didn't argue when he gestured at the scientists to unhook me. The Irion officials, standing behind the ambassador, helped hasten my freedom.

Charles coddled me on the way back to Dedare's spaceship, "We'll feed you, as soon as we're back. You must be hungry."

He acted a bit too friendly, in my estimation. After a moment I recognized why. He should've anticipated this problem. After all, he was the diplomat.

Back at Dedare's spaceship, and happy to discover my friends and mother had been thawed, I received numerous hugs and started eating.

"Syl, did they hurt you?" asked Mom, after giving me a minute.

"No, although I was certainly scared. I had no idea

why they were subjecting me to all that equipment." I stared at Hart. "I really needed you there to try and explain the technical bits. No one spoke to me—probably because no translators were available."

I chewed for a moment. "Perhaps the most annoying aspect is why this incident happened at all. Why wasn't this settled before we left Mars?" I glared at Charles.

Mom jumped in. "Obviously, the Irion diplomats didn't get the news back to this planet."

I didn't argue, but I wasn't convinced. Irion hadn't just discovered Mars in the last couple of weeks.

"Has everyone been unfrozen?" I asked Dedare, to change the subject.

"No. The captain will do the remainder—part of his duties."

"Well, let's move," I said, anxious to encounter a nonthreatening part of Irion.

So we all trooped off to our new home.

Chapter Ten

Our new accommodations were on the top floor of Dedare's flagship hotel in the capital city of Irion. Named after that capital, the *Sath-Satre Golden Hotel* stood taller than the surrounding buildings and filled an entire block. I decided I'd possibly seen the hotel glistening in the sunlight on my way to my examination at the spaceport. Our floor had four apartments. Dedare, his brother, and daughter resided in the largest, while Hart, Mom, and I had the smaller three, as we'd expected.

I wondered who used to live in these apartments? Perhaps the previous manager, but what about the other two?

"Belongings will be here soon," said Dedare. "Dinner main floor, one hour. Much to discuss."

"Sounds good. Thanks," I said.

So we Martians investigated our new homes. Mine turned out to be a suite that included an attached bedroom. A spacious living area accompanied a tiny kitchen. If the other suites were similar, I suspected we'd be taking most of our meals in the hotel facilities—which suited me and, definitely, Hart's culinary abilities.

The colors of my rooms focused on light green with a hint of gold. While checking into every nook and cranny, I noticed the background aroma. Apparently

Irion cleaning fluids had a cherry override.

My boxes appeared, so I started unpacking. Thankfully, the majority of the walls in the bedroom and kitchen were covered with attractive storage closets, with additional storage on one wall of the living room. Before I'd finished arranging my belongings my watch beeped to let me know it was time to leave.

"Before meal, Syl's office," said Dedare, pointing to a door after he arrived. The three of us had gathered in the lobby to wait for him.

We trooped into my new office. On the shiny wood-like desk sat a couple of pieces of equipment and numerous small items.

"Hart, translators for injection," said Dedare, pointing at one of the larger items.

"Those are UTs you want me to inject into everyone?" asked Hart.

"Yes," answered Dedare, picking up one of the pieces of equipment and handing it to him.

Hart's eyes sparkled—his scientist and doctor parts had dually engaged. After taking a minute to familiarize himself with the equipment, he motioned to me. "I think the best place for an injection is the upper arm. Since you're right handed, let's use your left, just in case."

In case of what? However, I didn't have the nerve to ask what he meant. After Hart injected the universal translator, I became the center of attention because of my recent allergic reaction. With no immediate response, Hart injected Mom, Dedare, and himself.

Dedare took off his translator pendant and spoke to us. "Understand what I am saying?"

Now our lives would be a little easier.

"Delightful," commented my mother. "Who're we able to communicate with? Do both parties need a translator?"

A good question! I gave Mom a wide smile and a thumbs up. I received a puzzled glance from Dedare at my motion—a topic for a later discussion, apparently.

"One translator works for any group," said Dedare, after a moment of reflection.

A sigh of relief escaped from my mouth; communication would be easier, while running a hotel. The science, behind the concept, eluded me, though.

"Hart, take equipment," said Dedare. "Other Martians will need translators."

Dedare's suggestion pleased Hart. "Sure. I'll get Syl to help me find our comrades."

"Eat now," said our new boss.

We followed Dedare into the main restaurant—an assumption on my part, as I didn't as yet know how many restaurants the hotel had—and were shown to a table that seated more than four.

The restaurant had a light and airy openness. Cheerful wall hangings and table coverings of red and yellow contributed to the ambiance. The tables were well spaced and a fifth center leg made each chair sturdier.

Mom picked up the menu—at least menus were a common item between our two worlds. "Dedare, I can't read this," she complained.

"I will order food tonight. This menu does not yet contain Martian items, so one of Syl's first duties, with Hart's help, will be to create a bilingual menu," said Dedare, pulling a machine out of his pocket and handing it to Hart.

"Document reader you worked on," explained Dedare.

"Good thinking," replied Hart.

Dedare ordered food for each of us from a jittery Irion. While we waited for our dinners, Hart puttered with his new toy, and the rest of us discussed what we'd seen on the way to the hotel.

Then Mom got a gleam in her eye. "Perhaps I'll need one of these readers, Dedare. Most likely reading Irion publications will be a necessary preparation for my history of Sath Enterprises."

"Excellent concept. Many ideas remain to be explored."

No kidding! I began to think we'd all done minimal analyses before we'd left Mars.

A voice interrupted our conversation. "May I join you lovely people this evening?"

I stood and gave Sweety a hug. "Wonderful! There's lots of room."

Sweety sat, and then she said, "Sylvia, you look amazing!"

"Thanks. The trip didn't bother me a bit. Syl, on the other hand, has stories to tell."

A glance from Sweety indicated a conversation in our near future. "Who's this?" asked Sweety, pointing to Hart.

I expected Hart to jump in and introduce himself, but he was unusually mute. "This is my good friend, Hart Adair. I'm sure I've mentioned him before."

"The scientist," said Sweety, standing and offering her hand. Hart shook her hand but just gave a grunt as greeting. "Being a planetary scientist, if I remember correctly, means you must be in heaven on this new world," said Sweety.

Hart didn't respond, so Dedare said, "Hart is now the scientific consultant for Sath Enterprises. I look forward to his innovative thoughts."

Again Hart had no response, so I asked, "Are you staying in this hotel?"

"Yes, for about two months. Enough time to see the sights and experience Irion." She glanced around the dinner table. "Although I've done a fair amount of sightseeing in my life, this whole adventure on Irion has excited me in new ways. I hope to spend time with all of you so I can view the planet through your eyes." She glanced at Hart, after she uttered those words.

Something's going on, I decided, and I had a good idea what. Instead, I asked, "How will you be returning to Mars?"

"My ship will return to Mars at the end of her holiday. Sweety is booked," said Dedare.

"Wonderful. I don't know how much off time I'm going to have, but we should certainly try and get together. Hungry?" I asked. Sweety nodded. "Could we order Sweety some food, Dedare? I'll figure out the billing later," I said.

"All-inclusive," replied Dedare, before he got up to find our waiter.

I gave Sweety a curious glance.

"I wanted to prepay as much of the cost of my trip, as possible. Of course, I'll have other charges like museums and such, I imagine, but I wanted the major items covered."

"A brilliant move," said Hart. "We're all venturing into the unknown."

Then he stopped talking and a flush came over his

face. Before I had a chance to jump in and embarrass Hart—what are friends for—another Martian walked up to our table.

"Ambassador Clarke, how are you feeling after the trip? Have a seat," I babbled, gesturing at our table. "Where are you staying?" For some reason, he made me uncomfortable after my ordeal with Customs.

"My assistant and I are at this hotel until Dedare gets our new embassy offices and rooms arranged. There's an office building nearby with our required space, so we just need to wait a bit."

Dedare came back, and glanced at Charles. "Hungry?" he asked.

"Yes, I'd love dinner."

Dedare took off again.

"Ambassador, do you know everyone here?" I asked.

"Again, please call me Charles." He smiled around the table. "I believe the only person I do not know is this young lady," he motioned to Sweety.

"I believe we met at the Premier's Christmas party last year," replied Sweety, "where they had that floating wine fountain sparkling in the center of the ball room."

Although Mars had become independent from Earth, our leader continued to call himself Premier. Another issue Parliament needed to address.

Sweety and Charles reminisced about the party, while the rest of us discussed our accommodations. Dedare rejoined the table, after returning from ordering food for Charles.

I didn't know why, but everyone around this table—at least the Martians—had a flushed look. A thought popped into my mind. "Hart, is Irion's gravity the same as Mars?"

"No. Irion's is about fifteen percent lighter," said Hart, tilting his head and frowning.

I rubbed my forehead. "Now I understand why I feel more energetic. Of course, I'm also quite excited about our new adventure." I glanced at Dedare. "Were you tired on Mars?"

"Yes. Coline and I discussed the problem, and decided to take longer rest breaks each day."

"Well, I guess I'll have to take shorter rest breaks." My statement got a lot of laughter but, before anyone had a chance to comment, our food arrived.

During our meal, we quizzed Dedare about various aspects of Irion life. I found it difficult to formulate questions, and Mom was unusually quiet, but Hart and Sweety made up for the rest of us.

While Hart and Sweety babbled, I analyzed my reluctance to speak. I realized I'd become shy because of my attraction to Dedare. Now that we'd arrived and settled on Irion, my mind had allowed my emotions to catch up.

During our coffee course, which turned out to be various kinds of tea, two Irions joined us.

Dedare made introductions. "This is my daughter, Reena Sath, and my brother, Sain Sath." Reena and Sain sat down after introductions were complete. "Syl, Sain is the head of security for all my projects, so you will be dealing with him if any hotel security issues arise."

"That's good to know." I took a long look at Dedare's brother, and I liked what I saw. Although I'd had minimal contact, so far, with Irions, Sain appeared in good physical shape and had a relaxed manner.

Although I suspected his stance would change given a security issue, he exuded confidence and, I must admit, oodles of maleness.

"Tomorrow, Syl, you will meet your hotel staff. Reena is one of your employees. She works part time in the amenities shop," said Dedare.

"Amenities?" I asked.

"Souvenirs, toiletries, necessities," replied Reena. "I love working there. Everyone I meet is happy."

Such a sweet child. "Have you worked in any other areas of the hotel?" I asked.

Before Reena answered, an Irion female arrived and interrupted our conversation. "Dedare, problem with a guest."

Dedare stood. "Problem?"

"He does not like his room. He is one of these *new*…people."

I don't think she spit—do Irions even have saliva—but she sure gave the impression of wanting to.

Dedare gestured at our table. "Tareera Weth is the sister of Reena's mother. She runs reservations at this hotel." He turned and looked at me.

"Time to get started with my new job," I said, glancing around the table.

Chapter Eleven

New job and new staff—what more could stress me out? Oh yeah, disgruntled guests.

Although I'd traipsed through the hotel's lobby on the way to my new office earlier this evening, I hadn't had time to study the surroundings.

The lobby didn't strike me as unusual—perhaps because the Irions were a humanoid race. The color scheme of red-dark blue seemed dark for a guest's initial impressions. Most human lobbies were as bright and sunny as possible. Glancing around I thought I spied a concierge station. Doorways led off in various directions—something to pursue later.

In the meantime, a human male stood at a long, shiny-silver counter. Not speaking, he seemed to be having a staring match with the lone female Irion employee. This was happening at what I assumed was the Reception front desk.

"How can I help you, Mr...." I asked, jumping into my new position as hotel manager.

"I need a different room. Do you work here? You look like a Martian," he replied.

"Yes, I'm the manager of this hotel. My name is Sylvestine Amera, and I'm recently arrived from Mars." Such a weird thing to say, *manager*, on an alien planet, but I needed to get used to it—promptly.

"My name is Mr. Branson. I'm a descendant of

Richard Branson." His demeanor implied I should be impressed. With his average height and fair coloring, his physical expressions were easy to read.

I nodded, like I understood his reference. Later, I'd get Hart to explain what the word *Branson* meant. "Let's go up to your room and you can show me the problem."

"Problems," he muttered, then said nothing further until we entered his suite—much similar to mine but smaller, as befitted a hotel room.

"There's a fridge, as you see, but nothing else. I need a microwave oven to heat the food I brought. I prepared for my stay," he said, tossing his longish black hair.

*Interesting problem!* I opened a waist-high door situated under a long counter, confirming the fridge. Nothing else in the way of kitchen facilities seemed obvious from my quick study of his room.

"Rest for a moment. I must confer with my colleagues." I motioned to Dedare and Tareera to accompany me outside Branson's room.

"Dedare, I imagine you want your guests to eat in the restaurant rather than bring their own food." Hotels needed income—a fact of life.

"No problem," he replied.

I decided Dedare had cracked a joke! Tareera looked like she wanted to say something, but she withheld her comments—at least, in my presence. I had no illusions about Dedare's sister-in-law. "Okay, so what we need is a small piece of equipment that heats food. Do you have anything similar?" I asked.

"Yes," answered Dedare. "Tareera, ask Sain to bring the *tink* from our apartment. Then gather dishes and utensils."

Tareera scurried off, and Dedare and I reentered the suite.

"Mr. Branson, your food heating problem should be rectified in a moment. What else can we help you with?"

"I don't like how the bed is made, and I can't understand the controls in the washroom."

"Show you," said Dedare. He strode to the washroom, and Branson and I followed. I needed to understand these facilities myself. I'd yet had time to even use my own washroom.

After Dedare finished his explanations, we returned to the main room. I said, "I'll bring housekeeping here tomorrow and you can show them how you'd like the bed made."

A second later, we heard a bell. Dedare opened the door and Sain entered with a small piece of machinery. I motioned to the counter top; Sain dumped it there, and then rummaged around to find a socket. The appliance and attached cord were strange—triangular shapes rather than rectangular.

"Is this a microwave?" I asked.

"I do not know *microwave*," said Sain. "This heats food." He showed Branson and me how to work the machine.

During Sain's demonstration, Tareera arrived with kitchen supplies.

"Now you have everything you need," I said to Branson, who seemed uncharacteristically silent. "Housekeeping will pick up any dishes you use and replace them every day. You can update me when we discuss your bedding tomorrow. In the meantime, have a great evening." I needed to disappear before Branson came up with other ridiculous requests. Bed not made properly...really?

The four of us left Branson's suite, and I gestured for Sain and Tareera to go ahead. I wanted to talk to Dedare.

I let them walk out of earshot, then said, "How many more surprises am I going to encounter? How many other Martians did you transport?" An urge to stomp my foot came upon me.

"Why upset?" asked Dedare.

I sighed, probably not a good idea to take my stress out on my boss. "I like to be prepared for possibilities. Surprises unnerve me."

"You handled yourself well. You do like surprises, otherwise you would not have taken this journey."

Dedare understood me better than I understood myself. "Yes, you're right. I apologize for my irritation. Sorry." I shook my head. "Now, let's get back to the others. I want to say goodnight and head for bed. I anticipate much confusion and many management decisions tomorrow."

Back at the restaurant, no one had left, but there were only sporadic conversations. Our stressful trip and arrival day had taken a toll on everyone.

Much to my surprise, Coline appeared. Dedare rose from our table, and the two of them walked a short distance away to confer. After a quick conversation, Dedare rejoined us.

I wondered about the topic of the conversation. If it was about the hotel, then I should've been invited to join them. Too nervous to ask on my first day on Irion, I let the situation slide.

However, Hart, my buddy noticed my discomfort. "Everything straightened out with your guest?"

"Yes, which is good, because I need an early—"

"No," interrupted Tareera. She and Sain had joined the dinner table after we'd all left Branson.

I glanced at Dedare, expecting a comment, but he remained quiet. So I asked, "What's the problem?"

"Not enough front staff for early tomorrow," said Tareera.

"How did this happen? Someone sick?" I asked, while I studied Tareera.

She made a motion with her hands, but said nothing.

Why hadn't she mentioned this problem before? "I guess I'm going to get a really early start. Tareera, you can show me around Reservations and the front desk at six tomorrow morning." I might as well start giving orders to my staff , and see how they responded.

"Let me help," said Hart.

"Not a bad idea, my friend. Tareera can fill in with the front desk staffing." I nodded at her. "Then you and I can take a walk and you can explain all the machines we find." Human machinery unnerved me, so I expected Irion gadgets to up my anxiety.

"Daughter, I can assist you, too," said Mom, concern evident on her face.

"Excellent. Tag along with us and figure out the work flow of the hotel. This will help your history research, and you may notice things I don't." Tactful I could be...sometimes. "Everyone's participation is greatly appreciated." Then I yawned. "Well, I guess that's enough relaxing for me. I need to—"

"I will help. I know the hotel."

Sain and Dedare, jumped in with a *no* and a *yes* at Reena's statement. For a teenager, two guardians would be difficult, I surmised.

Sain and Dedare stared at each other for the longest uncomfortable moment—uncomfortable for the Martians, at least. Eventually, Sain nodded and Dedare said, "Yes, you may help, Reena, but bed now."

Reena jumped up, rubbed their heads, and then bounced out.

Charles said, "I, also, must get some sleep. Putting together the Martian embassy will take a lot of energy. Sylvia, perhaps we can talk tomorrow?"

Mom nodded.

"Good night, everyone," said Charles.

The crowd began to disperse until only Sweety and I remained. "I could help too, you know. I'm not just a pretty face!" said my best friend.

Sweety always made me laugh. "Yes, you're more than able, but I think going out in the world, and making discoveries about Irion society, would be the best option. You'd help me understand a lot more, a lot faster." I studied her face. "By the way, were you eyeing Hart?" I tried to keep a smile off my face.

"I have no idea what you're talking about. More importantly, there's something between Mama A and Charles."

Thinking back, I thought Sweety had caught onto something, but I only said, "I need some sleep."

Chapter Twelve

The quiet lobby welcomed me just before six am. Such a refreshing calm soothed my nerves. The ambience made me realize I needed to re-introduce meditation into my daily routine. Getting to this point in my life had involved numerous stressful, never before encountered, activities, so I needed regular stress relief in order to function.

These thoughts occupied my mind until Reena appeared. "Thanks for getting here so early," I said. "Have you seen Tareera?"

"No. She does not live in the hotel." Reena twirled. "I am happy to help."

She certainly gave the impression of happiness. "Yes, I know you are, and I appreciate that. I need an Irion perspective." However young it might be.

Then Hart popped out of the elevator and joined us. Mom appeared, a moment later. "Where's the party?" asked Hart.

His statement confused Reena, but we needed to get moving, so I didn't explain. "Has anyone seen Tareera?" Mostly a rhetorical question as I tried to formulate a plan without her involvement.

We chatted a bit and waited a couple more moments. Eventually, I said, "Mom, would you mind helping out at Reception? We're short staffed today, as you know."

"Of course, dear. I'll be able to meet many new people." Mom gazed about the lobby of the Sath-Satre Golden Hotel and sized up the environment she'd be immersed in.

I turned to Reena. "Please introduce us to the Reception staff, and then get Mama A settled into helping out. After Mom's happy, we'll start a tour of the hotel, with you as our wonderful guide."

After introductions, Hart and I discussed our plan of attack while Reena got Mom settled.

After a few minutes, Reena joined Hart and myself. I asked, "Would you mind introducing us to everyone on this main level. I need to understand their duties and responsibilities. Hart will concentrate on any machinery we come across and study the work flow," I said, to update Reena.

"Yes, ma'am," said Hart. The tasks interested him but he wanted to bug me about them anyway.

Reena's gaze popped back and forth between the two of us, but she didn't utter a word. I had no idea what information she'd understood from our banter.

Dedare's daughter spent a good portion of the morning introducing us to my new employees. When we became confused regarding their duties, Reena helped our understanding. Most positions were straightforward, but a couple taxed the translator. For example, picker-taker eluded me. Hart quizzed Reena at length, and finally discovered picker-taker managed what we called room service on Mars. Simple words, with a mountain of misunderstanding.

Then we were introduced to a *nimble*.

"Ms. Amera, I would like you to meet Dial Deen. She is my father's *nimble*." Dial Deen had the usual limited amount of female head hair and sported colorful clothing—more colorful than I'd seen on Irion so far. Mind you, how much had I seen?

"Reena, you've been a great help, and your explanations have been quite clear, but what's a *nimble*?"

"Hotel liaison. Connection with my father for all hotels."

"Like a general manager?" I asked.

"Simpler," said Dial. "Any requests, any hotel manager makes, I coordinate and pass on to Dedare. Assistant."

"What about Coline Tare?" I'd wondered more than once about his duties during his stay with Dedare on Mars.

"He is Dedare's nimble for all other enterprises," said Reena.

Strange chain-of-command—I'd have a few questions later for my boss.

Our next stop included a tour of the kitchen, restaurant, and lounge. The kitchen was attached to the rear of the restaurant and lounge, for obvious reasons. The work flow appeared efficient, but one area eluded my comprehension.

"Reena, what's in that room?" I pointed to a door we'd started to pass by. It had caught my attention because of the strange door markings. My brain had received the images of large and small bones scattered about.

Reena hesitated, and then gave the equivalent of a sigh. "All calcified remains on Irion must go to a priest for disposal. This is our Bone Room."

At least the translator had given me words I

understood. "Human, sorry, I mean Irion and animal?" I asked.

Reena laughed. "Only animal. A priest arrives regularly to gather the residue from our kitchens."

An uncomfortable Reena made me drop the subject.

The second to last group of employees remaining on the main floor were ensconced in a windowless room populated with computer terminals or, at least, some kind of electronic equipment.

"What's this?" I asked Reena.

"Reservations hub. Reservations are taken for all Sath Enterprises' hotels. Quite busy."

"How many hotels does Dedare own?" asked Hart.

"I do not know, maybe twenty? Would you like to meet everyone?" She gestured at the staff hunched over their equipment.

"Another day. This looks like a busy time and I don't want to interrupt," I replied.

The dreary room hummed with conversations. Although I received the impression of cheerful exchanges between staff and potential guests, I really didn't like the room's ambiance—not a pretty place to work. Of course, I may have misunderstood Irion color schemes and their meanings.

"Syl, do you supervise these employees?" asked Hart, bringing me back to reality.

We both looked at Reena. Although Dedare had yet to give me any idea of who I actually supervised, I suspected, the total would include everyone who worked at the Sath-Sartre Golden Hotel.

"I believe the answer is yes," said Dedare's daughter. "I may be wrong."

I made a note to ask Dedare in-depth questions about my duties and responsibilities. I imagined many tasks unique to Irion would surprise me on more than one occasion. "Reena, I guess the only area left to visit on this floor is your Amenities shop. Lead on," I said.

From the look on Reena's face *lead on* hadn't translated well, so I gestured to Amenities. She introduced us to the manager of the bright and cheerful red-hued shop and the two employees currently on staff. Given their reactions to Reena's words, I knew they were fond of her.

The manager, Siska Teen, then asked, "Why are you not in school?"

I whirled and studied Reena, "I thought this was your day off?" When she wouldn't look at me, my suspicion was confirmed.

"Reena, I appreciated your help this morning, and I'm going to need much more in the near future. However, your schooling is important. Thanks for everything today. You really helped Hart and me understand this hotel and Irion but go to school *now*."

In an obvious cheery mood, she bounced off.

I sighed. "Siska, I appreciate your mention of Reena's absence from school. If anything else happens—like she's not where she should be—please let me know. I need to look after my employees, especially the young ones." I studied the shop for a moment, many inexplicable items accosted my eyes. "Siska, is there anything you'd like to discuss about your gift shop?"

"Yes. Many topics." A tall, female Irion, she exuded calmness and elegance—a perfect combination to keep young employees in line. And it wouldn't hurt her dealing with her customers, either.

"Let's meet this afternoon in my office, say two o'clock? I have no time right now. I have something I need to deal with." I'd spotted Tareera and my mother at the front desk, staring at each other.

After our goodbyes to Siska, Hart and I walked away from Amenities.

"Syl, I'm going to take off. I've seen every piece of machinery possible on this floor, and I need to do a little research."

I waved him away—abrupt perhaps, but he didn't notice.

As I got closer to the front counter, I recognized Mom's anger. "What's the problem?" I asked.

"Tareera says I can't do any investigating in this hotel." The constrained fury on Mom's face surprised me.

"Really? Tareera, please wait in my office," I ordered. She may not have heard about the duties each Martian, employed by Dedare, would have on Irion.

"But…" Bewildered, Tareera didn't have any other words.

"Wait in my office, *now*." My annoyance grew. Her loud three-toed stomp, as she walked away, didn't surprise me.

"What happened?" I asked my mother, after the two of us were out of earshot of anyone.

"I'd finished with Reception, since they were finally fully staffed. So I decided to start my research regarding this hotel. While I talked to the restaurant servers and kitchen staff, Tareera marched in and told them to return to work. Then she told me to leave. I followed her to the front desk, and then you came along." Mom took a couple of deep breaths. "It's a good thing you arrived. I was about to have words with her."

I would've loved to have overheard their exchange. However, I only said, "Probably not a good plan. I'll take care of this. Why don't you have a cup of tea or something, then continue your quest to understand everything about Dedare's empire?"

We both laughed at my choice of words. Mom disappeared—back to her rooms, I assumed—for a bit of quiet time.

Needing to deal with Tareera, I headed for my office, at a slow pace, as I got my chaotic thoughts in order.

After I sat down behind my desk, I asked, "Where were you this morning? You were to start at six and show me around the hotel." Although Reena had been wonderful, Tareera's no-show still irked, and I needed to know why she'd been missing.

"Home for paperwork. I did not realize I was expected," she replied.

"Really? Then I believe you forgot our conversation from the restaurant last night. Listen carefully, in the future. As for Ms. Amera, why were you harassing her?"

"A hotel guest is not allowed all access." If Tareera were human, she'd just put her nose in the air to claim her superiority.

"The restaurant is available. Why shouldn't a guest talk to the staff?" I asked, ignoring the fact she'd called Mom a guest.

"She talked to many staff, including the kitchen. Guests cannot."

"My mother's not a guest. She's an employee of Sath Enterprises and, as such, she's allowed to go anywhere she wants. I think you owe her an apology." Not only my mother's blood pressure had risen.

"She stays in this hotel, she is a guest," countered Tareera.

"She *lives* in one of the top floor suites. She's Dedare's historian and is writing about Sath Enterprises. Hart lives in one of those suites, as do I." A deep breath or two helped settle my anger, a trifle.

"I will talk to her." Tareera squirmed in her chair, as any human would. Hopefully, she finally understood my point.

"Be respectful. And if you're not going to be here during your regular shifts, you must let me know." I needed to reinforce the fact she reported to me. We glared at each other, but Tareera wisely refrained from speaking.

"Tareera, show me where to find the employee schedules." Now that I finally had her attention, I needed information. We spent a couple of hours going over the schedules, how they were created, and what effect the eight day cycle had. An eight-day *week* would take getting used to, and how would we Martians fit in, I wondered?

I let Tareera leave, and my thoughts wandered and envisioned a streamlined schedule.

Interrupting my ruminations, Dedare called about a lunch meeting. More than ready for a break, I settled with him in the restaurant and ordered food.

"Do you have anything you wish to discuss? Many things are on my mind," I said. "After all, it's my first day."

"Proceed," he replied, drinking from his glass.

Although unsure from his response whether he had anything to discuss himself, I asked, "Who was the previous hotel manager? Why is he or she no longer here?"

Dedare took another sip of water before answering. "Tareera's husband. Complaints from staff and suspicions of wrongdoing. Asked to leave."

Interesting. "What did the staff complain about?"

"Bad scheduling, preferential treatment, irritability."

The first two I understood. "What do you mean by irritability?"

Dedare studied me before answering. His look was a little disconcerting but natural, I supposed, after all, we were talking about his hotel. "Not friendly, rude."

"Rude is certainly not a good attitude for anyone involved in the service industry." How to continue? "Tell me about the wrongdoing," I blurted out. I cringed after asking my not-so-tactful question.

"Items missing." All three topics Dedare mentioned were certainly enough to remove any manager.

"How did Tareera feel about her husband losing his job?"

"Unhappy, but stayed." Dedare focused on the food he'd been served.

I'd momentarily forgotten. Tareera was Dedare's deceased wife's sister.

We ate, without speaking, for a few moments. Then Dedare added, "Tareera wanted the manager's position."

"Why didn't you give her the job?" Another

wrinkle, and a possible explanation for her no-show this morning?

"Not suitable. Fine with reservations."

I wondered why Tareera wasn't suitable as a manager, but I decided a new subject would probably be better. "I know you liked the Mars Best's slogan. Do you require implementation in your hotel?"

Dedare took a moment to formulate his answer. "Nothing written down for now."

Okay, I could live with that. "Dedare, your staff wear uniforms, shall I?" Truth be told, I didn't think shiny green suited my coloring.

He smiled. "No. You should look exotic, yet approachable, to alien visitors. We will have more non-Irion guests. Wear your Martian clothes. They will encourage and welcome alien visitors."

While I decided on my next topic, I studied the restaurant and spotted Mom at another table with Charles, the diplomat. Where had they had run into each other? Then my meal beckoned, so I turned away. "Dedare, we need a discussion about my actual duties. At the moment, I'm trying to meet everyone, and decide what they do and how I'm involved."

"Good plan." Dedare continued to eat.

His answer really didn't enlighten me about my responsibilities and his expectations. "For example, I spent a goodly length of time this morning having Tareera show me the schedules for the hotel. Do I, as the hotel manager, do all scheduling, or do the department managers schedule their own employees?"

I received a strong glance from Dedare. "Good question. In the past, the hotel manager did most of the scheduling. Perhaps a reason favorites were played.

You and I should decide which areas you, as the hotel manager, should begin to schedule. Change later."

"I'd like to start with the most visible areas, like the restaurant, lobby, and concierge. This will give me a feel for how the hotel runs, starting with guest arrivals."

Dedare thought for a moment. "Leave the front desk for Tareera, but add the Reservations room for yourself. Amenities is up to you but I believe Siska has everything under control. Your decision. The other areas are appropriate."

I let his suggestions swirl in my head, and then said, "You're right. Good places for me to start."

"The other managers will organize the scheduling for their areas, and the completed schedules should come to you for review. I will send a communication."

We ate in silence, while I contemplated the massive number of details I needed to uncover about the hotel and how it worked. Finally, I asked, "Anything in particular you want me to do this afternoon?"

"Continue as you are. Learn about the hotel. Yours to manage."

I loved Dedare's words. One of my life goals had been to manage big and important hotels. Although I knew I'd run into situations stretching my comprehension—after all, one inexplicable world awaited me—Dedare had given me a large charge of energy toward fulfilling my goal.

On my walk to my office, after lunch, I decided to devote a small amount of time learning the software on my computer. I called Hart to give me a hand—we'd each been given a phone/storage device similar to our Martian coms.

"What do you need?" asked Hart, after bursting through my door.

"I want you to show me how to use all the software on this computer," I said, pointing at the machine on my desk.

"Perhaps Tareera could help," Hart said, not exuding any pleasure at my request.

"She could, but I don't trust her. Apparently, she wanted my job and is not pleased with my presence. To make matters worse, her husband was the previous hotel manager and got fired."

"Ah, I understand." Hart pulled up a chair—in a better humor already.

I took a lot of notes, for the next hour, while Hart deciphered the programs on the computer. Then Siska showed up for our meeting. "Hart, please continue. Siska and I'll go into the lounge."

I'd found the lounge yesterday, attached to the restaurant. This afternoon, Siska and I were the only guests. We sat at a small table and ordered drinks.

"How long have you worked at the hotel?" I asked. Whether we received alien visitors or not, I needed to understand the Irions and their society to make the hotel work.

"Ten cycles. At first, after school." She kept her body still and her hands in her lap.

Although certainly no expert on Irions, Siska appeared young. I thought perhaps my indicator was her skin—the thickness of hers appeared to be between Dedare's and Reena's. "You must like your job, to have stayed so long."

She looked down at the table, and then picked up her drink. "I like Dedare—not everyone."

Not really a surprise. I hoped she'd be receptive to any of my future changes. "Tell me about any problems you're having with the Amenities shop. Are you getting your product in a timely manner? Are there other items you'd like to carry?"

Siska took a moment. Familiarity with the translator's idiosyncrasies was a big problem for everyone.

"Not many problems. Workable. I would like more tourist items." A small smile appeared.

"Good point, and I agree. I may be able to think of some you don't carry. Souvenirs of Irion will be particularly important for alien visitors. I'll need to study your products, though, to see what's missing. We should also decide which non-Irion amenities to carry for the Martian tourists, and Dedare's told me he's also expanding to other worlds."

With interest from Siska, we discussed the areas new to her. Finally, we stood and started back to Reception. As we arrived, I heard the familiar raised voice of Branson.

Damn, I knew I'd forgotten something. "Mr. Branson, I'm sorry. Getting Housekeeping up to your room, so you could show them the problem with your bed, slipped my mind. Shall we go now? Is this a good time?"

He snapped his fingers. "The bed's not important; what you need is a new chef. I had brunch in your restaurant, and all the food was soggy. I sent my first meal back, and tried another. Equally mushy. You must remedy the cooking."

"Of course. I'll go and look into the situation immediately. Will you be here for dinner?" He nodded.

"Then let me know later how your evening meal turns out."

Branson didn't say another word, but stomped in the direction of the hotel's front door.

What was I going to do? I didn't know how to cook!

Siska seemed to understand my reluctance. She patted my shoulder and gave me a push in the direction of the kitchen.

Before I got very far, I noticed Sweety sitting in the lobby. "What're you doing here?" I asked.

"Well, Hart and I were on a tour when you summoned him. I'm waiting so we can continue our explorations when he's finished."

"I'm so sorry. I didn't even ask Hart if he was busy." *I'm such an idiot.* "I'll tell him he can go but I need to talk to the chef, first." I again headed to the kitchen. A moment passed before I realized Sweety followed, but I decided to say nothing.

Located in the innards of the hotel behind both the restaurant and lounge, the kitchen also connected to an inner elevator catering to room service.

I recognized one of the kitchen staff from my earlier visit. "Is your chief chef here?"

She pointed to a burly Irion working over a stove. "Name Virem."

He watched as we approached. "Chef Virem, I'm Sylvestine Amera, the new manager of this hotel."

"Everyone knows." He turned back to his preparations.

Well, he certainly didn't act like a new friend of mine. How should I handle this? "You know other Martians now stay at this hotel?"

Virem turned back and gave a nod, and then I noticed he couldn't take his eyes off Sweety.

"I've had a complaint regarding the cooking of Martian food," I said.

Reluctantly, Virem turned his gaze to me—for the longest time.

I'd hoped my statement would get his attention, but his staring unnerved me.

"Perhaps you could show me how you cook Martian food." I didn't know how else to begin.

Virem turned around and for a long moment all we saw was his back. I whispered to Sweety, "I don't know how to cook."

"Agreed. You're a terrible cook. Let me handle this," she whispered. She thought, for a moment. "Chef Virem, my name is Sweety. Would you show me what you do when you cook Martian food? For example, when you make a sandwich."

Without a word, he opened a tall cabinet and took out a loaf of bread. He plucked two slices out of the bag, and plunked the bread on a plate—at least something was similar—then used a spray bottle to cover the slices with a mist.

"What does that bottle contain?" asked Sweety.

"Water. All Irion food is sprayed before preparation."

Considering Irion's climate I understood his action, but no wonder Branson had complained. I wondered why none of us had noticed the food we'd been eating had been treated with water. Then I realized, so far, we'd only eaten food that didn't mind a bit of extra water.

"Syl, I can handle this. Go back to Hart and get

him to meet me here when you're finished with him." Sweety's loud laugh echoed through the kitchen, and then she turned to Virem, "I'd like to show you how to cook a few Martian items. May I?"

The bilingual menu climbed higher on my to-do list. What a first day, so far!

As I walked away, I glanced back; a smitten Virem gazed at Sweety.

Arriving at my office, I discovered Hart pulling at his hair. "What's the matter?"

"Some of these computer programs are so alien. I don't know what they're trying to do."

"Why didn't you ask Tareera? She would've loved to help." We both laughed.

"Although I had a premonition of what her answer would be, I did ask, actually. Apparently, she knows nothing about any software except Reservations," said Hart.

Yeah, right. I predicted more trouble from Tareera, in my future. I didn't voice my opinion, but Hart read my thought. "Anyway, keep trying. Change the passwords if you can. By the way, Sweety is teaching Chef how to cook Martian food."

"Oh, ah," stammered Hart.

"She's a good cook. Many a meal she's made for me, but her teaching could take a while." I sighed. "I must apologize. I didn't even ask if you were busy when I called. I'm so sorry." I decided not to mention the fact I'd found out they were together at the time. "So let me buy the two of you dinner tonight to make up for spoiling your day." Hart nodded. "Until then, I'm going to investigate more of this hotel."

Leaving my office, I glanced back. Hart stared at

my office wall with unfocussed eyes. I knew what, ah who, was on his mind. Then I walked over to the Amenities shop, and discovered Reena.

"Working this afternoon?" I asked.

"Not scheduled. I came by after school to see if anyone needed help."

"Then you're the perfect person. I want to visit all the kinds of hotel rooms we offer. Could you make a list of the types, then check the computer to find out which ones are empty?"

"Not hard," said Reena.

"Why don't we use my computer?" I pointed to my office, and Reena took off. "Do you need her help, Siska?" I asked.

"No. We are not busy. I am making a list of Martian items we should consider. Meeting tomorrow?"

"Of course. How about eight am?" I asked, grateful for a cooperating, interested employee.

"Yes, good time. Keep an eye on Reena, good girl, but young."

Back at my office, I discovered Reena and Hart having an animated discussion. "Why would you start a program that way? Makes no sense."

I interrupted, "Hart, these are Irions not Martians. Who says our way is best?"

"Yeah, yeah. Just a little frustrated. However, Reena's given me a few ideas on how to proceed. Thank you, by the way. I couldn't have understood some of these programs without you."

Reena beamed, and Hart relaxed, a bit.

"Good, Hart. Let Reena have the computer for just a moment—we have a project and she needs to make a list, then we'll be out of your hair."

Hart vacated my desk chair, and came over to stand beside me. Reena plopped onto the chair and started to type.

"The first part of my day was quite good—gaining an understanding of Irion machinery. However, their ideas on computer software are bizarre. I have to say it—Alien!" Although his last comment sounded negative, he had a grin on his face.

"You came here for the challenge, and I know you're capable. I'm sure Reena will be glad to help, whenever necessary. However, right now, Reena and I'll be wandering about the hotel. Work for a bit, if you like, but take some time to relax and then meet me for dinner. Okay? Oh, and don't forget to tell Sweety."

Hart smiled and pulled out his com to make the call.

Reena spoke, "The computer is now yours, Hart. Do you need further help?"

"No, I think I'm okay. Your instructions were concise."

Hart's compliment pleased Reena. Then we took off to visit the available accommodations in the Sath-Satre Golden Hotel.

The rooms, with their mostly blue color schemes, ranged from tiny to suites—although none were as large or complete as our permanent residences.

I'd been too tired on my first day on Irion to notice the beds were square-shaped, rather than rectangular. Although the rooms were tastefully decorated, something seemed off. Then I recognized that no item, in any of the bedrooms, had a shiny metal surface. I thought I'd glimpsed shininess in other places in the hotel, but none came to mind. Many objects on Mars were encased in, or made of metal. I was accustomed to my eyes catching reflections. Each room did boast a TV-like object, but I decided to let Hart discover its workings. Would this machinery be useful to Martians and other alien species?

The Sath-Satre Golden Hotel had more room styles than I'd anticipated, but finally my day ended. I had a wealth of information to process.

Outside my suite, I said, "You've been a great help today, Reena. What's your schedule for tomorrow?"

"More school and some off-school projects." She gazed at me. Clearly, she hoped I'd need her help so she could skip school.

"Well, have a great day. Tell me about it later." I wouldn't fall for her intelligent brown eyes and cute smile.

Reena waved while she walked across the hall to her own home. Inside my suite, I collapsed on my bed. A two minute power nap grabbed my attention.

The com interrupted my dreams of aliens and knife-wielding dinosaurs. "I'm with Hart in the restaurant. Are you coming for dinner? It's getting late," asked Mom.

I glanced at my watch. I'd been asleep far longer than anticipated. "Give me five minutes."

Rushing into the restaurant, I said, "Sorry, everyone. I fell asleep—I don't know why." I dropped into a chair.

"Something about the first long day on a new job, perhaps?" said Mom.

"Something like that," I replied. Looking around the table I noticed Hart and Sweety, and also Charles. Then I heard a sound. Looking behind me I spotted

Dedare, Sain, and Reena. "Join us. There's lots of room." A little presumptuous, on my part, since we were in Dedare's hotel.

Reena ran up and took the chair beside me. I decided to be flattered. "I'm going to order dinner—I'm starving," I said.

"Are you always hungry?" Reena asked.

"Yes, she is. Syl loves to eat," said Sweety. "She just can't cook." My favorite Martians laughed.

"Who are you?" asked Reena. Clearly, she didn't remember meeting Sweety the previous evening. Reena must have been overwhelmed by all the new strange faces and mannerisms.

"Sweety, my name is Sweety, and I'm Syl's friend."

"Sweety, Sweety. Strange name," commented Reena.

"That's not exactly her name, Reena, but I understand why you're confused. My best friend here," I said, pointing at Sweety, "calls everyone Sweety, so that's why we changed her original name to Sweety."

The Martians laughed while the Irions digested my words.

"I might have to curtail my enthusiasm for that endearment on Irion," said Sweety.

Much laughter ensued. "Hart, you and I need to work on creating a bi-lingual menu. Your little reader will help."

"No problem. I'd really like to know what's available before I start picking items out of the air."

"Out of the air?" asked Reena.

"Oh, Hart means guessing." I turned to Dedare. "Hart and I'll need a list of which Martian foods you brought along, so we can update the menu." I thought for a moment, "And which Irion foods we can tolerate."

"Yes," replied Dedare.

"Good. I need to get a printed menu available, as soon as possible, for our Martian guests." Speak of the devil, Branson appeared out of nowhere and startled me. I decided to jump in before I heard any complaints. "Mr. Branson, how was your day?"

"Much better. My dinner was well prepared, and I had a good day touring Satre. I wanted to let you know. Good evening."

A pleasant Branson took a moment for my brain to accept. Everyone watched silently while he walked away. After he was out of earshot, I asked, "Hart, so who was this ancestor he expected me to know about, some Richard Branson?"

Hart, my fountain of knowledge, smiled and said, "Richard Branson was an English businessman born in the twentieth century. He's best known as the founder of the Virgin Group—more than four hundred companies which included the music label, Virgin Records. Then he created Virgin Airways, an Earth airline. After a time, Branson created a space tourism company, Virgin Galactic, and later collaborated with Mars Unlimited to establish the early human colonies on Mars. Branson believed in space exploration."

"So, this Branson thinks of himself as an explorer?" I asked.

"I'd think so. He has a deep pocket, or so the rumor goes. Which kind of makes sense with Richard Branson being his ancestor," said Hart.

"What is *deep pocket*?" asked Dedare.

"Someone with lots of money." Seeing Dedare's

confusion, Hart added, "He can keep pulling money out of his pocket because it's big and deep."

Dedare smiled.

"Well, the Sath-Satre Golden Hotel can always use guests," I said. "Even somewhat challenging ones." We all laughed. "By the way, what does Satre mean?"

Hart gasped. "Satre is the capital of Irion, and the city we now live in."

My foot firmly in my mouth, I tried to excuse myself, "I think I knew that, but I haven't had a chance to even leave the hotel, let alone explore the world outside. I'll add exploring Satre to my list of things to do on my day off." I glanced at Dedare.

"Later," he said.

Many more days like today, and I'd need a day off. So I hoped his comment meant we'd discuss the topic later. Our meals started to arrive and we all dug in—the long day had taken its toll on everyone.

"Sweety, your cooking lessons with Chef Virem obviously went well since Branson had no complaints," I commented.

Questioning looks came our way. "Sweety and I went to the kitchen to investigate how the chefs prepared Martian food, after Branson complained about his brunch. Since I'm a dud in the kitchen, Sweety offered to show Chef Virem our culinary practices. Apparently, all went well." I smiled at Sweety. "I think Virem's a little smitten."

"You might be right," said Sweety, stealing a glance at a staring Hart.

I ignored the two of them. "Dedare, any chance we can steal Chef from Mars Best-Tycho Basin? I think he'd adapt to Irion quite well."

Dedare laughed. "No, I have other plans. Please do not tell any other Martian on Irion, but I intend to open a hotel on Mars, and I hope Chef will join Sath Enterprises."

"Oh, that sounds like a wonderful idea, and Chef would be perfect with his past experience." I laughed—*past* was such a relative term. "Simon will never hear it from us." I turned to my mother, "What did you do today, Mom?"

"Learned an awful lot about Dedare's businesses—not enough to start writing yet, but enough to find areas I'll need to research. Quite an enjoyable day, except for Tareera." Mom frowned.

"Problem?" Dedare missed nothing.

"I'll tell you later. I have a few hotel topics to discuss, so perhaps we can adjourn to the lounge after dinner?" I suggested.

"Yes," said Dedare.

Mom asked, "Did you have a good day, Dedare, with all your businesses? You have a fascinating mix. I'm just beginning to learn about them."

"I conducted much business, but I also went to visit my wife's *petti*."

Breaking the awkward silence, I asked, "Forgive me, Dedare, but what's a *petti*?"

He looked at Reena. "*Petti* is a resting place. My mother is situated in a lovely garden. May I take you there some day?" asked Reena.

"Of course. I'd be honored. However, remember, you cannot miss any school."

Dedare and Sain looked at Reena and me, but the only one to speak was my mother.

"Skipping school is not a great idea, Reena. Syl

tried once, but never did again. She understood, after the first time, there'd be consequences." Mom smiled and changed the subject, like only a mother would. "I heard you were a great help to Syl today, and I'm sure you will be many times, in the future."

Then I recognized a blushing teenager—Reena's face turned a shade of blue much like a sparkling ocean.

Charles interrupted our conversation. "Sylvestine, some issues still remain regarding Customs. You may have to speak with them again."

"Why? I thought everything had resolved." I wanted to get up and pace.

"I agree. So did I. However, I received a visit from an Irion ambassador. A few officials would like to speak with you as they consider you a subversive since you didn't travel to Irion in the sleep chambers."

I glared at Charles—some ambassador he was. Why wasn't he on my side? "Did they think I plotted a takeover of Irion during our trip? You know I have an allergy to the stasis drug."

"I will take care of this," said Dedare.

"Well, Syl, you will have to meet with—"

"I will take care of this." Dedare interrupted Charles.

Charles remained silent.

"Syl, time to adjourn to the lounge. Sain, please join us." Dedare gestured at the table. "Enjoy the rest of your meal. Good night."

I'd finished eating, so I wasn't particularly bothered by his abrupt summons. After the three of us settled at a table in the quiet lounge, I asked, "Dedare, is there anything like wine I could tolerate? I need to relax."

"I brought many cases of wine from Mars. I knew you liked the beverage. Let me order you a glass."

Dedare ordered for the three of us, and then we settled down for our conference. "Syl, please start," said Dedare.

I pulled out my pocket computer. "Okay. First, I now understand I'm in charge of the Reservations room? Is that for all Irion hotels?"

"Good question. Yes, the room in this hotel is for all of Sath Enterprises' Irion hotels. When I expand to other planets, we will need to decide how to proceed. In the meantime, this room is your responsibility."

I wanted to be tactful but couldn't quite find the right words. "In that case, we need to do something about the working environment. The Reservations room looks like a dungeon. Perhaps an exaggeration, but renovations are definitely needed." I crossed my fingers and hoped I hadn't gone too far.

"What do you mean?" asked Sain. Dedare gestured at me to answer.

"The room is dark and dreary. At a minimum, the wall between Reservations and the front desk should be changed to be mostly windows. More light is needed for the staff, and I think gazing at a working hotel would improve morale. And the walls are painted in drab colors—a most cheerless working environment."

Dedare looked at Sain, and then said, "Excellent idea. We will start on the renovations tomorrow. What else?"

"I believe the staff in your Reservations room would also benefit from time on the hotel's front desk. They'd gain experience dealing with guests person to person, not only on the com."

Dedare smiled. "Well thought out. I will talk to Tareera. She will need to coordinate schedules with you since you do the schedules for the Reservations room."

He stared at me for a long moment. "Tell me about the problem with Mama A."

What approach should I take? The truth was probably best. "Tareera decided Mom was a guest and should not have access to many areas of the hotel. I explained the situation and Tareera backed off. She really doesn't seem to want any Martians on Irion and is being reticent with information. That's as tactful as I can be, Dedare."

"Do not worry. I understand Tareera and will speak with her." Dedare recognized my skepticism. "If you have further problems with my wife's sister, let me know," said Dedare.

For some reason, his reassurance made me uneasy. Were family dynamics different on Irion? Mom needed a hint about this new research topic. "Dedare, is there anything you wish to discuss?" What did he think about my first day?

"More items?" he countered, instead of answering my question.

In for a penny, in for a pound. And I needed to stop using my mother's expressions—they always caused trouble on translation. At least this time, I'd only thought the words. "One more. This lounge is not busy."

"Never popular," said Dedare.

"May I make suggestions to increase its attractiveness?" Too much for one day?

"Of course," said Dedare, and Sain sat up straighter. My creative juices kicked in. "Let's consider exotic, and transform the lounge into one you'd find on Mars. We want curious Irions."

"Interesting," said Dedare. "How?"

"Starting with a new name. What do you think about *The MarsLight Lounge*?"

Dedare smiled. "Excellent. What else?" Sain entered information into his com during our conversation.

"Renovations that include lots of lights, blue probably, and stars on the ceiling. We need music. The room should vibrate—this is way too quiet. The music should probably be Irion, but we could throw in some Martian music, occasionally. Maybe Reena could help choose music for a younger crowd. And we should have a lounge menu with some Martian-like items adapted to Irion tastes. Also, do you have competitions like sports? And electronics to play those recordings on? Stuff like that. What do you think?" I babbled.

Again Sain and Dedare exchanged glances, but for a longer time than previously. I'd probably overwhelmed them. How much could they understand in one burst of enthusiasm?

"I think you are extremely creative, Syl. I am glad I convinced you to come to Irion. Your ideas are wonderful," said Dedare.

We all smiled, and I relaxed. So far, I hadn't stepped over any boundaries.

"Sain is not only my security chief. He is also in charge of upgrades. I want the two of you to work together to make your suggested changes. We both agree the lounge would be improved and attract guests with these modifications."

Agreeing without words, as only relatives could. A

skill I'd like to gain.

"You two remain and have an initial discussion regarding priorities. I must take my leave. I have calls to make," said Dedare.

A pleasant and productive discussion with Sain ensued. He promised to put my suggestions into drawings, and we decided to meet tomorrow afternoon to discuss his ideas on implementation.

"I have other issues to discuss, but they can wait. You look tired," said Sain.

"An eventful first day. Yes, I do need a good rest. I have an early start tomorrow."

"Let us leave."

We took the elevator up to the top floor. Sain waited while I opened my door, then I turned back to say goodnight. He rubbed my right cheek. His action surprised me—perhaps Reena would offer some enlightenment.

"Goodnight Sain. We'll meet tomorrow."

He nodded then walked across the hall to his home.

I started to turn back to my door, but noticed Sweety had popped out of Hart's room.

"Smooching already?" she asked.

"What do you mean?" Too tired, my brain wouldn't decipher her words.

"Rubbing a cheek is an Irion way of kissing," said Sweety.

"How do you know?" Her statement annoyed me, for some reason. "Sain probably just wanted to know how human skin felt."

"I find out things, and that was definitely a smooch," replied Sweety.

"Apparently, since you've already found Hart's

room." I sighed. "Sorry, sorry, Sweety. I've had a long day, and what you and Hart do is none of my business. You're both my best friends, and I think I'll just shut up." My head hurt.

"You're forgiven, Syl. Your day must have been stressful."

"Agreed. However, I want you to know I appreciate you dealing with Chef. Branson is happy, so every other Martian will be."

"Oh, Chef is a softy. Now, you be careful with the Irions. Kissing on the second day on a new planet is such a first, even for you."

Sweety walked away while I stared after her. She entered the elevator and I still stared. I needed a good night's sleep. With all the thoughts running through my brain, I had no expectation of success.

## Chapter Thirteen

Contrary to last night's apprehension, I had a great night's sleep. I awoke refreshed and eager to learn more about this world—my new home. I grabbed toast and canned fruit from my tiny kitchen to sustain me through the morning until I could sample one of Sweety's new lunch recipes.

The front desk staff greeted me in a bright and cheerful manner. Well, maybe not Tareera, but I ignored her scowl. I settled in my office, and stared at my computer until Hart showed up around seven. Although Irion had approximately the same length of day as Mars, they broke their day into more hours, but we coped with the conversion.

"Hart, this computer stymies me. Even with my limited knowledge, I understand why you, who have much more knowledge than I, were confused yesterday."

"Uncertain might be a better word," said Hart. "I just needed a nudge in the right direction, and Reena helped."

Guys would never let on they didn't know mostly everything. Oh, well, I hadn't expected any change in that foible, even on a different world.

"Yes, Reena's quite helpful." I studied at Hart. "Now, we need to work on menus for the restaurant, but first show me again how to work the reservations' software, please."

Actual mastery of the reservations' software would come with practice, but after a short refresher, my comfort level rose. However, designing the bilingual menu proved a challenge for both of us.

"We can't finish the design until we find out what Martian items the restaurant can create," complained Hart. "We need to know which categories they fall under. You know, appetizers, entrees, and such. And we need to get a better understanding of the Irion food items."

"You're right." So I called Sweety. "Do you have time to help Hart and me design a menu? We're missing a lot of information, and I think your help would be invaluable."

"Of course. I'd love to. But let me grab a bite to eat from the restaurant and I'll be at your office shortly."

I'd forgotten she didn't have a kitchen in her room and relied on the hotel's services. Perhaps her room needed an upgrade.

Hart and I fiddled with menu design while we waited.

"Did you know they don't have take-out boxes? So I couldn't really bring my breakfast here," said Sweety, after breezing into my office. "Something to think about, Syl. Now what's the problem?"

"Dedare sent me a list of the Martian foods he brought along, but I have no clue which dishes Chef's going to make," I replied. "So we don't know what to add to our new menu." I sighed, "I do have guesses based on what we've eaten so far, but I'm no cook."

"No, you're not," said Sweety. "You have many other fine qualities, though. Who else would be offered the chance to manage an alien hotel?" She grinned. "Now, show me Dedare's list of foods. I need an idea of what we're working with."

Sweety hummed as she read the printout I handed her. "Okay, this is what we need to do. Hart and I will visit Chef, or whichever of his assistants is available this time of day. We'll work to create numerous Martian menu choices, and Hart will take pictures of them, and of course sample everything."

Hart beamed. He loved to eat as much as I did.

"And I'll investigate the machines in the kitchen while I'm waiting to give my opinion on the food," said Hart.

"Sweety, you're fantastic! Pictures are a great idea. We'll need them for the Irion items, too—to spruce up the menu." I thought for a moment. "Don't try and create every Martian recipe in one day—just a sample for all three meals. We'll create a temporary printed menu each day, until we reach a final version." I paused for a moment, and then asked, "Sweety, do you think you'll be able to help us for a few days? I don't want to interfere with your sightseeing."

"Being a tourist can wait. This is an interesting challenge and I'll have good company," said Sweety. "And since I'll be learning about Irion, it's almost like being a tourist."

The tips of Hart's ears glowed, but I decided tact was in order. "You have no idea how much I appreciate your help. As much as I'd like to do everything myself, I'm not superwoman."

"No problem. Everyone knows how much you like your new position, however overwhelmed you'll feel—especially, for the first little while," said Sweety.

"You got that right." I sighed. I'd known I'd be challenged, but I hadn't realized the depth of my lack of knowledge.

"Well, Hart and I need to go to the kitchen. We need a few recipes to add to your dinner menu for tonight." Sweety grabbed Hart's hand and dragged him off, all the while waving goodbye to me.

No reluctance on Hart's part I observed. I turned back to the reservations program on my computer; it sorely needed further study.

A noise at my door broke my reverie. I walked over and pulled it open. "Siska, come in, please. I really must leave my door open, so I know when someone's arrived."

"Did the chime not sound?" she asked.

"I just heard a little noise." I watched Siska put her hand on a knob at the side of the door. A faint tinkle tested my hearing limits.

"Should be louder," said Siska. "Maintenance." She made a quick call in a low voice, but her words were beyond the hearing of my translator. "Fixed soon. I am here for our meeting."

"Of course." I returned to my desk, and Siska sat in the chair on the opposite side. "Have you thought about discussion topics?"

"Yes," she replied, in a cheerful voice.

"Before we start, I'd like to tell you something. Dedare and I've discussed the motto of my previous hotel. Essentially the hotel will provide everything any guest asked for, and if we can't, their stay would be free. Of course, we will have restrictions."

"People like free things, any way they can," said Siska, grinning at me.

Apparently, some traits didn't apply only to humans. "You understand, that's great! Somehow we want to implement the motto in this hotel. Do you have any ideas? Specifically in regards to Amenities, of course."

"Interesting question." Siska took out her hand computer. "I have a list. I will send it to you."

"Is this list appropriate to supply any requests a guest may have?"

She nodded. "Yes. You should receive the information soon."

"What does the list entail?"

"Possible things guests could ask for in Amenities—forgotten when packing. Also many tourist items. And ones we do not yet carry."

"Now, that's exactly what's going to help us implement the policy. Of course, Dedare and I are keeping this a little hush-hush, for the moment."

"Hush-hush? This does not translate."

I mentally smacked myself. I needed to talk to Hart about updates to the universal translator; if it was even possible. "Hush-hush means we're not letting the policy become general knowledge. We want to figure out the implementation first."

"Sensible. Like my list?" Siska squirmed in her chair.

"Let me look." I spent a couple of minutes on my com. "Excellent work, Siska. This is exactly what I need." Thinking for a moment, I then asked, "How do you order product for Amenities?"

"I send a list of current requirements to the hotel nimble. After a short time, I receive the items."

Nimble, of course. "Okay, this time send your

whole list to the nimble—not only the items you normally order, but also the ones you think we should add to anticipate guest needs." I thought for a moment. "Now we need to figure out the Martian items required. You start a new list, and I'll add updates. How does that sound?"

"Excellent plan. Send a list soon." Siska stood and then came around my desk. She put her hand on my forehead. "Thank you for being considerate."

I didn't know how to respond. However, before I had a chance to make a fool of myself, Siska left. I really needed to understand Irions, and sooner rather than later. To be fair, I hadn't been here long, but I decided my previous experience with Dedare and Coline on Mars had made me expect Irions would react much like Martians. Perhaps Dedare had adapted to our lifestyle and skewed my perception. None-the-less, my Irion knowledge needed to be kicked up a notch. Restless, I pedaled out of my office, without a clear purpose in mind.

Noticing Simon, the general manager of my old hotel, talking to Tareera at the front desk raised a few questions in my mind.

"How're you Simon?" I asked. Before he had a chance to respond, I said, "Thank you, Tareera. I'll chat with Simon in my office." I pointed to my door, giving Simon little choice but to follow. I ushered him in and glanced back at the front desk. Tareera glowered and stared at me. No surprises there.

"Simon, how's your stay been so far? Are you enjoying our facility?" A strange feeling of superiority emerged—a notion I needed to study, at a later time.

"An adequate hotel. The restaurant menu doesn't

accommodate Martians, but my room is comfortable. Currently, I'm taking in some of the highlights and culture of Satre." Simon studied my office. I had no idea why.

"Excellent. Chef is creating more Martian recipes, so the restaurant menu will continue to grow. As for Irion culture, I envy you. Until I have some time off, I can't engage in any sightseeing." I really did want to learn about Irion culture; the knowledge would help me run the hotel.

The big question being why was he really here? "How long are you staying on Irion?"

"A couple of months. This is a working holiday. Some of my visit time is personal, some work related."

"Well, if you have any problems, please don't hesitate to contact me." I stood, and Simon got my message and took his leave. His previous attitude, on Mars, still annoyed me, but I needed to let go of my anger. No longer his employee, I had my own life to live.

I gathered my thoughts and decided the time had arrived to tackle the Reservations room. After I stepped inside and glanced around, I found Sain measuring and taking pictures. I don't think he'd told the staff about our plan, since I thought I detected some apprehension. My reading of the situation may have been wrong, though.

So, to do my job, I stood at the front of the room, and motioned everyone forward. "Is it possible to switch your incoming communications to voice mail for a few moments?" I asked, as they gradually approached.

A female Irion, at the front of the group, said,

"Yes."

"Please do so. I'll be quick with my information, so you can get back to work and keep our guests happy." Soon she rejoined the group clustered about me.

"I'm sorry I haven't spoken with everyone yet, but this is only my second day on the job. My name is Sylvestine Amera, and I'm the new manager for the Sath-Satre Golden Hotel. As you can imagine, a staff this large is overwhelming." I sensed a receptive mood. "I want a quiet conversation with each of you, but it may take a few days to accomplish. In the meantime, we're implementing a few small changes. You've noticed Sain taking measurements and pictures, I'm sure." I waved at Sain. I don't know if I amused him, but the Reservations room staff smiled.

"I suggested to Dedare, the owner of this hotel, this room was too dark and enclosed. So Sain will be arranging to renovate this outer wall and install windows, so you can watch the running of the hotel. Does everyone understand what I mean?" A few heads nodded.

An Irion stepped forward. "I am Miseena; supervisor of this watch."

Interesting choice of words. "Do you understand what will happen?"

"Excellent idea. Better is we turn our positions to face the new windows," said Miseena. "I do not think the activity outside will distract."

"Good idea. And the guests will see how busy you are. Any other ideas?" I asked.

I glanced at the employees. Miseena moved her head. I took her action as a no, since no one had responded.

"I'm sure, though, you will have many in the future. Please feel free to discuss innovations and let me know your thoughts." I paused, and then added, "As a further idea, the walls are terribly drab. As a non-Irion, I don't know what pictures, posters, or other adornments you have or like, but I'm sure you can create an interesting and cheerful Reservations room."

Time would tell what my suggestions might inspire.

Then I took the plunge. "I'd like to offer another suggestion, but no one is bound by it. Reservations staff—in this room—would benefit by taking a turn on the Reservations front desk." I pointed outside, but they understood my gesture. "Face-to-face experience is excellent training."

Before anyone had a chance to respond to my suggestion, I asked, "Now, who helps me with scheduling? Remember, I'm learning everything," My statement received a few laughs.

"I do," said Miseena.

I smiled. "What I need to find out is who would also like to work on the front desk. If you would talk to everyone, that'd be great. Remember, working on the front desk is not a requirement of employment. When you have the appropriate details, you and I will need to coordinate scheduling with Tareera, as she's in charge of the front desk."

Miseena gave a slight bow. "I will do this. I would like to say these are positive steps."

The room's atmosphere did have energy. I waved my arms about. "If anyone has questions, please visit me. Thanks everyone. You know where my office is." I scooted out the door and back to my office; I needed alone time to think and process this recent encounter.

Hart and Sweety arrived to interrupt my thoughts. "Syl, we're here to work on the menu. We'll need your computer, of course" said Hart.

"Great. I need a break anyway," I said, and stood. "Sweety, did you teach Chef more recipes?"

"Actually his assistant, but the knowledge will be passed along, I'm sure. I'll work on further recipes tomorrow—only so much can be learned in one day. We overwhelmed the poor cook, as it was."

I laughed. The vision of a young Irion bedazzled by Sweety, and then throwing up his hands, amused me.

"Agreed. That's why Hart's printing a temporary menu. We'll need to reprint each time you get creative with the kitchen. I imagine the next few days, maybe weeks, will be intense, for all of us. You don't mind helping, do you?" I kept asking Sweety this question—my guilt on interrupting her holiday weighed on my mind.

"Not at all. However, right now, I'm out of here. I have touristy things to do." She glanced behind her. "Dinner, Hart?" A little pink-faced, he nodded. "See you guys later," said Sweety, as she swept out of my office.

"Syl, this should only take me a few minutes to format and print. Would you take care of getting them to the restaurant? I need to visit one of Dedare's factories today."

"Thanks for doing this, Hart. A few more times might be necessary, though. We need to produce an interesting menu for Martians and Irions alike. We want customers to flock to the restaurant."

"Sure, of course. I could teach you how to

assemble everything; it's not hard. Even a technophobe like you could master the steps."

Hart always made me smile. "Let's start tomorrow on erasing my issues. I'm kind of busy today—my second day."

We both laughed. Hart left and I went out to the front desk. A couple of Irions waited to book a room but no problems were evident.

After a moment of thought, I knew what my next step needed to be. I popped into Amenities. "Siska, are you busy?"

"Not much." She sat at a side desk sorting papers.

"Would you mind showing me around more of the hotel? I've seen the kitchen, restaurant, all the room types, but I need to see more."

"Where?" she asked, studying me.

"Do you have exercise facilities in the hotel?" I had no idea why that notion popped into my mind.

"No. Irions exercise at home." Confusion spread across her face.

Had I stepped into a taboo subject? Had Dedare and Coline used our facilities on Mars? "I'd like to see Housekeeping. A very important part of any hotel." What next? "Do you have hotel tour guides?"

"I do not know *tour guide*."

"A tour guide is someone who accompanies guests to tourist sites and cultural activities. They spend time with the guests and introduce them to areas they could explore further."

Siska made a negative motion. Finding out completely how Irion hotels were run would be a major challenge, I decided. "Okay, let's start with Housekeeping."

So we took off to Housekeeping, after stopping at the restaurant and delivering the latest menus. In addition to Housekeeping, we went to Recycling, Laundry, and Maintenance.

Three of the areas held no surprises, but not so much Recycling. Apparently, the Sath-Satre Golden Hotel recycled one hundred percent. Nothing left the hotel that hadn't been processed into a useful item, or organized for future processing. Food waste was composted for the gardens—they had machines that accelerated the process—everything else went into a special large bin, except for the bones.

Mars hadn't yet developed complete recycling, so I needed Hart to investigate—especially since the explanation I'd received of what happened to the large bin entirely confused me.

Finally, we arrived back at the front desk. While Siska and I discussed what I'd encountered, Dedare appeared. He greeted both of us. "Lunch, Syl?"

"Yes, I'm starving." I turned to Siska. "Thanks for all your help."

"I enjoyed our excursion," said Siska. "If you wish to visit other areas, let me know."

Dedare glanced at both of us, weighing our exchange and then he gestured in the direction of the restaurant. After we settled in our seats, I noticed the updated menus. Dedare grabbed one and studied the changes.

"The menu is clear and concise," said Dedare. "The Martians will be able to figure out what to order, and the pictures will help Irions, also."

"A temporary version. Hart and Sweety will be working on the menu for the next few days, as Sweety teaches your kitchen staff more Martian recipes." Sweety already had some of my favorites on the menu. "By the way, perhaps you should offer Sweety a job in the hotel. She's spending lots of her own time in the kitchen."

Dedare looked through the new menu again before he answered. "Yes, her culinary teaching is helpful. What else would she do?"

"She may not want a full time job as she's here as a tourist but, after her kitchen experience has finished, maybe a hostess in the restaurant—part days, of course."

Hostess turned out to be another topic I needed to explain.

"An excellent position for Sweety. She is sociable," said Dedare. "A greeter is not something we normally employ, so Irions would consider her exotic."

I took a deep breath. "Dedare, I'm making a lot of suggestions for change. Are you all right with this? Or do you want me to accept the Irion way?"

"If I did not like your ideas, I would not agree. You are refreshing for everyone, but especially the hotel. The changes should bring in curious guests."

I relaxed a little. We ordered, as the waiter hovered.

"Syl, a few complaints," said Dedare, while we waited for our meals.

"About what?" I didn't like the word *complaint* after only two days as hotel manager.

"Most are already fixed. For example, a Martian complained about no proper menu. I explained you had arrived at the same time as he, and you had scurried—a good word—to create one for tonight. You beat my expectations," Dedare said, pointing at our new menu.

"Good. I'm trying to be proactive, but this hotel is a bit alien." I laughed. I thought I was funny. "Time is required to dig out the potential problem spots for an interspecies hotel."

"I understand. That is why I hired you as manager; I saw potential in your abilities."

His words pleased me, more than I'd expected. "Thank you. I do have other topics to discuss, but let's leave them for later this evening. I need time for further research. Any other complaints I need to address right now?" I hoped not.

"One. Reservations are missing. Tareera says you erased them."

Tareera lived up to my expectations. "I suppose I could've deleted them, but why would I? We need guests."

"Do not worry. I am having this issue looked into. However, I wanted you to know the situation existed. The information may help you deal with Tareera."

"Thank you for telling me," I responded. Our lunches arrived and we attacked them—or at least I did. So far today, my body had consumed a lot of energy.

"What have you been busy with this morning?" I asked.

"Buying. I like buildings and factories," said Dedare.

He amused me in so many ways. "More hotels?"

"No. Not on Irion, but perhaps on other planets in the future."

"Tell me about some of your non-hotel holdings." I listened in fascination while we ate. Dedare had quite eclectic interests. In addition to hotels and manufacturing facilities, he apparently had an interest in spiritual topics and animal husbandry.

As I was about to question him about those topics, I glanced up. Dedare's brother stood in the restaurant doorway. "Must be time for my meeting with Sain. I'd better run."

"Talk later," said Dedare.

"My office?" I suggested to Sain.

"We need your big table to lay out these plans," he agreed. His arms were full.

After I'd seen my office for the first time, I'd had no idea what I'd need with a big conference table, but I was about to find out.

Sain plunked down a pile of big sheets of paper, or the Irion equivalent. He rummaged through them and found the one he wanted. "Reservations room. Please advise if this meets your expectations."

I saw inside and outside views. The wall facing the front desk now had windows, and the work desks had been turned to face the new light source. "This looks great. Fast work, Sain. The staff will be able to glance outside, and the guests will be able to view Reservations. Exactly what I had in mind."

Sain touched my hand. I decided he was pleased with my comments. "The lounge is more difficult. Some of your concepts I do not understand."

"Let me see what you have." Perhaps an Irion-Martian miscommunication.

Sain pulled out another blueprint, for want of a better word, and spread it on top of the other papers.

I poured over the diagram but the drawing perplexed me. "Sain, what is this?"

"This is a drawing of the lounge with your

requested changes." He pointed out a few areas.

Then I realized their version of a blueprint-type drawing was not what I'd expected, or ever experienced. They incorporated three-dimensional figures and objects and somehow, four dimensional ideas—how the lounge would look as the day wore on—at least, that's what I thought the sheet tried to portray. Confused, I asked, "Sain, what is—"

My doorbell rang much louder than previously. Siska had obviously motivated Maintenance. "Come in," I called out.

Reena walked through the doorway and gave us a bright smile. "Hello, Manager Syl, are you busy?"

"Hi, Reena. Your uncle and I are going over changes to the lounge. Please join us." I pointed at the conference table.

She walked over and studied the top drawing.

"Sain, perhaps you'd explain the proposed changes to Reena. I'd like her help with our design because we want to make the lounge a place for younger people too." I contemplated Reena's age. "Perhaps not as young, but Reena will have wonderful ideas, anyway." I didn't know who was more pleased with my statement.

Before Sain had a chance to speak, I asked, "You aren't skipping school, Reena?"

"No," she said, adding a laugh. "My off-school project this afternoon involved hotels, and my father owns many. So I was not required to participate."

I smiled and gestured at Sain.

"We are going to transform the lounge into a room called The MarsLight Agora—with a Martian theme," said Sain.

"What does Agora mean?" I asked. The word was new to me, and I had no help from my translator.

"Lounge. We want Irions to understand the function of the room," said Sain.

I nodded. "An excellent idea using the word Agora, and MarsLight will indicate the alienness." I glanced at the blueprint again. "Sain, what changes are you proposing from my initial suggestions? Some I recognize, but please start from the beginning for Reena."

"We are going to make the walls red and sparkly. My image of Mars," stated Sain.

"Then the tables and chairs should match," said Reena. "And pictures of Mars on the walls should increase interest."

"How about we rename the menu items, even the Irion ones, to reflect something about Mars?" I asked.

"Menu?" asked Reena.

"Well, we need a menu. Customers need to know what food and drink is available. How do they know what to order?"

"Standard," said Sain.

"That's about to change. Nothing is standard when we need to include aliens." Sweety and Hart's workload had just increased. "We can make the menu all Marsy, to increase Irion interest in the Lounge."

"Marsy?" asked Reena.

"What I meant was the items on the menu could be named after places and things on Mars. With these tidbits, Irions may become more interested in going to Mars. Dedare would like that," I said. "More tourists to transport."

Reena clapped her hands. "Yes, Father would be

happy. What else do we need to discuss?"

"We need music, particularly live music, in the lounge. Is this possible?"

"We have music," said Reena. "Not Martian music."

"I don't think that's necessary. Irions may misunderstand and there aren't many Martians here anyway. Do Irions have different kinds of music?"

"Many," said Sain.

"Perhaps the MarsLight Agora could feature a different type each day. Would it be appropriate to have one of the corners of the lounge dedicated to musicians? Perhaps a stage?"

"Think," said Sain, scribbling on his drawing.

"Why don't you two talk to Dedare? Hiring musicians for the lounge would involve further expense. You should be able to explain the concept to him better than I."

"Manager Syl, I mean Syl, many good ideas. I am so glad you are here," said Reena. She ran around my conference table and put her hands around my waist. I looked at Sain. He gestured to reciprocate—at least that's what I thought he meant—so I did. Reena didn't complain, just squeezed harder.

"Reena, perhaps you would assist Siska. She helped me out today, so she may be behind in her Amenities work. Only if you have no school work, of course," I added.

"Excellent," said Reena, "Later." She skipped out the door of my office.

"I can't keep up with her energy," I commented.

"A problem," said Sain. "But guardians manage. As for school teachers and hotel managers, I am sure they cope in their own ways."

I laughed. Sain was such a character. "Agreed. Do you have enough information to update your drawings?" I asked.

"Yes. Many items to discuss with Dedare. Will I see you this evening?"

Oh, oh. Perhaps Sweety's assessment regarding Sain would prove correct. And to confuse me further my body started to respond to his nearness. I shook my head to clear my emotions and senses. "Ah, I should be in the restaurant later for dinner. Perhaps then?"

Sain picked up his papers and left.

Before I had a chance to contemplate the situation with Sain, my doorbell rang. I decided the noise might just become annoying. "Please enter," I called out, shelving my irritation.

Miseena came in holding a sheaf of paper. "Time for scheduling?" she asked.

"Yes. Actually, this is a good time. Have you talked to all the Reservations room staff?"

"I made a few calls to those not on shift, but I now have answers as to who would like to work the front desk. Unanimous. Excellent idea."

"Great. Let me get Tareera, and the three of us can plan the coordinated schedules." Pleased with everyone's acceptance, I gestured for Miseena to sit at my conference table, and then I went outside. Tareera stood at the front counter, so I waved at her and she followed me into my office.

"Tareera, you know Miseena, of course." They made some kind of head motions. "I'm implementing a new procedure. Those of the Reservations room staff, that wish to do so, will be taking shifts on the front counter. Therefore, the three of us need to cooperate on scheduling the two areas. Tareera, please print off your current schedule from my computer, then we can get to work devising a new coordinated schedule."

I sat at my conference table beside Miseena, but Tareera continued to stand.

"I do not like this concept," she said. "Reservations staff do not need to be on front desk."

"Now they do. The experience will be positive for everyone involved. I'm sure your staff will love to join the Reservations room and talk to people from many places." If the Reservations room was any indication, the front desk staff would reciprocate wholeheartedly.

"No," Tareera said, and stormed out without a backward glance.

"Well, that was difficult," I said, after studying her retreating figure. Perhaps I wasn't the manager I thought I was.

"Difficult," agreed Miseena. "When Tareera agrees, we can schedule again." She studied me. "Manager Syl, some of her staff may not want to join the Reservations room."

"Perhaps not but we must give everyone the option, Miseena. An excellent experience."

She patted my head and left.

What a day! Had I said something to offend Tareera? Miseena would've informed me, I was sure. Oh well, I'd discuss the situation with Dedare later.

Before I had a chance to start a new project, my com rang. "Sylvestine, I need you to come to the Martian embassy," said Charles.

"Whatever for? I'm pretty busy." My problems were piling up and I didn't need another. "Is this about immigration again?"

"No. This involves you and your mother," said the ambassador.

My mother? Alarm bells rang. "Okay, I'm on my way." My head hurt. "What's going on, and where's the Martian embassy?" Not terribly coherent or logical thoughts.

Charles spewed out directions, but didn't answer my question about the situation. I decided I needed to tell someone where I'd be. Who should I inform? Siska popped into my mind and so I spoke with her. I needed to look into the chain of command—perhaps an assistant hotel manager would prove beneficial.

My walk to the new Martian embassy, located only a short block away, did not release any tension in my shoulders. They were the bane of existence, and in times of stress, I looked and felt like a hunchbacked senior with shoulders up to her ears. Following the ambassador's instructions, I proceeded to the third floor and Charles' assistant led me into the ambassador's office. Charles stood at my entrance, and then returned to his desk. I found my mother sitting on a couch, so I sat beside her.

"Mom, what's wrong? Are we being deported?" She shook her head, clearly upset. Evidence of tears graced her face—most unlike Mama A.

Charles cleared his throat. "Sylvestine, your mother and I have information to impart you may find upsetting. Do you wish anyone else to be present for emotional support?"

"Mom's here. Who else would I need?" My confusion grew.

"This is a difficult situation. Your mother and I

have been acquaintances for a long time," said Charles.

"Really? Then why didn't I know about you until recently?" I swiveled my gaze back and forth between them.

"My words were badly spoken. I knew your mother decades ago. We were close. Then I got transferred to Earth, and we parted company," said Charles.

"So?" His statements didn't enlighten me.

Charles sighed. "I just found out—from your mother—that our previous relationship produced a child."

"I'm happy for you, but what does this have to do with me?" Charles had a relationship with Mom? Well, their dating was news to me, but I hadn't expected my mother to be celibate forever after my birth—or was it before my birth? Anyway, not a topic I liked to dwell on—no offspring did, I imagined.

I glanced over at Mom and saw more tears. Then the light dawned. "You're my father?" The bees in my head were having a field day.

I turned to Mom. She nodded; her eyes glistened, but she didn't speak.

"You never told me," I said.

"I never expected to see Charles again. He'd gone back to Earth—to stay, I thought. And you never seemed to want to know about your father. You asked once, but only once."

"You have no idea the thoughts that have gone through my mind over the last many years." I looked at her. "I thought you wanted to hide the identity of my father, for some reason. Sometimes you act very strangely, Mom."

"I know, I know. I blame my artistic nature." A

164

tentative smile graced her face. She really was a sweetheart.

After taking a long look at Charles, I stood. "I need to do some thinking; I'm not good with personal surprises."

Mom also stood and held out her arms. I did hug her, but not very enthusiastically.

Charles left his chair and came around his desk.

"Fortunately, or unfortunately, I have a lot to digest. Your hug will probably come later," I said to him, and exited the embassy with a distinct lack of grace.

Chapter Fourteen

"I have a headache. I'll be in my rooms," I spewed as I passed the front desk. "Call me if you need me." The trip back from the Martian embassy had not cleared my mind.

Sitting in my living room, I stared at a blank wall. I'd received a huge shock, and my mind found the situation slippery, to say the least.

Sometime later I heard a knock. I trudged over and opened my door to Sweety and Hart.

"We need to talk," said Sweety, rubbing her arms and glancing at Hart.

"Not now. Maybe later." My tight chest made me want to hide from the world.

"You've been alone for two hours. Now you really do need to talk," said Hart.

My watch confirmed the time lapse. "I needed to think about things," I said, somewhat sullenly.

"Yes, you did—no question," said Sweety. "We ran into Mama A, and she told us about the, ah, ah, situation. You need to talk to her, Syl, she's hurting."

"I know, but it's not easy suddenly having a father, and at my advanced age." The stress of a new family relationship on top of the stress of a new job on a new world had definitely taken a physical toll today—I had no energy to spare for idle conversation.

Sweety grabbed my shoulders and spun me around.

"Let's sit down," she said. "I'm getting sore feet standing out here. After all, I spent a good deal of time on my feet today doing all that cooking."

I gestured them in. I didn't want company, but I couldn't turn my best friends away. "What I need is a drink," I said, after we settled in my living room.

Then my doorbell rang. Who else wanted to bother me?

"I think one of your problems is now solved," said a grinning Sweety.

Sometimes she made the strangest pronouncements. Answering the door, I found two of the concierge staff each carrying a crate.

"Manager Syl, Dedare would like you to have these. May we put them inside?"

"Ah, of course." What had Dedare sent? I stepped back to let them enter.

Sweety popped up and gave something to each of the guys after they deposited the crates in my tiny kitchen. They thanked her and left.

"What's this?" I asked. "What did you give them, Sweety?"

"*This* should be a couple crates of wine, and I gave those cute guys a little tip," said Sweety.

"Wine? I needed some, but how did Dedare know?"

Neither Sweety nor Hart responded.

I glowered at them. "You told him about the situation, didn't you, before you came up here?"

"We may have mentioned we were going to see you," said Hart. "Dedare was concerned you weren't feeling well."

Dedare did have a considerate soul, albeit an alien

one.

"Okay, okay, I give in. Somebody pour me a glass." I shook my head, "I really did have a headache, but it's easing. You guys are the best, and so is Dedare."

Sweety and I sat, while Hart arranged the glasses of wine. Sweety made us clink glasses, but I wasn't exactly sure of her reasoning.

"Syl, this is difficult, but I do think discussing the situation might help you understand," said Sweety.

"I have no idea what to discuss. I now have a name for my biological father—obviously, someone donated—but Mom never offered any details. Today, she insisted I never wanted to know anything."

*Donated* didn't sit well with Hart, but Sweety laughed. "I think more than donation was involved," she said, "at least that's the indication I received from Mama A."

"What? What do you mean?" I asked. Sweety obviously knew more than I did about my current crisis.

"Well, your mother blushed and muttered something neither of us could hear," said Sweety, while Hart gazed around my living room, ignoring our conversation.

"All I understand, Sweety, is she and Charles had a fling decades ago, then he went to Earth to be an ambassador. Mom didn't figure she'd ever see him again."

"Makes sense. How could she tell you much about him when he left before you were born. I bet this shocks him, more than you—he never knew he had a child."

"Oh. I guess you're right, but I wouldn't give him a

hug. I gave Mom one when I left the Martian embassy, but I couldn't think. I mean I really couldn't think—my head buzzed with angry bees." Why did I call them angry?

"Shock and stress," said Sweety. "Now drink up. We promised Mama A we'd bring you down for dinner. Food conquers all—especially my recipes!"

I managed a weak laugh. "Okay, I'll go to dinner, however awkward the meal may turn out, but I'd like to finish this glass and perhaps another before we go down."

Sweety gave me a knowing glance.

"I really was churlish, I guess you'd call it, to Charles, and now I feel bad. I don't know how to handle my situation." Shocked, I thought out loud, "Maybe I have a step-mother, step-siblings?"

"Would that be such a bad thing? Anyway, you're full of common sense. You'll figure out how to handle things." She leaned over and hugged me. "As for wine, two glasses is nothing for either one of us. I don't know about Hart, but he can be our designated driver, err, I mean, walker."

Hart shook his head and declined to comment.

Sweety always cheered me up. What she saw in a non-socialite like me, I had no idea. None-the-less, I loved her dearly. So we ignored today's revelation, and chatted about various hotel staff and other Irions we'd encountered in our wanderings. Hart listened to us babble and finally suggested dinner.

I didn't argue. I knew I had to face everyone, eventually. There'd be no hiding from the world.

In the restaurant, Mom, Dedare, Reena, and Sain populated our favorite table, and were half way through their meals. The three of us sat down and decided on our own dinners.

Dedare ordered Sweety and me a glass of wine. "Anyone else?"

"Yes, please," said my mother.

Sweety patted my shoulder, as if to say, "She's as stressed as you are."

Mom had probably never expected to encounter Charles again. What decisions she must've had to make on her own—before and after my birth. I stood and went around the table to her. "This must be as hard for you, as for me."

"Not trivial," Mom replied. The Martians laughed.

I hugged her and said, "We need a long discussion but not tonight. I'm tired and need to process my thoughts."

"I want all the details after you guys have your discussion," said Sweety.

"Daughterish person, be quiet," said my mother, blowing a kiss to Sweety. "I think it's time to start a novel," she added.

Laughter broke out from myself, Hart, Sweety, and my mother.

"Funny?" asked Dedare. Sain and Reena were perplexed, as well.

"A lot of humans, when dealing with emotional crises, like to write things down. This helps them understand their feelings," explained Sweety.

"And Mama A has started a lot of novels," said Hart. We glanced at her and tried not to laugh again.

"You are teasing," said Reena, "Is that correct?" Reena bobbled her head back and forth while we exchanged our quips.

"Tension is released by teasing. And I believe I explained Mama A and Syl's emotional crisis," said Dedare.

"Yes, you did, Father, but I do not understand. I will not comment further until I research," said Reena.

Dedare attempted to defuse the situation. "Sweety, various sources tell me you were helpful in my hotel today."

"I enjoyed dealing with Chef and his assistant. They had no idea how to prepare Martian food, and I love to cook, so teaching them was easy. And Chef is such a sweetheart."

"Invaluable instructions." Dedare massaged his forehead. "My error in overlooking this aspect of hotel management—a mistake to expect Irion chefs to understand alien food."

Dedare took a sip of his drink before continuing. "Sweety, a proposal."

I almost choked on my food, but Sweety bounced in her seat.

"After talking with Syl, I would like to offer half-day employment. I understand you wish to explore Irion, but I would like you to help us make this hotel comfortable for Martians. Mornings or afternoons, your choice. I would like you to continue to teach the kitchen, as I am sure Chef will appreciate your instructions. On the days when you are not busy creating recipes, and this is Syl's suggestion, we need a hostess for our lounge—which will be renovated soon—or was that a hostess for this restaurant?"

A confused Dedare glanced my way. I'd suggested too many changes in such a short time.

Before I had a chance to respond, Sweety said,

"From my explorations, both venues need a hostess. Syl, that's a great idea! I love being a hostess—so many people to meet and, now, aliens to boot. Dedare, I accept! I'll wander over to your office tomorrow, and we can discuss details."

Sweety touched her glass to Dedare's.

Ignoring my current confusion about life, I proclaimed, "Everyone, a toast to Dedare's newest employee!" We clinked glasses, and I beamed at Sweety.

Reena interrupted our congratulations. "Sylvia Amera, may I call you Mama A?"

"Of course, dear," said Mom. She collected children everywhere—even alien ones.

"I do not understand what your honorific means, but I will research. Manager Syl is your daughter?" she asked.

"Yes," said Mom, "as you are Dedare's daughter."

"Manager Syl has just discovered her father?"

Ah, teenagers. I jumped in. "Yes, you're correct. We should discuss this tomorrow at a more appropriate time. Perhaps we can meet for lunch?"

"But…" said Reena. After catching a glance from Dedare, she subsided.

"Dedare, a question," said Hart, diverting attention from Reena and me. "I went to one of your factories today, in my fact-finding mode as your scientific advisor, of course. I might be wrong, but I thought I saw bombs being made in the Scireif facility."

Dedare gazed at Hart, for a long moment. "Correct. We make bombs to outfit our spaceships."

"Why? What's the problem? Why do you need bombs?" asked Hart.

His question surprised me. Hart was usually the soul of tact.

"In the past, Irion came upon a hostile species. We did not have any defensive weapons and so our scout ships were destroyed. We are primarily explorers but, because of the incident, we decided our scouts needed protection."

"Sensible," said Hart. "How many exploration vessels do you have?"

"Our diplomats will be upset if I answer your question," said Dedare.

Hart understood Dedare's comment, and since diplomats were a sensitive subject with me, I didn't push for any explanation.

Reena asked, "May I ask another human question?"

She received nods from various people.

"Manager Syl, I think I understand your current situation. Why do you not accept your father?"

Sweety patted my shoulder to encourage me to breathe. "Reena, we'll discuss this at lunch tomorrow," I said. "Remember?"

"My apologies. I am sorry for bringing this up prematurely. I must leave, I have schoolwork to attend to—my guardians are sending me glances to remind me of such."

I wasn't convinced that was the information Dedare and Sain tried to convey. "I applaud them. Have a nice evening studying," I said. We watched Reena walk away. Such a sweetheart and such a teenager when it came to her emotions.

"I remember you as a teenager," said Mom. "In fact—"

"Not now, Mom," I interrupted. "I need to talk business. Shall we retire to the lounge, Dedare?"

"This location is appropriate," said Dedare. "All employees, so we can speak of business."

If that was what Dedare wanted, who was I to argue? My energy had been depleted anyway. "Okay. As some of you may have heard, we're combining the Reservations room and the Reservations front desk."

I glanced around our dinner table and saw a couple of confused people. "The Reservations room takes bookings for all of Dedare's hotels on Irion. The Reservations front desk helps people register for their room in this hotel and also make reservations for future stays. Tareera is in charge of the front desk." Weariness tugged at me. It'd certainly been a long day.

"Miseena, from the Reservations room, and I attempted to coordinate schedules with Tareera, but she refused. We have a problem."

"She complained to me this afternoon," said Dedare. "However, I believe your idea is excellent. Reservations will run smoother, on all levels. I have found a place for Tareera in another facility."

My relief astonished me. "Well, then we'll need another manager for the Reservations front desk."

"For the interim, you would be best, Syl, since you supervise all reservations areas. Try managing both for a few days. You will come to understand how to run the areas efficiently, and you will recognize how to delegate or rearrange the management flow," said Dedare.

Sweety topped up my glass, while I attempted to breathe. Dedare had just added a great deal of responsibility onto my plate.

Deflecting the attention I saw around our dinner table, I asked, "Has anyone discovered anything new today? New to Martians, I mean." I looked around the table. "Sweety, how about your tour? How was that?"

Before she had a chance to respond, one of the front desk staff approached our table. "Manager Syl, an alien wishes to register."

"You've dealt with Martians, you understand the procedures," I said, not too tactfully.

"Not Martian. Skuttem," the panicked Irion told me.

What kind of alien was a Skuttem? "Dedare, what's this? What haven't you told me?" I wanted to throw my hands up in disgust—managers needed warning.

"I am sorry. I did not expect a Skuttem so soon. Let us both deal with the situation."

"Okay, everyone, later," I said as I stood. Dedare and I left the restaurant and walked to the front desk.

A strange looking alien stood glaring at anyone he noticed. With four limbs, he approximated an Irion or Martian, but the yellowish-pink scales covering the visible parts of his body gave me a brief hiccup. Coarse black hair, about six inches long, streamed off his head, and a sleeveless floor length green cape covered the remainder of his body.

"Room, I need room," he spewed. A bit of spittle glistened in the air.

"Of course," I said. "What do you need?"

"Basic room," said the Skuttem, picking at his scales.

"Do you need a separate bedroom?" I asked, as I watched his less than pleasant physical movements.

"No." For some reason, the alien didn't look at us. He turned around and studied the lobby. His gaze wandered from the ceiling to the floor.

I hoped I hadn't misunderstood his request. The single staff at Reception, after all it was our dead time, alternated her stares between the Skuttem and me. "Please provide me with an available room," I said.

Soon I had a room key. The alien followed Dedare and myself to the elevator. He rubbed his hands over the shiny blue surface of the door.

"This is a means of getting to your room in a prompt manner," I explained. I hoped I'd correctly interpreted his facial expression.

"Short?" His eyes went from the elevator to me and then away again. The Skuttem had mastered skepticism.

"Extremely short," I answered. I hoped I'd interpreted *short* properly. Maybe he was calling me *short*—after all, he beat my height by about four inches.

The Skuttem followed us into the elevator and didn't move a muscle, as far as I could tell, while we moved upward. At the appropriate floor he exited without a word, and then he followed us down the hallway.

"This is your room; here is your key," I said. "Please try your door."

We watched while he used his key, then the three of us walked into the room. No electronic keys for the Sath-Satre Golden Hotel—something to discuss with Dedare and Sain, at a later time.

After a couple of moments of silence, while our new guest studied his room, we eventually heard, "Adequate. I will talk with you tomorrow regarding my dietary requests. Go. I need rest," said the Skuttem.

Dedare and I retreated, and the new alien shut the door in our faces.

"More dietary requests?" I asked when I finally had a chance to breathe.

"I am sure Sweety will accommodate. She is adaptable. Let us return to our rooms and rest. It has been a long day."

I couldn't argue. Fathers, mothers, what more would tomorrow bring on my out-of-this-world journey?

Outside my suite, Dedare paused. "May I enter?"

I nodded, and the two of us sat in my living room. Dedare beside me on my couch.

"Thank you for the wine. A glass or two makes my day manageable. You might want to transport more since I don't have time to make my own. I will pay you, of course."

"You make wine?" asked Dedare.

"Well, I made wine on Mars—kits of course. Much cheaper than buying bottles. I like to think wine keeps me young. Although, at this current time, I'm not feeling very spry." And I really wasn't.

"A long and challenging day," said Dedare. He took a moment, and then said, "Syl, I am happy with your progress. You have made our hotel guests content, and the management chain will begin to flow better. As the days pass, more will change, but understand I am most appreciative of your efforts and skill."

I relaxed for the first time today.

Dedare poured himself a glass of wine and took a sip. Then he commented, "Syl, I would like to stroke your face."

Surprised, I asked, "Why?" I had no idea how else

to respond.

"Fond of you, and a way of expressing my feelings," said Dedare.

I took a couple of deep breaths. "Sain touched my face last night."

"Yes, we discussed." Dedare softly rubbed my cheek.

After a moment, I had an urge to kiss the palm of his hand. I gazed into Dedare's sparkling eyes, and I decided my idea wasn't so bad.

Chapter Fifteen

Over my breakfast of toast and peanut butter, my thoughts turned to last night and how this alien world toyed with my emotions. Of course, a new *father* had tremendous impact. I had no idea how to deal with the concept of a father figure in my adult life. How much bonding time would Charles want? After all, I was no longer a child he needed to help raise. And then there was Dedare. How attracted to him was I becoming? I had to admit the notion of an alien lover intrigued me.

Enough with the emotions—I reminded myself I had a hotel to run.

Happy to see the initial Reservations room renovations proceeding, I walked through the door and searched for Miseena. Nowhere in my view, I asked the first non-busy staff.

"Miseena starts in one hour. She overlaps two shifts," said the young Irion.

"Would you send her to my office after she settles in? We have scheduling." I waved and left the room.

Outside the Reservations room, I stopped to speak with Sain. "This is a promising start." The wall had been enclosed on both sides to minimize dust and noise.

"The staff will soon have more light. The renovation will not take long. An excellent idea."

We both gazed at the progress. "Thank you, Sain. You may regret your compliment, though. I have more thoughts regarding changes." Ideas bubbled through my brain.

"Amusing, but not unexpected," he replied.

I wasn't sure what he meant by amusing, but I didn't pursue the topic. "If you need to discuss anything, we could get together this afternoon. I have a busy morning."

Sain nodded, patted my forehead, and left to talk with one of his workers.

Back at my office, I settled down to drink a cup of tea. Much to my delight, my office boasted the Irion equivalent of a tea kettle.

Still slurping my hot drink when Hart and Sweety appeared, I asked, "Are you guys joined at the hip?" I sighed and waved my hand around. "Never mind me. My life has overloaded my brain. What can I do for you?" I pointed to the chairs in front of my desk.

"Wrong question." Sweety grabbed a place to sit. "What can we do for you?"

"Right. Brain freeze." I picked up a copy of the restaurant menus. "Sorry, Sweety, but it appears our menus, for both the restaurant and the lounge, need to include a new alien species. A new guest, a Skuttem, arrived yesterday. Now, I have no clue whether Skuttem is a species name or an individual name, but I'm leaning toward species from what Dedare mentioned last night."

"Tricky—I don't know how to cook Skuttem," said Sweety. "I mean I have no idea what they eat."

I had to laugh at the idea of Sweety cooking the Skuttem—no matter had annoying he'd been.

"No Martian would. We've never even heard of the species. I agree it's a challenge, but I know you can charm this guy—and he needs a lot of charming. Why don't you get the front desk to call him and you can set up a meeting—perhaps in the kitchen?" I suggested.

"First thing I'm going to do is call Dedare and ask what Skuttem food is available. Let's hope he has something," said Sweety, "or you're going to have a very hungry and upset guest."

At that moment, I didn't think Dedare topped her friends list. "Yes, please do. I'm sure he's organized food for the Skuttem, as he did for us. In the meantime, I have questions for Hart."

Hart gazed after Sweety as she left my office. "Mars to Hart," I said. "Okay, perhaps Mars isn't particularly accurate."

"You need something?" Hart asked, in a testy voice.

I needed to stop teasing my unusually sensitive friend. "A couple of things. For your own interest, you might want to investigate Sain's renovations. I'm no expert, but their building technique appears different from what we'd do on Mars. I'd also like to know about the composition of the windows he's installing—I don't think they're glass."

"Interesting. Anything else?" Hart typed into his com.

I needed his attention. "Yes. Words are missing from my translator. I'm sure that's natural, but how do I update?" Perfect translation probably wasn't possible, but there had to be a way to add new words.

"That's simple enough." Hart went over to my computer and hooked up something. "This is an adaptor. Just press it to your arm where I gave you the injection, and the software will take over. My apologies, but I just received this new hardware this morning."

I pressed it to my upper arm, but I didn't feel a thing. "How do I know if the updates went through?"

"Say one of the missing words," said Hart.

"Hush-hush." Then I heard my computer say, "Updated."

I smiled. "Easy and helpful. My communications, especially since we have a new alien species, should progress in a smooth manner." I thought for a moment. "Actually, how was I able to talk to the Skuttem last night? He's the first I've encountered."

Hart said, "Dedare uploads rudimentary alien languages as soon as he receives any information. Perhaps each morning updating your translator should be a priority. That way you get a heads-up on surprises."

I nodded. It was useful information to have. "Anything else I should know about?"

"Not really. I'll give you a lesson or two in putting the menu together, but perhaps tomorrow would be best. I want another stab at it first. There may be some idiosyncrasies of Irion food that help shape the menu. Who knows? Anyway, I'd better catch up with Sweety and be a photographer. She's probably getting Chef in shape, and the new alien, of course."

"You're right. Sweety's efficient when she puts her mind to anything. I'll talk to you later. In the meantime, I'm meeting Reena for lunch, so I'd better not forget."

"Such a sweet teenager." Hart smiled. "I'd better look at Sain's renovations before I find Sweety—the updates sound interesting." He waved and went through my doorway, almost colliding with Miseena.

Hart's positive mood always improved mine.

"Manager Syl, you wanted to see me?" Miseena asked.

"Yes, I did. We have scheduling to work on but, before we start, I have a question. What do you think the staff should call me—Syl, or Manager Syl, or perhaps Ms. Amera, or even something I haven't thought of?" I had no idea how chain-of-command and status operated on Irion.

"Ma'am, you are most approachable so I do not think you want a serious title, but some authority is appropriate. Manager Syl suits you best. Familiar, yet a level above."

"Miseena, I've only been here a couple of days, but I've been called many names, and I've been called on to do many things. I've been feeling like a fish-out-of-water—which I am—but your suggestion is well thought out. We'll go with Manager Syl."

"Fish-out-of-water?"

Another update for my translator. "Not quite settled—not quite understanding everything in an unfamiliar environment." A massive understatement.

"Understanding will come with time. We have scheduling?" Miseena distracted me from my anxiety.

"Yes, of course. You may not have heard, but Tareera is no longer employed at this hotel. Dedare gave her another position in his empire, after she complained about me."

I swore Miseena tried to hide a smile.

"In the meantime, I'm in charge of anything to do with Reservations—Reservations room or front desk. You and I need to do the scheduling for both areas—at least for the interim."

Miseena gestured to my table. "Here?"

"Good idea. Would you print off the schedules for both areas from my computer? It's a little beyond me." I needed more instruction from Hart.

"Soon you will have no problem." Miseena spent a couple of minutes on my computer, and then we had our working data.

"Tomorrow, perhaps you could show me how to print off the schedules." I needed to study the difference between Irion and Mars. "However let's start scheduling. We don't want to fall behind." Optimizing the schedule occupied a good deal of our time.

"Are we done?" My head hurt from learning all the new staff names and the convoluted schedule an eight day cycle produced.

"Almost," said Miseena. "You mentioned having the front desk be included in the staff switch."

"Good question. Can I give you another job?" As the day had progressed, I'd been more and more impressed with Miseena.

"I am happy to help with reservations. If you asked me to help in another area, I might question your wisdom."

We both laughed. "Would you talk to everyone who works the front desk and determine if they also want to work in the Reservations room? They are under no obligation, of course. We'll add them when we next schedule," I said.

"I will do this," said Miseena. "Anything else you require? I should return to monitor our workload."

"I think we're finished. You've been a really great help today," I said. "Thank you for everything."

She smiled and gathered up the schedules we'd

worked on. After Miseena left, I glanced at my watch—the morning had flown. However, I had one more project before my lunch with Reena.

No guests gathered at the front desk. "I'm Manager Syl," I said to an Irion I hadn't seen before.

"I am happy to meet you. I am Trina," she replied, focusing on my face.

Quite a chipper person, most appropriate for her position. "I'm sorry, Trina, I haven't been able to meet everyone yet."

"You have much responsibility. We are happy you are here as manager. Everyone is talking about your changes."

Interesting. "In a good way, I hope?"

"Yes. Changes were needed. How may I help you?"

Such a customer service type of question from a friendly, cheerful face. "My question may be strange, but is there any kind of book or publication put in every room describing available guest services?" I asked.

"Do you mean the *xertl*?" asked Trina.

"I don't know." I shrugged. "Do you have one available?" Another word to add to the translator.

"Yes." Trina rummaged under the front desk and produced a thick document.

"Is this how it's presented?" A tacky, amateurish, and dull colored object greeted me.

"Yes. Resides in a drawer in the main area of each guest's room."

Obviously I needed another look at the rooms to see what else I'd missed. I took the *xertl* for further study and went back to my office. I made a cup of tea and then started my examination.

A short time later, my doorbell rang. "Come in," I called out.

Reena opened my door.

"Oh, hi. Lunch time already?" I'd lost track of time.

"Yes. I waited for you in the restaurant."

My glance at my watch told me time had indeed flown. "Sorry, I forgot to check. You were smart to come and find me. I've been studying this book, with the aid of Hart's reader, of course."

"Is this our room book?"

"Yes. Updates are required with all the aliens starting to visit." I decided not to mention the amateur presentation.

On our walk over to the restaurant, Reena quizzed me about Martian room books. Although similar in nature to the Mars Best room book, the Irion document didn't list a room service menu. According to Reena, guests called the restaurant to see which items were currently available. An interesting idea, but not terribly customer service friendly, I decided.

While we waited for our food, Reena and I discussed other questions arising from my study of the *xertl*—although I think Hart's reader fascinated her more.

After delivery of our food, Reena asked, "Your father, why were you not happy to encounter him?"

I knew she wouldn't forget the main reason for our lunch meeting.

"Not unhappy, Reena, surprised. I've never known my father, for more years than you've been alive." My heart started to pound.

"But he created you?" Reena's voice rose.

"Yes, he and my mother are my genetic parents. However, I'm an adult, and I've already created a life without Charles. Effort will be required to integrate him into my activities. We don't have common experiences." Much confusion on all sides.

"Understandable. I did not think you would reject your own father. Will you keep me updated?"

Reject my father? Understandably, a teenager with two male guardians, and no mother, might want to understand my situation. Hormones abounded in human teenagers, and I suspected the same for Irions.

"Of course, Reena. I'll let you know how things go. Now, what're you doing this afternoon?" I wanted to redirect her focus.

"Amenities. Usual shift."

"After you're through, would you show me places I found in the room book—the ones I haven't seen yet, like the chapel." I didn't want to miss anything inside the hotel—outside would come later.

"Certainly. Exciting," said Reena.

We both glanced up when Dedare joined us.

"Favorite ladies, how are you?"

Reena grinned. "Father, everything is good. I will be helping Manager Syl after my shift in Amenities." She stood. "My work starts shortly. I must clean up." Reena waved, and then she took off at a young person's speed.

We both glanced after her, and Dedare's face softened and expressed his love.

"As I said to Sain, I don't know where young people find so much energy," I put in.

"Exhausting. How is your day?" he asked. "More surprises for me?" Dedare caught the attention of our server.

"Well, if you insist."

However, my joke fell flat.

"What does *insist* mean? I do not understand."

"The translator is trying to interpret my humor—apparently an impossible task. What I tried to imply was I do have more ideas, but I wanted to express the concept in a humorous manner."

"Please tell me, I won't laugh," said Dedare.

Now, either he joked, or he still didn't understand what I'd tried to say. "I spent a good deal of time this morning with Miseena, putting a reservations staff schedule together. She's going to talk to the front desk staff and see if any of them want to rotate into the Reservations room, like we're doing the other way around."

"Excellent idea."

"Yes, well, I think Miseena should take care of all parts of our hotel regarding reservations. We can make her a manager or supervisor of some sort—I'm not sure of the staff titles in our hotel—because she seems to know everyone and to have good relationships with them."

"Efficient. I wanted you to meet the staff and get a feel for the hotel, and you are doing that well. You realize you said *our hotel*. This pleases me."

Dedare dropped his hand on mine. Surprised, I studied his face. Before I had a chance to interpret his expression, I noticed my hand beginning to twitch. Then I recognized a tingling beginning in my arm. My body had responded to his touch, much to my surprise. We stared at each other until I said, "Who should I talk to in Human Resources to get Miseena's promotion arranged?" I gently pulled my hand away. I decided to ignore my physical response—at least for the moment.

"What is Human Resources?" Dedare glanced at my hand resting on the table top.

"Human Resources, on Mars and Earth anyway, is a group of company employees who hire needed personnel for the various departments of a business. How does this work in our hotel?" Correctly, Dedare had noticed I'd started to think of the Sath-Satre Golden Hotel as my own.

"Each department manager does their own hiring."

"Do you have guidelines for new positions and salaries? Who determines if a new position, an extra position, I mean, is needed?"

Dedare smiled. "The hotel manager controls those items—after consultation with me—especially when the manager is new."

Someone thought he was funny, but I wasn't amused.

Dedare continued, "You can make Miseena the overall Reservations manager, if you desire, and I think the idea is sound. I will help with compensation—especially since I believe you do not know what you are receiving yourself."

I lost my ability to speak for a moment. I hadn't given my salary a thought since we'd arrived on Irion. "I'm going to look back on these first few days and decide I had no clue what I was doing."

"Fooled me," said Dedare.

I laughed. He really was a sweetheart. "Okay. Next topic is Hart and Sweety."

Dedare straightened—in surprise, I thought. I suspected my words gave him the impression there were issues. He gestured for me to proceed.

"Nothing's wrong. I know Sweety now works for you part time, and Hart does so full time, but I keep asking Hart to help with various projects. Is this a problem? Maybe you have enough for him to occupy all his time?"

Dedare made a motion with his hand. "I understand your need for Hart's technical expertise. However, he assured me he will teach you how to accomplish these tasks as you become more acquainted with the equipment. I do not foresee any problem."

"Good. I'd been concerned about overstepping my bounds." Too much, too soon?

"Never. No bounds," said Dedare, staring at me.

No bounds? Interesting answer. However, I ignored the thoughts in my head. "I've discovered another problem."

"Serious?"

"No. I shouldn't have used the word problem—just another project now that we're having alien guests."

"Restaurant?" asked Dedare. "Sweety talked to me about the Skuttem."

"A similar issue. Each of our guest rooms have a book describing the hotel and the various guest services options."

"Yes, normal. You had one on Mars."

I hesitated. "Yes, well, the one for this hotel needs a massive update. For example, we need a section for each species, in their own language. Also the book needs to be spiffed up."

"Spiffed up?" Dedare didn't look around for his non-existent translator, but I knew what went through his mind.

Apparently, I really loved English colloquialisms. "Made to look shiny and fancy and expensive, like our guests are getting their money's worth by staying here."

"You mean classy." Dedare's eyes twinkled just a bit. What had prompted his amused expression?

"Yes, classy and inviting. Since we need to update the *xertl* for new alien species, the time is right to revamp the whole thing."

"Anything else?"

"No, that's about all I can manage for one morning." For once, we both laughed at the same time. "I need to get back. I have meetings for most of the afternoon." As I stood, my shoe encountered an object under the table. I reached down and pulled out a cloth doll resembling an Irion.

"What's this?"

"A child's toy. I will remove." Dedare held out a hand.

I took a step back. "You can't. This is most likely a child's prized possession. I'll take it to Lost and Found."

From the look on Dedare's face, my words didn't compute. "Lost and Found is a place where you archive items found around the hotel. So when a guest asks if we have a certain possession, we can return the object."

"New project. No procedure."

Another project, indeed. I gave Dedare a slight bow, and he replied with a smile.

After I exited the restaurant and started walking to my office, I noticed our one and only Skuttem berating one of my front desk staff. I increased my pace.

"What's the problem?"

"Master Tyre wants to prepare food in his room,"

replied my quivering employee.

"If I remember correctly, your room does not have that option." Tired of the Skuttem, I hoped his stay would be short.

"That is what I am trying to tell this person," he spit out. His actions mimicked last night's when he looked everywhere but at me.

"Would you like to upgrade to a room with the appropriate facilities?" I asked. "Your cost will be greater, of course."

"Yes, yes," spluttered the Skuttem.

After the same issue with Richard Branson, I'd had Sain update a couple of rooms with minimal kitchen facilities to be able to anticipate future requests.

I nodded at my staff. She pecked into the reservations system. "We have a new room," she said, after a few moments.

"Let me arrange for the concierge to help you move your belongings," I said. "Anything else?"

"Yes, many. The restaurant food is inadequate," said Master Tyre.

"Didn't you converse with a Martian named Sweety today about that very topic?"

"Yes. I explained what I like to eat, and I sent her recipes. I like to think I am a good cook," said the Skuttem.

*Of course you do.* "Sweety'll be teaching Chef and the other cooks, so I'm sure you'll have an excellent dinner this evening. If not, please let me know." A sigh escaped. "How else may I help you?"

"I need an escort," replied the Skuttem, glancing around the lobby.

I tried not to burst out laughing. Where would I

find a Skuttem, hmm, a worldly woman? "What do you mean?" I asked, with a degree of tact. Actually, I wasn't sure Master Tyre was a *he*. Or, for that matter, even what sexes the Skuttem had.

"I need to be shown around this city. I do not know what is available or where to start."

My amusement subsided. "Ah, you need a tour guide. I will find someone suitable for the day after tomorrow. This'll take time to arrange. Anything in particular you'd like to see?"

"Common areas," said Master Tyre.

"No problem," I said. Although, finding a suitable tour guide might be a challenge. Reena had walked over from Amenities and joined us, but she hadn't said a word.

"Now, if there's nothing else I can do for you. I'll—"

"No, you cannot," shouted the Skuttem. Everyone in earshot turned our way.

"What's wrong?" I asked. I had no idea what'd upset him, or why he wouldn't look at me. "Have I done something to displease you?"

"Your hair, foul," Master Tyre responded.

"Meaning?" asked Reena. We all studied the hair sticking out from the Skuttem's head.

"Color denotes a Skuttem criminal. When convicted, the hair color is changed on the perpetrator, and then all know." He directed his gaze back up to the ceiling.

Reena jumped in from of me. "Manager Syl is no criminal but we will cover her hair. Sufficient?"

Master Tyre made a motion, with his hands, we took for agreement. Then one of my quick thinking front desk staff led him to the concierge to take care of transferring his belongings to his new room.

"Manager Syl, let me take care of this," said Reena, after she turned to me. "Shall we meet for dinner? I will bring a hair covering that should keep Master Tyre happy."

"You're the best," I said. What a bizarre experience I'd just had and not one I could've predicted.

Reena smiled and took off.

After my heart rate approached normal, I walked to the Reservations room. Sain stood outside eyeing the progress of the wall.

"Looks great and it's almost finished," I commented. I needed a new topic for my brain.

"Renovations should be complete before you start work tomorrow." Although I still struggled with Irion facial expressions, I interpreted Sain's as pleased.

"Excellent. Minimal interruption and I thank you. We don't want our guests unhappy, or our employees, for that matter." One project almost successfully completed—one down and about a million to go.

"Syl, I updated my plans for the lounge, do you have time for study?"

"A little later. I need to talk to Miseena, but we shouldn't be long. When she leaves my office, you can join me."

Sain nodded and turned back to his workers.

Inside the Reservations room, I caught Miseena's attention. After she finished her call, she came over. "Do you have time for a meeting? I have something to discuss," I said.

"Let me log out of the call system." She did so, and

then we walked the short distance to my office.

We sat at my desk and I said, "Miseena, you've been very helpful the last couple of days, thank you. You've lightened my burden."

"Help was required. This is a new world for you. You act strangely but we are becoming familiar with your mannerisms. We now know what most of them mean, and can adapt."

What mannerisms did she refer to? "Thank you, I think."

Miseena laughed.

"I have an offer for you," I said. "Now that we've combined both reservations areas, I'd like you to be the manager of our new Reservations department. You'll do a great job, you're perfect for the position."

A wide grin appeared. I also spotted moisture in her eyes.

"This is an honor. I may need help. Managing two areas, with all the scheduling, will be a challenge."

"If I didn't think you could do it, I wouldn't have made the offer. I'll be happy to help, but I don't think you're going to need much from me. By the way, Dedare and I still need to discuss your salary, as I'm not familiar with that aspect of Irion hotel staffing."

"Dedare has always been fair with compensation. There will be no problem. I am pleased by your decision, Manager Syl. A difficult one, I am sure."

"Not really. You're competent and everyone likes you." I gave Miseena a big smile.

Miseena had no words. Eventually she said, "I must go to work. I have much to do. Thank you, thank you."

She seemed to float out of my office—gracefully,

of course.

At least one thing went well today. I needed to reflect on the Skuttem; he was going to be a huge challenge. What kind of hair covering would Reena come up with?

Sain poked his head through my doorway and asked, "Now?"

I gestured him inside. "Let's sit at the work table."

After we settled, Sain said, "The reservations window wall will complete this evening. I compliment your idea. I have received positive responses."

I nodded and basked in my great wisdom, for a very short moment. "Show me the Lounge plans. I'm excited." A grin broke out on my face.

Sain rolled out an Irion blueprint. "I used your updated ideas and came up with these drawings."

We discussed his plans in depth. "Sain, I think you read my mind. This is exactly what I'd envisioned. Wonderful!"

Pleased, he sat back in his chair.

"Are we going to have issues with Dedare over these changes?" I asked.

"I do not believe so. I will show him the plans today, but I imagine I will be able to start on the changes tomorrow—unless security issues engage me."

I'd been mulling over the topic of security since my arrival. "How often do you and I meet to discuss hotel security?"

Hesitation appeared on his face. "Never. Why?"

"I think we should. Ah, after all, I'm the manager and need to be up on all issues relating to this hotel."

Words escaped him. Finally he said, "I will discuss this with Dedare. Will you be at dinner?"

"Of course." I tried not to smile. I kept pushing the Irions out of their comfort zones. However, I really did think, as manager, I should be consulted regarding hotel security.

Sain took his drawings and left. Before I had a chance to rise from my worktable, Reena and Siska appeared.

"Are you ready for the Sath-Satre Golden Hotel Grand Tour?" asked Siska.

Her question gave me the vision of capital letters on a marquee. "I certainly am. My knowledge of the hotel needs to be expanded. I want to know everything."

"We can fix your gaps. Amenities is covered," said Siska.

"Great! Then two knowledgeable women, please present your delights," I said, getting up from my table. Glad Reena had engaged Siska for our tour, I relaxed a little.

Passing by the front desk, I spoke to Miseena. "Do you know how to reach me, if you have any problems?" A question I should've asked on my first day, not days later. Sloppy, Syl, sloppy.

"Your com contact has been programmed into ours," replied Miseena, trying not to smile. Of course Dedare thought of everything. Miseena gave a little wave. "Enjoy your tour."

Apparently, my life and actions were an open book—a little unnerving since I hadn't been on Irion long. However, I reminded myself, we Martians were the aliens.

Our first stop didn't surprise me. I'd found out about it in the room bible. "Why does the hotel have a

chapel? Surely, there are many situated around Satre."
*Wasted hotel space* popped into my mind.

"A lot of travelers do not have time to go off site. Since we talk to God every day, this chapel provides access," said Siska.

She had a point. A hotel needed to offer convenience.

No church goers currently occupied the chapel. A raised dais dominated one end, and the remainder of the area contained small rectangular pools of water. The walls and ceiling were neutral, and the only splash of color came from the vases situated around the dais.

"Siska, why are there pools of water? And why does the chapel not have benches or chairs for the supplicants?"

I knew enough Irion physiology, by now, to recognize Siska tried to hide a smile. "Irion has many wet areas, and much food is grown on water. Thus our chapels evolved to be outdoors. We sit naked in water pools and meditate. Most chapels are small and used for a particular family group adjacent to housing."

So that's why Dedare wanted a water pool in his room in the Mars Best hotel. Thank goodness, the hot tub I'd had installed had satisfied his religious needs.

For some reason, Siska decided I exhibited horror at the thought of naked Irions, so she added, "In the hotel chapel, since people are from many different areas, we usually wear a simple garment."

A bathing suit type covering, perhaps. My glance around the chapel triggered more questions. "Siska, do Irions have more than one religion?"

"Yes. Send information?"

"Please do. I'd like to learn about the differences."

I thought for a moment. "Do all your religions use this chapel? Or just one denomination? Are services with a priest provided?" Assuming they even had priests.

"You ask a lot of questions," commented Siska, "but do not stop. We do have scheduled services for more than one religion. I believe Dedare's assistant takes care of the details."

Which assistant, I wondered?

"Since Martians, and other aliens like the Skuttem, now stay at the hotel, I think we need to modify the chapel to accommodate other species. Assuming they have need of a chapel." I didn't know about the Skuttem, but I didn't foresee Martians sitting in pools of water. Sain's future included additional renovations.

"Never considered," said Siska.

I thought I detected the equivalent of a frown on her Irion face.

"Not exactly your department, but something to add to my list." I made a note on my com. "Now, what's next?"

"Our growing areas," said Reena. "Favorites."

"Gardens? I love to garden. Lead on." Having a hotel garden surprised me.

We started at the Hydroponics lab—down in the bowels of the hotel. High light levels and humidity assaulted my senses, but I marveled at the magnificent room. Many-colored plants were visible, and they tended to hold a purple-blue palette, unlike a human green.

"Reena, this is fantastic! Do we use these items in the restaurant?" Before she had a chance to respond, I said, "Introduce me to whoever is in charge, please."

I couldn't contain my excitement. I'd loved

growing plants during my youth, but we'd had limited space in our apartment.

An Irion approached. "Lain, this is Sylvestine Amera, our new hotel manager. Manager Syl, this is Lain Tisis, who is in charge of growing vegetables, flowers, and other plants," said Reena.

I offered my hand in greeting, and after a short hesitation Lain responded, "Manager Syl, how nice you visit Hydroponics. How may I assist?"

"I want to know all about this area, and anything else you're responsible for. Hydroponics will be one of my happy places."

The four of us stood still for a few seconds grinning at each other. They all seemed to understand my *happy place* comment.

"In addition to Hydroponics, I am also responsible for our roof-top garden," said Lain.

A roof-top garden! "Do you grow enough vegetables and herbs to supply the hotel's needs?"

"Not yet, but close. A challenge to balance the growing in Hydroponics and the seasonal roof-top."

Seasonal? I didn't even know what seasons Irion experienced—something to ask Hart.

Lain gave me a tour of the Hydroponics lab. Most of the vegetation proved new, but some I recognized from our meals.

Then the four of us traipsed up to the roof.

What a wondrous sight! Sparkling in the orange-tinged Irion sunlight were numerous plant areas. Raised beds with sprinkler poles were visible and tall trees surrounded the edges. Fruit trees, perhaps.

"Lain, this's wonderful! Are hotel guests allowed up here?"

"We have a small area, in the center of the rooftop, which anyone is allowed to visit. Let me show you." Admittedly not large, the location consisted of a sparkling fountain surrounded by low wooden benches and pots of flowers. Very tranquil.

"This'll be a wonderful place to relax," I said. "I'll be back, whenever I have a chance."

"You are welcome," said Lain. "You manage this area."

"And that makes me happy." After a final glance, I said, "Now my tour guides are anxious to show me other areas. I'll visit soon, and I think we need to talk about planting Martian vegetables."

Much to my surprise, Lain gathered my hands in hers. "We are happy you are here," she said.

Taken aback, I wasn't quite sure how to respond, so I gave her a hug. She seemed delighted and hugged me back. Then Reena, Siska, and I went on our way. I'd quiz Reena later about Lain's action of clasping my hands.

My tour guides took me through Engineering. Some of the machines were inexplicable, but I decided another day would be appropriate for sleuthing. I had information overload, and I probably needed Hart along to understand the mechanics. He'd be delighted.

"Do we have anything else?" I asked, starting to feel the fade.

"Last stop, the hotel offices," said Siska.

The end neared.

We wandered through several hallways. By this point, confused about the layout of the hotel, our arrival at the hotel offices pleased me.

Reena and Siska went inside. I held back and

glanced around the unfamiliar passage we'd taken. The offices were tucked away in a corner of the hotel new to me, and I felt a little disoriented. I turned away and joined Reena and Siska in the office.

"Manager Syl, nice to meet you again," said Dial Deen, one of Dedare's assistants.

"Reena and Siska are showing me around. Did I not see you in a different area previously?"

"Yes. I have two offices, different functions."

"Okay. What do you do here?" Two offices triggered a few warning bells.

"Supervise the office staff."

Not a ton of information. Was she being difficult? Although tired, I decided not to pursue the subject. "What functions do the staff have in this office?"

"The Sath-Satre Golden Hotel is Dedare's flagship, so we do the ordering of all supplies, purchasing of hotel equipment, and everything needed for all hotels under Dedare's ownership. Quite a challenge."

A glib Dial irritated me. However, nothing out of place caught my eye.

"Who's your supervisor?"

"I report to Dedare."

How had this arrangement come to be? Because she ordered for all hotels? As I turned to speak to Reena and Siska, a movement caught the corner of my eye—a shape disappeared around a corner. "Did anyone see who that was?" I asked.

Neither Reena nor Siska had even had a glimpse of what I'd had so they were no help. Something about the figure, though, made me think I knew the person and they shouldn't have been anywhere near here.

The three of us walked back to reception. "Siska,

thanks for your help. I now understand the hotel a lot better. Reena, your perspective proved invaluable." I yawned. "Since I believe all of us should have been on our way home by now, I'm going to say goodnight. Siska, I'll talk to you tomorrow. I'll see you at dinner, Reena."

Reena nodded.

"Good. Then I'm going up to my room and ruminate on everything you've shown me today." If napping equaled ruminating, I had the situation covered.

Reena and Siska wandered off, and I studied the lobby—since the day had been all about digging out information.

The young Irion on the front desk interrupted my reverie. "Manager Syl, I just received a message informing a priest is on his way to the Bone Room, and would like to meet you there."

"When?" I really wanted a nap.

"Soon. He is in the hotel somewhere."

Probably just finished a service in the Chapel, I thought. "Okay, I'll go back there now." I trundled through the busy kitchen to the Bone Room. Since I found an unlatched door, I stepped inside.

No priest awaited me, so I had a chance to study the room in a little more depth than I'd previously had time for.

Quite a cool temperature assaulted my skin. I'm sure this helped preserve the bone remnants until their collection. The walls, of the approximately eight foot by eight foot room, were covered with shelving and closed purple boxes about one cubic foot in dimension. Other than the purple, the room had a drab brown and black demeanor.

I started to shiver, so I decided to go back outside and wait for the priest. Walking toward the door, I heard a click. Glancing around the room, I couldn't imagine where the sound came from.

Brushing the noise aside, I grabbed the door handle but it refused to budge. I yanked and jiggled the knob to no avail.

What a bummer. It must be stuck. I pulled out my com, but I had no signal. There went that option. I tried yelling, but with no response. The Bone Room must be heavily insulated.

Finally, after a considerable time yelling and pacing, I collapsed in a corner. I found some kind of tarp to pull over my body for a little insulation.

****

"Syl, Syl, wake up," someone muttered. The words didn't quite fit in my dream, but I opened my eyes anyway.

"Hart, Dedare, what are you guys doing here?" Hart put his hand on my wrist, while Dedare lifted me into a sitting position.

"Rescuing you, of course," said Hart. "Why are you the only one to get into these predicaments?" He felt my forehead, and then nodded at Dedare. "We're going to help you stand. If you feel any pain or dizziness, let me know right away."

Slowly I rose to my feet. I wobbled a bit but the sensation didn't last.

"I feel fine," I said. "What happened?" Physically, I may not have been weak, but my brain had slowed.

"You got locked in the Bone Room," said Hart.

"How did you know? How did you find me?"

"You didn't show up for dinner, so Dedare and I went searching. We thought you'd fallen asleep in your suite, but you weren't there."

"My suite? How did you get in?" Given my propensity for long days and naps, not a bad place to start looking.

"Dedare has his magic keys." Hart laughed.

Hotel owners would have such a thing—maybe I needed a set. "So what did you do when I wasn't home?"

"We retraced your steps. Reena told us she'd left you at the front desk, so we started there and found out about a priest meeting you in the Bone Room. So that was our next stop. Finding the door locked concerned Dedare, so he opened it, and here we are. Now let's get you outside. You need to warm up."

The two of them helped me through the door. "Back to your suite?" asked Hart.

"No, I need food; something hot like soup. I'm really chilled."

Dedare turned and gestured. Miseena popped into my view. Why was she here?

"Housekeeping, blankets, please," said Dedare.

"Yes. Manager Syl, I will be right back." She took off at a run.

I looked at Hart and Dedare. "Miseena is concerned," said Hart. "She was at the front desk when we inquired as to your whereabouts. She insisted on joining us."

Such a sweetheart. I started to shiver, then Dedare put his arms around me—a welcome warmth. Soon Miseena returned with a couple of blankets and a heating pad. Dedare wrapped one blanket around my shoulders, and Hart took the other items from Miseena.

"Thanks, Miseena. These're much appreciated. I'll be fine, and I'll see you tomorrow," I said. "We'll have much to discuss."

She gave me a reluctant nod, and then she abruptly patted my forehead and turned away.

I had no clue what her gesture meant. "Okay, guys. Thanks for all your help, but I need food," I whined. Hart and Dedare hovered while we walked to the restaurant.

Because of the hubbub at my entrance, I said, "I'm fine, just a little chilled. Some hot food will cure all my ills."

Mom and Sweety held their tongues, but the number of glances between them and Hart and Dedare would've filled a short novel.

After my temperature rose sufficiently, and my stomach had been satisfied, I said, "Apparently, I had an adventure today."

"Darling daughter, how did this happen?"

I frowned, "I don't know. After a wonderful tour of the hotel with Reena and Siska," I directed a big smile Reena's way, "I stopped at the front desk to study the lobby. There I received a message a priest wanted to meet me at the Bone Room. I figured I had an opportunity to learn more about Irion, so I went." I shivered. "The next thing I knew the door had shut and locked. Thankfully, Hart and Dedare came to my rescue. A pretty chilly experience." And not one I wanted to repeat.

Mom coughed. "Dedare, do…"

"The situation is being looked after," Dedare said, after a glance at his security chief, Sain.

"Of course," said Mom.

Then Reena changed the subject. "Hair covering," she said. She gave me an item similar to a beret. I tucked my hair up inside and modeled the soft green covering to unanimous approval. My blanket slipped off my shoulders, and I decided to let it be. I'd warmed up considerably.

"What is this?" asked Dedare.

"Master Tyre did not like the color of Manager Syl's hair. Reminded him of a criminal on his planet. I found a covering," said Reena.

Dedare had no words, so I jumped in. "Dedare, if you have new aliens about to arrive, would you tell me? I'll try to research and forestall any problems like this." I sighed. "Although, it'll be a difficult implementation—who knows what'll cause offense?" I shook my head. "On the bright side, I'll need more berets to match my Martian clothing."

Mom perked up. "Some of us are taking tomorrow as our day of rest. I can do some shopping for you."

A day off? "Dedare, when is my day of rest?" I asked.

"Whenever you wish. Perhaps tomorrow would be appropriate, so the Martians can be together. Busy time for everyone with much acclimation. Relaxation required."

I flashed a smile—sometimes the translator spewed the correct words.

"If anyone wants purchases, charge them to me. We still need to formalize salaries, and banking, so balancing will occur later," said Dedare.

That'd work, I decided. "So who all's taking tomorrow off?" Happily, Mom, Hart, and Sweety would join me.

"Be your guide," said Reena, "I know interesting areas."

"Great idea!" said Mom. So we spent time discussing what we wanted to explore to help Reena plan our day.

"By the way, Dedare, our Skuttem guest, Master Tyre, also wants a tour. I put him off until the day after tomorrow. Who takes care of excursions for the hotel?"

"No department." Dedare glanced at Sain.

"Should I tell Master Tyre he's on his own?"

"Don't do that," interrupted my mother. "I'll take him on a tour after we've had our own. I'll be more knowledgeable, and able to keep him happy for a day."

"Mama A, are you sure you want to do this?" asked Dedare.

"For a limited engagement—not full time." My mother had the choicest words.

"I understand. Since you are my historian, perhaps you can set up a small tour department for the hotel. Irion history is important, and we have many historical sites. I had not thought about this concept. However, I do not want you alone with Master Tyre."

Dedare gave me an unfathomable look. What were his thoughts?

"I will go with Mama A," said Reena.

"No," came in unison from Sain and Dedare.

"I will accompany Mama A," said Sain. "Security is my department, and this will give me the opportunity to research possible issues regarding tours."

Mom didn't erupt with any arguments—which told me a great deal.

While our discussion turned to what to visit

tomorrow, I glanced around the quiet restaurant. I spied Simon having dinner with Tareera. What could this mean? How did they meet?

"Syl, Syl, Mars, oops, Irion to Syl," said Hart, scattering my thoughts.

"Sorry, sorry. What's happening?"

"We finished planning our tour. Do you agree?" asked Reena.

"Sure, sure, sounds good."

My distracted answer let the Martians, at least, know I hadn't heard a word, but I'd go along with whatever they'd planned.

"Shall we meet for breakfast? Then we'll all be ready at the same time." They all readily accepted my suggestion.

Before we had a chance to retire, Charles said, "Sylvestine, your problem with Customs has been resolved, thanks to Dedare. They no longer need to question you."

I gave my father a big smile, and then did the same to Dedare. "That's great! I knew you guys would take care of me."

Referring to Dedare and Charles in the same sentence brought up a ton of overwhelming emotions. Dedare's nearness had begun to touch me on a regular basis—I couldn't ignore the physical sensations any longer. I had much to think about.

"I don't know about everyone else, but I'm tired and I need to get a good rest before our long, exciting day tomorrow."

"Sweety and I are going for a walk. Do you want to join us?"

I shook my head in response to Hart's question.

Then Mom and Charles made the same offer. Again I refused. After Reena left to do homework, only Dedare, Sain, and I remained. Their expectant glances made me pause.

"Guys, I need rest. I'm starting to feel chilled again, and my mind requires downtime."

Anyone in the galaxy could've read the disappointment on both faces. "I'll see you tomorrow," I said, as I left with as much dignity as I could muster.

****

Too restless to sleep after I returned to my room, the bare walls caught my attention. Painting would settle my mind, I decided. So I unpacked my paints and dabbed at a canvas for a couple of hours, and then I collapsed and slept.

Chapter Sixteen

More people than I expected showed up for our early breakfast.

"I hope no one minds," said my mother, "but I asked Charles to join our day trip." Mom locked glances with Charles.

"From what Sylvia mentioned, your itinerary seems perfect to increase my understanding of Irion culture," said Charles.

No one offered any objections, but the heads turning my way made me realize I needed to comment. "An excellent idea, Charles. Your perspective should be helpful."

He sat up straighter and smiled. My encouragement eased the tension I'd encountered when I'd joined the breakfast table. Then I gave Sain a questioning look.

"I would like to join your excursion. Added security may be useful, as most Irions have not encountered Martians."

A point to consider and I was sure looking after his niece played a major role in his decision. "I can't argue with your reasoning," I said.

I glanced at Dedare.

"I am here to see everyone off. This is not my day of rest, and I have meetings, so I cannot join you. Reena, what have you planned? Has anything changed from yesterday?"

Reena pulled out her com. "I thought the farms—both animal and plant—spaceship manufacturing, the planetarium, an outdoor church with a bell tower and view, and shopping."

"How are we travelling to these places?" I asked.

"I have allowed Reena the use of the hotel shuttle and driver," said Dedare.

"Wonderful," Mom said.

I studied Reena trying to decide how to proceed, and I required tact. "Perhaps we've scheduled a little too much for one day. I suggest we split up—half of us to visit the spaceship manufacturing and planetarium and half to experience the various farms. Then we can all converge on the church and bell tower. Afterward, we should have sufficient time for shopping. What do you think, Reena? Any objections from anyone?"

My suggestions met with complete approval. We discussed how to split our group, and then we all left on the shuttle.

I made a mental note to find out how many shuttles were available. Since the hotel didn't normally give tours, of what use were shuttles?

We dropped Hart, Sweety, Mom, and Charles at the spaceship manufacturing building, right next door to the planetarium. After agreeing upon a pickup time, Sain, Reena, and I went to the closest garden farm.

The facility skirted the outer limits of the city. I recognized a few of the plants I'd seen on my hydroponics excursion, but the majority were new. "Reena, I'm noticing many plants we don't have at the hotel. Should they be added to the Hydroponics lab or rooftop?"

"We grow the ones most popular and required for

our restaurant menu. Lain would like more, but space is limited. We do buy items from this farm to supplement our needs."

I needed to get Hart to visit the hotel's roof top garden and see if he could discover a more efficient design. I envisioned multi-level beds on two sides of the roof top grabbing all available sunlight, but what did I know—Hart was the engineer. I suspected I'd just thought up another project for my favorite males. Sain, Hart, and Dedare would need to confer.

Then I noticed a section in the garden farm devoted to flowers. Moving closer, the spread of greenery delighted me. Different from the plants we grew on Mars and Earth, none-the-less they were exquisite. No color dominated amongst the flower petals, although the leaves carried a blue-green hue. Curiosity made me peer closer at the flowers. Much to my surprise, the petals were more triangular in shape than Martian ones, and only overlapped each other by a small amount.

"Does the hotel get flowers from this farm?"

"Yes," said Sain. "Sensible to acquire everything from one location. The orders go through the office."

Gradually all the duties were becoming clearer. Did the hotel have any documentation on jobs and who reports to whom, I wondered? Another item to discuss with Dedare.

After spending an hour at the farm, we took our shuttle over to the animal ranch. After a short tour, I asked, "Reena, are any of these animals meant for the hotel?"

I'd viewed different animals in various feed lots on the farm. Many small rodent-like creatures, and other larger animals, wandered about.

Sain responded instead, "They are butchered here, and then sent to a central facility where the hotels and restaurants buy what they need. All farms send their meat to the same facility in Greater Satre."

"How about the public?" I wondered about the location of this store. I'd be interested in seeing the various animal products sold in Satre.

"They are also supplied from the same location."

"What about the possibility of having Martian animals? I wouldn't mind fresh meat."

Sain said, "I have contemplated this idea. I think the main criticism will be possible contamination. Officials would need to decide. Slow process."

Same old, same old, I concluded.

"Time to rejoin," announced Reena. So we gathered up our driver and travelled to the planetarium. After picking up the other four of our party, we took off for our next tourist spot.

Jumping out of the shuttle, I studied my surroundings. The outdoor chapel consisted of numerous small, rectangular plots filled with water flowing from one row to the next. Why was the water moving? Then I realized each row of plots had been built at a slightly different elevation. Nestled between the terraced water plots were colorful low lying plants.

Although I wasn't a stranger to an Irion chapel, Mom, Hart, Sweety, and Charles most likely were, so Reena gave a short explanation.

"What's that tall building?" asked Mom, pointing to a structure about five stories high. Each of its four sides seemed about thirty feet tall.

"Bell tower. Living areas for the priests, an inside chapel, and a large bell at the top used to indicate a service about to begin," said Reena.

The area surrounding the tower included apartment buildings, so the officials had a ready congregation.

"Can we go to the top and see the view?" asked Sweety.

"Crowd gathering," said Sain, pointing at the tower.

"Tour time," added Reena.

We trooped over and joined the group of waiting Irions. A few trips in the tower's elevator were required to transfer the whole crowd. After everyone had arrived, we received a spiel from the tour guide.

Two hundred cycles old, the bell tower housed one of the younger Irion churches. Priests, who were recruited from church goers, lived in the tower for a few cycles. After they found spouses, they moved to adjacent housing. A life-long occupation, they continued their religious duties at the closest church.

With all the people hovering around the guide, a bit of crowd anxiety came upon me. I crept to the outer edge of the viewing platform for some much needed breathing room.

The top of the bell tower provided a spectacular view of the surrounding land. In addition to the farms we'd visited, I glimpsed winding rivers, yellow colored land areas, and buildings I thought might be manufacturing facilities. My speculative nature had a good time.

Behind me, the city loomed. Tall buildings shone in the sunlight and I glimpsed an elevated transportation system.

Someone bumped into me, as I gazed over the city. I turned around and saw Reena, but the rest of the crowd were strangers.

Again turning and gazing over the lands, I said, "Reena, this is spectacular. Are there other areas—"

Suddenly I lurched over the guard rail. And then both of my arms were grabbed from behnd—yanking my body back from the edge. Stunned, I settled back on my heels.

"Take a deep breath," ordered Sain, in a loud voice. "Then another."

For some reason, Sain's command annoyed me, which may have been his intent. I attempted to comply after I noticed both Sain and Reena holding my arms.

"Wha...wha...what happened?" I spluttered. The breaths I'd taken hadn't settled me, to any great extent.

"Someone pushed you," said Sain. "You were falling forward, so Reena and I grabbed your arms."

"Did you see who did this?" Even in my misery, I still noticed the strain in his voice.

"No. Looking the same direction as you," said Reena.

The rest of our group gathered round.

"What happened?" asked Mom.

"Someone tried to kill Manager Syl," said Reena, being a typical teenager.

"Reena! Don't upset Mama A," I admonished.

"Sorry, but true," she protested, a hurt look on her face.

When several voices rose in pitch and spoke at once, I'd had enough. "Stop. I'm not dead, you guys! Reena and Sain saved me." I took a deep breath. "Did anyone else see this happen?"

Heads shook, but Reena perked up after my remark about her and Sain.

"Anyone suspicious?" I asked. "Anything? I need to find the culprit." A mad had started, and I needed action.

"I saw Simon and Tareera in the crowd," said Sweety, "but that doesn't mean they had anything to do with your accident."

"Anybody else?" I asked. No response. "Okay, let's go look for them." My mind had latched onto Simon and Tareera.

Our group searched from the top of the bell tower to the bottom exit. At the base, we decided to expand our search area around the tower, but Simon and Tareera had vanished.

"Syl, you're shaky," said Mom. "Reena, Sain, is there a restaurant nearby? I think we all need sustenance and rest."

I didn't argue.

Sain loaded us in the shuttle for a short ride to a cute restaurant. The comforting establishment reminded me of a Swiss chalet—either because of the window boxes, or the shape of the building.

"After this, we're all going shopping, right Reena?" Sweety glanced my way.

"Yes. A market, close by, is filled with many native items and staples. My favorite shops are located there."

I sat back and attempted to relax. Maybe no one had tried to kill me—maybe someone stumbled, and I'd been in the way. However, thinking back, the push had been strong enough to make me think…what? That it could have been deliberate?

My com rang, interrupting my thoughts.

"Manager Syl, we have a problem," said Miseena.

"We need your help at the hotel."

"Okay, I'll be there shortly." I trusted Miseena, so I said, "Sain, I need to go back."

"I will go with you, and then the shuttle will return and take everyone shopping."

"You don't need to…" I stopped and regrouped. I had no need to be ungrateful. "Mom, will you pick up some berets, please. I need to keep our Skuttem guest happy."

"Anything else?" she asked. Her frown and hunched shoulders gave me a couple of clues about her mental state.

I whispered. "Perhaps some plain tops and underwear. I haven't had a chance to do any laundry, and I wouldn't mind having a few native items."

Mom nodded, but the concern didn't leave her face.

"It's okay," I whispered. "Sain will be with me." I raised my voice and said, "Okay, everyone, I have a crisis to solve. I expect lots of reports at dinner regarding your shopping successes. I'm most jealous."

Chapter Seventeen

Back at the hotel, Miseena hovered at the front desk. "What's the urgency?" I asked.

"We must go to the kitchen," my new Reservations manager said.

The look on her face defied my interpretation. "What's going on?" I whispered to Sain. He shook his head. We followed behind Miseena on the short walk to the food facilities. She led us to the end of a set of kitchen counters and pointed at the floor. A body lay sprawled face-down.

I had a good guess as to whom lay there, but I wanted to turn the figure over to confirm. Too awkward for me alone, Sain helped. Unfortunately, I'd been correct. Chef's body greeted my eyes.

Sain tried for a pulse, and then asked, "Miseena, have you called the medical responders?"

She moved her head from left to right.

"Call them, and also the police. Possible murder," said Sain.

Miseena scurried away. "Can you try to revive him?"

"Useless. His blood has ceased flowing." Sain stared at Chef. I had no idea what thoughts were going through his mind.

"How do you know?" I hadn't studied Irion physiology, and so I had no information to go on.

"His skin color indicates death. I must tell Dedare." Sain stepped away to make his call.

I stood over the body and mourned the loss of Chef. Chef had been most accommodating to the culinary needs of new species, and I'd miss him. The blue tinge of his skin had faded to a dark gray.

Who was the most experienced assistant chef? Should we advertise for a new chief chef? What would Sweety think about this development? Questions swirled in my mind, adding to the stress of my day.

Dedare and Sain walked into the kitchen. "Syl, how are you feeling?" asked Dedare.

"A little shaky since I've never touched a dead person before." I didn't know why that popped out of my mouth. "Of course, almost falling off the bell tower has also rattled my nerves."

Dedare grabbed my arm, and then asked Sain. "What happened?"

"Someone pushed Syl when we were all at the top. A large crowd had gathered, and we were listening to the tour guide."

"Sain and Reena saved me, Dedare. They were wonderful. After seeing Tareera and Simon close by, everyone is suspicious," I added.

Dedare stared at me, and then at Sain. Sain made a little motion with his head, and Dedare reciprocated—Irion communication between close relatives, I imagined.

A noise made me turn around. The kitchen filled with what I assumed were first responders. A bunch of them gathered around Chef, and shoved the rest of us out of their way.

Sain, Dedare, and I were a silent trio as we

watched the proceedings. Eventually, an Irion approached—an Irion wearing a formal black outfit covered with insignia.

"Dedare." The new Irion added a nod to his greeting.

Kind of cute, I thought, but who was he?

"Teeka." Dedare took a deep breath. "Detective Cole, I am sure you know my brother Sain, and I would like to introduce my new hotel manager, Sylvestine Amera."

"A Martian?" Skepticism infused his voice.

"Yes. I've recently arrived." I didn't like his attitude.

He studied me from head to toe. "Let me see your hands."

I really, really, didn't like his attitude, but I held my hands out anyway. He grabbed my wrists and flopped my hands back and forth. "You need to come to police headquarters. I see blood."

"Of course, you do." Idiot! "Sain and I turned the body over to determine its identity." What was he, some kind of stupid?

He glanced at Sain's hands. "I do not see any blood on Sain. You must accompany me." The detective put a bag over each of my hands, and then tied them together.

"Necessary?" asked Dedare. He knew me well enough to understand my fury.

"You may accompany us, Dedare," added Teeka Cole, after glancing at the two of us. He sighed. "Sain, also. Check hands."

Mollification for me perhaps.

Our sojourn at police headquarters turned out to be short. After scanning my hands, they determined I'd encountered the blood post-death, so I was allowed to leave. Of course, Sain had no blood on his hands. Some people had all the luck.

After we returned, Dedare, Sain, and I stood in the hotel lobby. No one knew what to say, so I took the plunge. "Dedare, we should probably discuss a new chef."

"Tomorrow. This day has been stressful. Dinner."

I glanced at my watch. "You're right. I am hungry—especially since I missed lunch. However, I need a short nap. Wake me in an hour, and then I'll be ready."

Apparently, Dedare and Sain were not adverse to their own break from reality, but I certainly welcomed mine.

Too soon I heard my door chime. Much to my surprise, Mom and Charles stood outside. I motioned them inside.

"I have your purchases," said my mother. "You missed a really great market. How did the rest of your day turn out?"

"Unbelievable, but I'll tell you at dinner." I took the packages and set them down in my living room. I needed to get to my laundry and soon. I had no excuse—the machines were nestled in a corner of my living quarters.

The doorbell rang again. Dedare and Sain waited outside. "Come in. Looks like we're having a party." I tried to smile, but my downtime had not totally alleviated my tiredness.

After greeting Mom and Charles, Dedare said, "Dinner. Reena and the others are waiting."

Soon we settled at our customary table and

ordered. Mom asked, "Okay, Syl, tell us about the crisis requiring your presence back at the hotel."

With much concern in my mind, I tried to decide how to start. In the end, I said, "I don't know how to make this any easier to grasp, so I'll have to be blunt—Chef was murdered today."

"Oh, no! Who did it?" asked Sweety. "Such a lovely man, and we got along so well." Tears threatened.

"First, the police thought I did. Sain and I turned the body over, and I got blood on my hands. However, after a short visit to the police station, they let me go. Somehow they knew the blood on my hands was put there after death occurred."

Hart shook his head. "That's not logical. You might have killed him without getting any blood on your hands."

"Hart! I was with you guys today, remember?" Duh! I gave him a disgusted look.

"Sorry, sorry. Trying to think logically," he said, waving his hands around.

For a moment, silence blanketed our table.

"Should I talk to the police," asked Charles, "reassure them you would never do any such thing?"

A little naïve on Charles' part, I thought. "Thank you, but no. The detective investigating Chef's murder is Dedare's friend, and he let me go promptly. I should be okay." I crossed my fingers. I'd had too many recent encounters with officials. "Everyone, tell me about your shopping today. I'm most envious."

After listening to wondrous tales of the many items discovered, I said, "Okay, next day off, I'm going shopping, and that's final." Particularly since my first day off hadn't been particularly refreshing.

A few smiles graced the faces around the table. I suspected I'd have company for my next excursion.

"Agenda for tomorrow?" asked Dedare.

"I'll be giving Master Tyre his tour. We visited a few interesting spots today, so I thought I'd start with some of those." Mom asked Dedare, "May I borrow the shuttle tomorrow?"

"Sain will accompany you," said Dedare.

"Possible security issues," added Sain.

Mom objected. "I'm perfectly capable—"

Interrupting my mother normally proved dangerous, but I plowed ahead anyway. "Dedare and Sain have good points. I know you want to be in charge until you get tour staff lined up and trained. However, you're a foreigner and, since we know so little about Irion, major problems could arise. Probably won't happen, but take their advice, mother."

Mom nodded, albeit with reluctance.

"I will arrange for a vehicle," said Sain. "The hotel shuttle should not be tied up. I have already received complaints about today's absence. Dedare, we will need to acquire more shuttles if touring becomes viable." Dedare and Sain exchanged glances.

"Mama A, after you make arrangements with the Skuttem, tell me what time you want to start tomorrow," said Sain.

"Thank you. I shall do that after dinner." Our meals had started to arrive.

Words were few, for a short while. The day had been memorable—for more than one reason. Eventually, Reena said, "Manager Syl, I enjoyed taking everyone on the tour today. May we do it again?"

"That'd be lovely. Let's talk later about activities for my next day of rest. Reena, during business times, continue to call me Manager Syl, but I'd like you to call me Syl at times like this. We're friends, I hope."

"Of course, Manager—I mean Syl. Having you at the hotel is the best."

Such a teenage moment. Reena sat beside me, so I leaned over and gave her a hug.

"What?" she asked, confused about my gesture.

Oops. Perhaps I'd crossed into forbidden territory. "A hug, Reena—a show of affection. If I have offended, please tell me," I said.

Dedare interjected, "Reena, a *quirtl*."

Reena studied her father, and I studied the both of them. What had I stumbled into?

"Everything is fine, Syl. Physical expressions are different for each culture," said Dedare.

His statement relieved a portion of my tension.

Reena hesitated, and then hugged me back.

I smiled and decided I'd need a better explanation of *quirtl* at some later time. "A great meal and, for the most part, a great day," I said. "Dedare, before I relax for the evening, I have a few things I need to discuss—hotel issues mostly."

"Adjourn to the lounge," he replied.

Dedare and I stood, and people began to disperse. "Sain, join us. I have hotel topics to discuss, and Syl should be involved."

In the lounge, we grabbed a secluded table. After discussing a multitude of topics including Miseena's salary, the hotel bible, Chef, and security issues, I ran out of energy.

"I'm exhausted," I said. "I need to return to my

room and chill out."

"Chill out?" asked Sain.

"Oh, you know, unwind, relax, drink some wine and forget everything that's happened today." I sighed. "What I mean is I need to recharge to prepare for another seven days of stress. Oh, sorry, I meant excitement!"

We all laughed, and then Sain asked, "May Dedare and I join you for a short while? We also need to *chill out*."

"I'd like that." I decided I meant my statement. Although I'd planned to spend the evening alone.

So the three of us sat on my couch, and I tried to understand a strange Irion movie they played on the equipment in my living room. Much to my confusion, but emotional satisfaction, the three of us majorly cuddled.

Of course, I had a hard time getting to sleep later, as I had a decision to make—they both interested me, in so many different ways.

Chapter Eighteen

Last night's good mood continued to the breakfast table the next morning. I wasn't the only one relaxed—Sweety and Hart sat close together and held hands under the table. We'd walked down to breakfast together. With their rosy glows, they looked so good together.

"Dedare, I need to meet with you today," said Hart, after we'd ordered and were awaiting our first meal. "I have subjects to discuss, business and personal."

Curious about Hart's personal subjects, I tried to catch his eye, but he avoided me and everyone else.

"Always," replied Dedare. The two of them agreed upon a meeting time.

"I, also, need time," I said. "Hotel business, of course." My list of topics grew longer and longer, as the days passed. Informative days, but only the tip of the iceberg, I imagined. So much to learn, and so many mistakes to make.

"Lunch," said Dedare. "I will come to your office. I have meetings all morning."

I had no idea how many businesses Dedare owned. I needed to find a quiet time to talk to Mom and find out how her history of Sath Enterprises proceeded. She'd be able to give me a clearer understanding of Dedare's holdings.

"However there's one subject we should discuss

right now, Chef's death. What do you think, Dedare, and you also Sweety, about Sweety supervising the kitchen, alien recipes and all, until we determine who should be the new head chef?"

"Good idea, as long as Sweety agrees. You came to Irion for a holiday, not to work," said Dedare.

"Don't worry, Dedare. I'm enjoying all my projects, and my time with Martians and Irions. This planet is so interesting I may extend my vacation." Her face acquired a dreamy look.

What did she dream about, I wondered? I needed to have some alone time—some girl time—with Sweety. We were way overdue.

A thought popped into my mind, so I turned to Reena. "A question about Irions," I said. "Why did Lain gather my hands together when we were taking our leave yesterday? I didn't know how to respond." I'd been ignoring a lot of Irion mannerisms, but I decided Reena, as an emotional teenager, would be the appropriate Irion to ask.

"A sign of respect," answered Reena. "Her hands around yours implied she had bonded with you. High praise."

I felt a big smile break out on my face. I'd started to fit in. And thinking about other situations, namely the Sath boys, I'd actually started to enjoy my life on Irion.

Despite the fact it'd been a most pleasant breakfast, the time to start my work day had arrived. Reena accompanied me to the front desk. "No school today?" I asked.

"No. Today is our ACTER day." Reena put her hands behind her back, and gazed at me.

"What is ACTER?" Another word to add to my vocabulary.

Reena grinned. She knew her explanation of an Irion tradition would confuse me. "The whole Irion year is divided into eight day cycles."

"Yes, but is that the same as your cycle that gives everyone the eighth day as rest?" I confused even myself with my question.

Reena interrupted. "Syl, I mean Manager Syl, let me explain, and then questions." She'd correctly deduced my confusion. "Our whole year has forty-six eight-day cycles."

I got out my com to do some necessary calculations—necessary for me, anyway.

"The first day of each cycle is called the ACTER day. We do not have school or work that day. Tradition."

"So your year has three hundred and sixty-eight days?" I asked. I vaguely remembered Hart telling me Irion took a little longer to circumvate their sun than Earth did its.

Reena moved her head to signify agreement.

I tried again. "How does this affect your normal eight-day cycle where the eighth day is a rest day?" My head hurt.

"Clarification. Our normal eight-day cycle is based on our day of birth. The ACTER eight-day cycle is based on the calendar year. Messy, but we have learned to organize work and play around these issues. Obviously, not all acquaintances or businesses can have activities or meetings which involve all participants."

My head continued to hurt. "So, for example, when Miseena makes up a schedule, she has to take both of these cycles into consideration?"

"Yes, complicated," said Reena.

I thought for a moment. "But if no one is supposed to work or go to school on this ACTER day, which is common for absolutely everyone on Irion, how does the hotel run, or any business, for that matter?"

Reena laughed. "I knew you would understand. You are smart. Simply, if a person wishes or is asked to work on ACTER, they take another day off."

And I thought my scheduling on Mars had been a headache. "I think I understand. So no one should be working since it's ACTER, but scheduling staff positions has already been accommodated. Then why are you here today, Reena, on your ACTER day?"

"I want to learn all about my father's businesses, and I thought I could help, if you have any questions. And you might be short staffed because of ACTER."

Touched, I gave Reena a hug. "You're right. I'll probably have many questions. Now, go and help Siska until I need you, but don't overwork yourself. And make sure you take a rest day, they're important."

Such a lovely child. If I ever had children, I hoped they'd grow up to be as sweet as Reena. "If I need help, I know where to find you."

Reena took off, and I checked my mental agenda. I went to the Reservations room and stood in the doorway. Miseena looked up, and I gestured to my office.

In a moment, Miseena settled opposite me at my desk. I said, "You're doing a great job with your added responsibilities."

"Thank you, Manager Syl. I am enjoying the tasks."

As tactfully as possible, I said, "I have one comment. This is in regards to yesterday's incident with Chef."

Tears started to form in her eyes. "A tragedy. Such a nice person."

"Yes. We're all going to miss him. What I wanted to talk about was how you handled the discovery. You were in shock, I realize, but do you think you should've called the medical responders before you called me? Perhaps Chef could've been saved."

"No. His bleeding had stopped. This I knew," objected Miseena, throwing me a glance indicating confusion.

"What are the hotel's procedures when an accident happens?" I asked.

"First call the responders," she replied. "Then call the hotel manager. However, I knew Chef could not be revived so I called you first. You are new so I wanted to keep you up to date and allow you to call the responders."

"Excellent, Miseena, excellent. I'm thinking, though, perhaps we should update the procedures manuals so the first item of business is to call the responders. Then no one has to make a decision whether there's any medical hope for the victim."

Clearly confused, Miseena sent me a questioning look. "What is a procedures manual?"

"Each position in the hotel should have a small manual describing all duties required. The employee then understands what's expected of them," I said, after a moment. Having her ask the question made me question my explanation, or perhaps the translator.

"We have no manual," replied Miseena. "Each

person is taught by their superior."

The back of my head started to ache—this'd be the day for headaches, I decided. "Because I supervise many managers, I need to teach each of them their job?"

"Only if you hire someone new," said Miseena. "Since you created my new position, we should discuss your requirements."

She'd correctly deduced my confusion. "Then the first procedures manual I produce will cover your position," I said. "Let me start writing it up, then we can discuss the contents. In the meantime, if you have any questions about your position, be sure to ask. I'm relying on you for scheduling the Reservations departments. Reena tried to explain ACTER and other issues, so I'm more confused than ever."

"I will let you know if I have questions." Miseena's smile indicated her understanding of my dilemma.

Happy after our discussion, I let my anxiety go. My to-do list had immeasurably increased, of course.

I called Hart. "Can you help me with my office computer? A couple of programs are defying my understanding."

"Sorry, no. Tomorrow is the earliest I can do. I have a ton of projects today."

"No problem." I really couldn't expect Hart to jump at my every whim. So I tackled the programs again, on my own, hoping for inspiration. When I got to the point where I'd started pulling out my hair, or at least ruffling it, Sain popped his head through my doorway. "Miseena said you wanted to talk to me."

"Come in. How are the Lounge upgrades going?" I

asked.

"I left the drawings with Dedare, but no response," said Sain. "Thus I have not started any changes."

So start nagging, I thought to myself, but how could I get Sain to do that? "Dedare is a busy man," I commented.

"As am I," said Sain. "Anything else?"

"No. Thank you for your time." A testy Sain surprised me. I wondered what'd triggered his mood.

I needed to re-examine my actions. Apparently, I'd annoyed Sain, and I had no idea why.

\*\*\*\*

"Syl, meal time?" asked Dedare, standing in my open doorway and interrupting my futile attempt at understanding a computer program.

After we'd ordered our lunches, I sat back and wondered how to start. "Dedare, I have suggestions and questions about the running of the hotel. Is now a good time?" After meeting with Sain today, I'd become a bit hesitant dealing with Irions—at least, my favorite ones.

"Certainly." He drank from his water glass.

I couldn't read his facial expression, but I heard no enthusiasm in his voice. Dedare apparently fell in the same annoyed department as Sain.

"Yesterday, Reena and Siska gave me a tour of the hotel areas I'd not previously seen. I found the chapel interesting and quite striking. Do you think the chapel should be a little more generic? By that, I mean welcoming to other species. We could add pews for Martians to sit upon, and something for the Skuttem—although I have no idea about their religions."

"Please research," said Dedare, "then I will be better able to decide."

A little noncommittal, but something I could work with. And he was correct. My information remained sketchy.

Our food arrived, so I took a couple of bites before proceeding with any of my other topics. "Dedare, do you think the hotel staff should wear berets to keep Master Tyre happy?"

"No. You are the only one who concerns him. Female Irions do not have hair of your color."

He had a point, but I'd look into the background of other species before they arrived—at least, if I knew about them beforehand. However, at this point, how could I research the Skuttem and determine what else Master Tyre may decide to complain about? Did information exist on our Irion coms?

"I love the hydroponics area and the roof top garden. Such wonderful places! Do you think we should start growing Martian fruits and vegetables?"

Dedare studied me. "A possibility. You must talk to Ambassador Charles. He will need to coordinate the research and present the option to our leaders. I am sure many issues need be considered."

"You're right. I'll talk to Charles." We ate for a few moments. "Is there anything you wish to discuss?"

"No, but I have a request—please enlighten me about human marriage. How different from Irion relationships?"

Interesting question, but why had he asked?

"I know little about Irion relationships, so I'll just tell you about human customs and not compare them." Simple to say, but Irion relationships began to swirl through my mind.

With interruptions and questions from Dedare, our

discussion took the better part of thirty minutes.

"Thank you. I now better understand today's issues."

Shocked, I asked, "What happened?" Why would Dedare be involved in human marriage?

"I cannot say. I promised to reveal nothing for a short time. You must be patient." A smug smile appeared. Apparently, he knew how impatient I could be.

"Okay, I'll bite my tongue." My mind filled with strange thoughts and questions.

"Why would you want to do that?"

I laughed. "Just a human expression meaning *I won't ask*. Of course, I'll be spending my time wondering."

"Humans have strange sayings."

"I'm sure Irions also do but the universal translator must filter them out or translate them." After taking a sip of water, I asked my final question. "Dedare, I don't understand the role of Dial Deen. Does she report directly to you? Or does she report to me, as the manager of this hotel?" I needed confirmation of what she'd told me.

"She reports to me." His glassy eyes surprised me.

"But…"

"She reports to me." Dedare stood. "I must return to my meetings. Meet again at dinner?"

"Of course. I enjoy our dinners." Dedare left the restaurant in a hurry. Was he annoyed? I shook my head. Aliens, impossible to read!

My afternoon passed with little interaction. I worked on the procedures manuals, but my enthusiasm had disappeared. I had no idea why my mind had filled with restless thoughts. I had a brand new world to understand.

Sain arrived and brightened my afternoon. "How was your tour with Mama A?"

"We will talk about the tour at dinner." No smile graced Sain's face.

Efficiently getting information from Irions often eluded me. "What can I do for you?" Irion males were exasperating or maybe only the Sath boys had that trait.

"I have details. Dedare gave his approval for the changes to the lounge." Sain rubbed his head. "I noticed his bad mood. What did you say?"

Somewhat annoyed with his assumption I'd created Dedare's bad mood, I racked my brain. "Ah, the only thing I thought he seemed irritated by was my question about Dial Deen."

Sain stood a little straighter. "What did you want to know?"

"I just wondered why she reported to him, rather than the hotel manager. Reporting to me seemed the natural hierarchy."

"No. She organizes requests from all hotels." Sain sat down in the chair in front of my desk. "There are many things you do not know about Dedare."

"Of course, I don't. I haven't known him very long. You, neither, for that matter," I said. Was this a personal issue?

Sain reached across and took my hand. "Dedare has had many personal relationships. Dial was one. Together for a long time, he gave her this position as a token of respect."

I tried to get my hand back. I wasn't particularly happy with either of the Sath males at the present

236

moment.

"Do not be upset. Although Dedare no longer has any romantic interest in Dial, he still considers her a friend." Sain placed his other hand on top of mine.

I tried to understand the situation. Not so different from humans, I decided, but I wasn't sure how happy I was about Dedare's numerous past relationships. On the other hand, why did this concern me?

"His relationship with Dial was in the past," said Sain, correctly interpreting my discomfort.

"Why was Dedare so cranky?" I pulled my hand back—successfully this time.

Sain gave the Irion equivalent of a sigh. "You are trying to change too much, too soon. Dedare has many enterprises, and needs to focus on all, not only this hotel."

And my numerous ideas for change had probably overwhelmed Dedare—even though he'd professed to welcome them. *Well, he'd just have to get used to me— I had a new playing field to romp in.*

"Sain, your tactfulness is refreshing. I'll consider what you've told me. See you at dinner." Now was not the time to bring up my new idea about updating the roof top garden.

He got my hint, and left.

I sat down at my worktable and started reading what I'd written yesterday for one of the procedures' manuals. After my eyes started to glaze over, I knew my restlessness had resurfaced—I needed exercise.

Grabbing my oversized bag and throwing my com inside, I locked my office. As I passed the front desk, I noticed Miseena. "I'm going on walkabout for an hour. I've got my com, if anyone needs me."

Miseena gave me a tentative smile but didn't speak. Had she understood *walkabout*?

After I exited the swooping entrance doors of the hotel, I stopped. I'd never truly taken time to study the grounds of the hotel.

The marvelous in-and-out driveway was wide enough to accommodate many vehicles, and the layout allowed a large number of guests to arrive and leave, simultaneously. The immense flower bed, situated between the driveway and the street, brought a smile to my face. I recognized a good number of the flowers, from my previous tour of the farm and around the hotel, but many were new. I knew our hotel took up the entire block, so I had a lot to investigate. I tore my gaze away from the flowers, and glanced behind me. The arch over the driveway gleamed with glass and shiny blue supports, but what really caught my eye was the hotel's front façade. Gleaming with gold, even the windows seemed to exude a similar hue. Although I wanted to linger at the front, today's escape was to study the city surrounding the hotel.

With no idea where North and South were in relation to the hotel, I started to my left. There I found a whole block of shops. Walking in and out of them for about thirty minutes, I studied a multitude of objects. Most of the items were obvious, but a couple I'd need to discuss with Reena. Since I had no local currency on me, I bought nothing. I supposed I could've billed anything to Dedare, but I lived with my oversight regarding obtaining local currency.

In the next block west, according to my reckoning, at least, I found an open-air market. This was what I'd missed on our previous day tour. Delighted, I sat on a

238

bench to study my surroundings. The market occupied an entire block. The Sath-Satre Golden Hotel had lucked out being across a street from this amazing entity. Then I had a thought—had Dedare decided on the hotel's location because of the market? Which came first?

Regardless, I wanted to look around. The air surrounding the market filled me with energy. Where to start?

I noticed a small area filled with musicians. I walked toward them, and stopped to listen. Benches were available, but I decided to stand and study the players and their audience.

After listening to a couple of artists, my back began to twitch. I glanced behind me and noticed more Irions had gathered. If they were here to listen to the performers, they were too close for my comfort.

I felt a hand on my right arm. Startled, I glanced into the eyes of an Irion male. What did he want? Why did he touch me?

Then someone stroked my left arm. Looking around I discovered another Irion male.

I realized I'd been surrounded by Irions—both male and female.

Before I had a chance to freak out, someone spoke and the crowd dispersed.

"What are you doing here? Shouldn't you be working, or something?" Perhaps not the most tactful question, but Sain had unnerved me with his sudden presence. Actually, I should've blamed the crowd of Irions.

He grabbed my right hand. "Perhaps you should let the one in charge of security know when you leave the hotel."

"I'm not a prisoner," I objected. Being tied down and not in charge of my actions were two of my biggest red flags.

Sain laughed. "Not a prisoner. Irions are not yet familiar with Martians, perhaps?"

He had a good point. For some reason, I expected all Irions to react like my hotel employees—a little naïve, on my part.

I took a few deep breaths and tried to appear reasonable.

"I understand," I said. "Before we go back to the hotel, though, would you walk me around this delightful market?"

And that's what we did. And when I found anything I drooled over, Sain took care of the transaction.

Eventually, Sain asked, "Dinner?"

I heard the desperation in his voice.

"Yes, it's getting late," I agreed, after glancing at my watch. "I need to go home and clean up, though. An hour, perhaps?"

Sain nodded, and a few minutes later, he left me at my suite.

While sipping a fortifying glass of wine, Mom and Charles appeared. "Ready?" asked my mother.

"Come in. Let me pour you guys a glass of wine, and then we can go down." I wasn't ready to face anyone and certainly not Dedare. His mixed vibes confused me.

After we settled in my living room, I asked, "Charles, what do you think about growing Martian vegetables and fruits on Irion? The Sath-Satre Golden

Hotel has a hydroponics lab and a roof top garden, both of which would be ideal."

"An excellent idea, Sylvestine. I'll need to research this topic because there are many issues to consider. For example, the soil may not be compatible and..." He paused. "I'll consult with Hart."

My long-lost father took another sip of his wine. "We should be able to make this viable, but it may take time." He gave me a speculative look. "By the way, Sylvestine, what is your middle name?" asked Charles.

"Charleze," I said. "Why?"

"Just curious." A small smile appeared on Charles' face.

I stole a look at my mother. Her face confirmed my suspicion. I'd been named after my father. I'd suspected that, after learning about Charles, but I'd been reluctant to get confirmation from my mother. "We'd best go downstairs. You know how hungry and impatient everyone can be at this time of day," I said.

Surprised not to see Sweety and Hart at our table, I studied the restaurant. "Why are Hart and Sweety over there?" I pointed across the room. They always had dinner with us.

"They needed to discuss a few things," said my mother. "So they took an early private meal. Hart seemed a little out of sorts, though."

I shrugged. I hadn't spoken with Hart and Sweety lately about anything except work. "Anyone know what's going on?" No one volunteered any insights.

Okay, next topic. "Mom, how was your tour with Master Tyre?"

Before she had a chance to respond, Hart and Sweety arrived at our table. "We're going up to the roof garden. We'll be back pretty soon. Save some dessert for us," said Hart.

The two of them waved and took off, hand in hand. Their behavior struck me as a bit odd, but I ignored my impression and asked again, "So tell me about today's tour."

"Unexpectedly, we had an extra passenger. In addition to Master Tyre, Simon showed up. Apparently, Tyre invited him."

"How would they've met?" A human and a Skuttem?

"I have no idea. Sain and I decided we'd cope with the added client, so we didn't argue with Master Tyre. We did charge a bit more, though," said Mom.

We all laughed, and Dedare acted pleased with their initiative.

Sain gave a nod of assent. "Since only two were on the tour, security would not have been a major issue, so I gave my approval."

"Something seems wrong to me—Simon and Master Tyre together," I said.

Mom rubbed her forehead. "The tour went as well as expected, but some tension did intrude." Everyone looked at Mama A. "I never told you, Syl, but I had a few dates with Simon, way back when."

Simon? Charles I could stomach, but not Simon. My mind blurred. I didn't know what to say, or what to ask. However, I needed to make a stab at understanding. "How did you and Simon get along?"

"The relationship didn't go very far. He's a jerk, for want of a better word. He didn't take the situation well when I told him I didn't want to go out again." She took a sip of her wine. "Our relationship, which I think of as non-existent, was many years ago. Although I knew he was on Irion, he certainly surprised me being on our trip today."

Mom wasn't the only one surprised. By the look on Charles' face, the two of them would be discussing her revelation about Simon.

How close were Mom and Charles? I hadn't spent much time recently with either of them to gauge the situation. Were they rekindling their relationship?

Hart and Sweety returned from the roof garden, and grabbed a couple of chairs. "Thanks for helping me with the ring purchase, Dedare. I didn't know who else to turn to," said Hart.

Ring? I looked over at Sweety. She flashed a ring on her left hand, and grinned like a ridiculously happy person.

"Are you telling me…" My brain had gone numb.

"Yes, Syl. Hart and I are engaged. We're going to be married!" Sweety ran around the table giving everyone a hug.

"I'm delighted! You may thank me for introducing you." I grinned. "I suspected something was going on, but I didn't realize the seriousness of your relationship."

"Hart may have been a bit more serious, but I didn't say no," teased Sweety. "Hart is so sweet." She blew him a kiss. "I have much to plan."

A flushed, shell-shocked Hart kept his mouth shut.

"What happened?" asked Reena. The Irions tried to catch up.

Mom replied, "Hart and Sweety are getting married!"

"Married?" Reena looked at Dedare and Sain. They

glanced back, but made no comment.

"Marrying is a life-long commitment to be together," said my mother, trying to help Reena.

"Forever?" Reena's wide eyes darted back and forth.

"Generally, yes," Mom replied. "Of course, sometimes relationships break up, but this won't happen with Hart and Sweety."

"No, Mom," they said, in unison. Laughter rang around the table.

My mother added. "So where's the wedding going to be? Mars?"

"No, here on Irion. Neither of us have much in the way of family on Mars, and our friends are here." Sweety gave Mom, sitting beside her, another hug. "Will you help with the planning?"

"I'd be delighted. We'll have many things to discuss. Hart, you'll need to be involved," my mother said.

"Ah, I'll go along with whatever Sweety wants." Panicked-looking, Hart gazed at me. "Maybe Syl will help?"

Guys never wanted to be involved and just as well. In due time, Hart would get his instructions.

A thought popped into my mind. This was why Dedare had asked his questions about human marriage.

"I'll need to get back to Mars and arrange my personal matters, banking, storage, and such." Sweety glanced around the table at her new permanent comrades. "Dedare, you and I'll need to discuss any position I could possibly hold in your hotel."

Dedare offered his hands to both of them. "Of course. Congratulations."

Reena looked at her father—a discussion appeared imminent.

"Do you want to put an Irion spin on your ceremony, Sweety?" Mom asked.

"Maybe. Something to look into. Right now my mind is mush."

Hart and Sweety locked glances and then Hart said, "Sweety and I have many topics to discuss. We'll see you all at breakfast."

The situation delighted me—I knew they'd make a great couple.

The evening ended with a lot of smiles. Mom and Charles disappeared somewhere, and Reena did also. That left Sain, Dedare, and me.

"Anyone want dessert?"

Dedare said, "I am tired and need rest."

I glanced at Sain.

"Rest for me."

"See you tomorrow," I said. Alone, I went home to my apartment.

Chapter Nineteen

Hart and Sweety were the cheeriest people on Irion, I decided, when I arrived at breakfast the next morning. They grinned and hugged everyone. The sweet vision cheered me, and my spirits needed bolstering after my lonely evening.

"Syl, I have time today to help with your computer programs," said Hart. "I was too busy yesterday."

"No kidding, a pretty exciting day for both of you. I can only imagine the range of emotions you're experiencing."

Hart and Sweety gazed at each other for a long moment.

"Pretty intense," said Sweety. "However, let's discuss today. I want to focus on arranging my return to Mars, and I also need to spend time in the kitchen to get a better idea of who's capable of taking over for Chef. Not an easy decision."

Dedare said, "Thank you for your help, Sweety. Replacing Chef will be difficult. Please meet Syl and me for lunch, so we can discuss your findings. We will also discuss trips to Mars and pertaining issues."

Trips to Mars? Did I want to go back? So soon?

Hart interrupted my thoughts, "Syl, after I help with your computer programs, I'm going to study the proposed changes for the Lounge. Dedare asked for my advice because of my engineering background."

"Great! I look forward to your suggestions." I gave Hart a hug. Apparently, I wasn't totally in the dog house if Dedare had asked Hart to look over my suggestions.

"Reena, do Irions keep household pets?" Why this question popped into my mind, I had no idea. Perhaps triggered by the words dog house?

Everyone peered at me like I'd come from a different galaxy. Had I? A question I'd never had answered.

"What do you mean?" Reena asked.

"On Earth and Mars, we keep small animals in our homes for companionship. Critters like dogs and cats. Do you have those?"

Because of the perplexed look on her face, I showed Reena pictures of household pets on my personal com. I hadn't had a pet recently, because I'd lived in the hotel, but we'd always had one underfoot during my childhood.

"A *chirka*," said Sain. "A small animal acting as company."

Reena's eyes widened. "Irions have these. However, our living space is small so we do not," she said, gazing at Sain and Dedare.

"They're a lot of work," said my mother, hoping to ease the obvious glaring conflict. "And do not always like to be confined, at least, the ones on Mars don't."

None of the Irions said a word.

"Well, Charles and I are going to visit a few historical areas today," said Mom, continuing her diversion attempt. "I need lots more information for my book on Sath Enterprises, and Charles needs to further his understanding of Irion. Works for both of us, and

Charles has an ambassador vehicle and driver we can use. We'll be back for dinner."

Thoughts rummaged through my mind as I watched them leave. Were they spending a lot of time together? None of my business, I admonished myself, but my curiosity refused to submerge. Eventually, the rest of us vacated the breakfast table and went about our duties.

I did a quick run through Amenities. I hadn't really checked in detail what they currently carried. I'd made a lot of assumptions, but I needed confirmation. Then I proceeded to the front desk. No problems existed, but I did encounter Master Tyre as I was about to head to my office.

"Manager Amera, I would like a tour," the Skuttem said. "There are many areas I need to explore and your off-world perspective is unique." Master Tyre knew how to push the right buttons, unfortunately.

However, I really didn't want to spend any time with him. "I'm not sure if I can get away."

"I insist. You would make my stay on Irion comfortable."

He put his hands on his head. The action made no sense, but I said, "Okay, but it'll have to be tomorrow. I'm busy today."

"I have my own vehicle, so no need to acquire one," said the Skuttem. "We will meet tomorrow, after breakfast."

I nodded and turned back to the front desk. I wanted him out of my sight, so I waited, talking to Miseena, until he left. To distract myself, I went to my office. While working for an hour or so, my mind naturally turned to Hart and Sweety. Happy turned out to be a miserly word to describe how I felt about their proposed union—I settled on ecstatic. Friends with both of them for a long time, they'd be staying on Irion with me. We'd have many adventures together, and our futures were bright.

A knock sounded at my door. "Come in." When Hart entered I told him, "I was just thinking about you guys."

"Isn't Sweety great?"

"Hart, I've known her forever. She's my best female friend, and you are my best male friend. Of course, you're both wonderful." I gave him a hug. "However, I know what you're trying to say. I'm glad you two found each other." I grinned. "How did you decide Sweety was the one you wanted to spend your life with?"

He blushed a deep red. "I thought about her returning to Mars after her holiday, and I was devastated."

So sweet. "How did Dedare help?"

"A little old-fashioned but I wanted an engagement ring. I didn't have a clue if any existed on Irion, so I went to Dedare and explained the situation. I have to admit, the explanation took a bit. Apparently, they have jewelry, but engagement and wedding rings are a new concept. However, Dedare steered me in the right direction, and gave me cash to make my purchase. Cash against earnings, of course."

"We still need to understand a few things regarding income, money, and such, but time has flown so quickly." I shook my head. "Look at the two of you!"

Hart blushed again.

"If you tell me you still don't believe in *love at first*

*sight*, I'll smack you." Hart had once given me a scientific explanation as to why the concept wasn't possible.

Hart shrugged, and declined to comment.

Wise man.

"A gorgeous ring, by the way. However, I'm upset you didn't let me help you choose."

"Ah, ah…" His face started to lose color.

"I'm teasing, Hart. I probably wouldn't have been able to keep your secret, anyway," I laughed. "So I'm glad you thought of Dedare."

"He's a great guy. I'm so glad I came to Irion, and not just because of Sweety. You were very persuasive."

"I don't remember saying much of anything except mentioning the scientific possibilities."

"Ha, ha. Now let's get going on your computer programs. I have other things to do today."

We worked on half a dozen programs, and my comfort level rose. Then my mind started to shrivel. "I'm beginning to understand these programs, Hart, but I think I need time on my own with the software. If I have any issues, I'll let you know."

"You won't have a problem," he replied. "You're not as unskilled with software as you'd like everyone to believe. However, I'm always available." He got up from my desk, and strode to the door. "I'll look at the lounge blueprints today. Perhaps I'll see you at lunch."

After his comment, he abruptly left my office but that was Hart's way. His mind had turned to a new project.

Needing a break from my computer, I sat at my work table and studied the piles of paper corresponding to various procedures manuals, but my attention wandered. What had made Mom decide to go on a date or two with Simon? Mom had better taste. Of course, my judgment might be a tad cloudy after my experiences with Simon, the boss. Who else had Mom had relationships with?

Mom's love life was none of my business, I reminded myself. I had no tactful way to ask, anyway. However, I decided I was allowed to think about Charles, my biological father, so I called him. "Any news on the Martian fruits and vegetables, Ambassador?"

"Sylvestine, you know you can call me Charles or anything else, for that matter." A reproving glance came my way.

Was he hinting I should call him Father, or Dad? At the moment, my mind rejected those notions.

"As for Martian organics, I did send the word out but diplomatic circles move slowly. I'll let you know when I receive any responses."

"Sorry. I understand. The topic just popped into my mind, so I decided to call." Perhaps not my wisest decision.

"I'm happy to hear from you, anytime." He stared at me, for a moment. "How about dinner one evening? With your mother, if you wish."

"That'd be lovely. Do you have a day in mind?" I wanted to be gracious, after all we were related.

"How about in two days?"

"I'll update my calendar. However, please call and remind me. Perhaps another restaurant in Satre?"

"An excellent idea. I'll see which ones can cater to Martians."

"Thanks for your help regarding the veggies. I'll

talk to you soon." I closed my com, and tried to put my thoughts in order. One good note in my opinion, was that my attempt to reach out to Charles had succeeded. However, I had no idea what our next baby step would entail.

As for baby steps, what were my feelings about Dedare and Sain? Did I want a relationship with either one of them—and my mind rang with the weirdness of that question—or should I back off?

A call from the detective investigating Chef's death interrupted my personal relationships perusal.

"Manager Sylvestine, I need to speak with you again," said Teeka Cole.

"Sure, but what about? I thought you were happy with my answers and the test results." Was I a suspect again?

"Yes, happy. I have new topics." He rubbed his hand around his head.

New topics? His statement put me on edge. "How about today? I have time around mid-afternoon." Teeka would distract me from my procedures manuals, but I hoped he had benign topics.

"I will proceed to the hotel," Detective Cole said, and then ended our conversation.

Why would he want to talk to me again? He'd given me no inkling, but what could I possibly do to dissuade him? Complain to Dedare, since they were friends? Not a viable option, I decided. I had to admit I was curious about his reasons for visiting. Detective Cole had seemed particularly friendly. Perhaps an incorrect impression, on my part.

Before I had a chance to obsess about my situation, Dedare stood in my doorway. "Lunch?"

Pleased with his suggestion, I said, "Good, I need a break. I didn't realize so much time had passed." Sain joined us, but no other Martians occupied the restaurant. Before we ordered, I said, "I must apologize to the both of you. I realize I've made too many suggestions. I can be pretty pushy."

"Pushy? Meaning?" asked Dedare, clearly confused.

"Enthusiastic, I guess you could say." I studied the two of them. "Anyway, please accept my apologies. I'll try to reign in my ideas."

"I like your enthusiasm," said Sain. "However, Dedare is conservative."

I swear Sain tried not to laugh. I liked him more and more. Our personalities were similar, I began to realize.

Dedare gave Sain an icy glance. "I understand your background and how you like to improve areas and make them work at top efficiency. I do not always have time to consider your suggestions. Do not take my reluctance as criticism. You must follow up again to remind me. Apology accepted." Then Dedare glanced at Sain.

"No apology necessary. Your ideas are innovative, Syl. Understanding Irions better will help," said Sain.

I agreed with Sain's assessment. "So what should I do to up my understanding?"

"Have crazy ideas!" said Sain.

Grins spread around our table—even from Dedare.

Before we had a chance to discuss Dain's statement, Miseena burst into the restaurant. "Manager Syl, we have a call about a bomb targeting Martians."

My heart started to race. Martians? "Did the caller

say where the bomb was planted?"

She waved her right hand behind her back. "In the Lounge," she replied, holding back tears.

"Call your responders, Miseena. Sain, help her. Dedare, we need to go to the Lounge." Everyone turned toward me, surprised by my response. "Hart decided to take the updated blueprints to the Lounge for further study."

Everyone started to scatter, and then we heard a loud whomp. "That's a bomb!" I yelled. "Hurry, hurry!"

I scurried over to the Lounge. No flames or smoke were visible outside, so, tentatively, I opened the front door. Dedare pushed me aside.

"I'm not some weak female," I complained. After glancing at me, I understood Dedare had no idea what I meant.

"Follow," he growled.

Oh, I would, but we'd have words, at a more appropriate time. However, my foremost thoughts concerned Hart. I peered around Dedare into the Lounge. The air reeked a bit of smoke, but nothing else. "Hart, are you here?" I yelled.

"I'm in the back. I'm okay. Don't worry."

His voice didn't sound concerned, so I took a couple of deep breaths. Tentatively, Dedare and I entered the Lounge. Hart came out from the Lounge's prep area. Purple dust coated his clothing.

"Happened?" asked Dedare, looking at the small particles on Hart's shirt. "What?"

"I opened a cupboard door in the kitchen. Then I heard a loud bang and this dust spewed everywhere. My ears are still ringing." He put his hands over his ears, for a moment. "This dust is really sticky. Oh, and my face and arm were smacked." Hart poked at his exposed flesh.

Wordlessly, numerous Irions burst through the doorway of the Lounge, startling me. Two lifted Hart onto a portable bed, and then pushed him out of the Lounge. Other Irions grabbed Dedare and me and hustled us out of the room.

"Stay here until we verify the room is safe," said one of the responders when Dedare started to argue.

"Dedare, wait with me," I commented, trying to defuse the situation. "We need to determine Hart's status before we do anything." A few feet away, while we watched, the medical staff poked Hart and sampled his blood and the purple dust covering his clothing.

"Are you two causing trouble again?" asked Detective Teeka Cole, who'd arrived without our notice.

Before either of us had a chance to respond, Sweety ran into the lobby, and then over to Hart. Tears streamed down her cheeks. We couldn't hear their words, but we really didn't need to.

"Wait here," said our favorite detective. He strode off in the direction of the Lounge.

I spent my time glancing between Hart and the Lounge entrance. What'd just happened in our hotel? Had we really been bombed?

Soon Hart and Sweety approached, arm in arm. "I'm fine, Syl. Stop worrying. The dust is benign, apparently, and I only have a couple of scratches." He pointed to the pieces of yellow fabric on his cheek and arm.

"I'm so glad you're okay." I gave both Hart and

Sweety hugs—although I tried not to get too close to the purple dust.

"I need to clean this gunk off and change my clothes. My hair feels weird." He ran his fingers through his locks. "Then I need lunch. Sweety and I'll be back shortly."

"No," said Detective Cole. "The technicians need to search you for evidence, and then you can clean up. To give a little breathing room, I will wait to interview you until after the techs are finished, and you've showered and joined us in the restaurant."

No one found any reason to argue with our personal detective.

Teeka took Hart inside the Lounge, and then returned. "I also need food while we wait. Come along you two, I have questions." He pointed to Dedare and me.

We went back to the table where Dedare, Sain, and I'd tried to have lunch—a lifetime ago.

"What happened?" I needed to know how to protect my hotel.

Detective Cole admonished, "I ask the questions. Why did the two of you hustle over to the Lounge?"

"Miseena came to us and said she had received a bomb threat targeting the Lounge," said Dedare. "Syl mentioned Hart had decided to check out our planned changes. A second later, we heard a loud sound, so Sain and Miseena ran to call responders, and Syl and I went to search for Hart."

"What did you find?" asked Detective Cole.

"Hart answered my call-out, and emerged from the serving area covered in dust. No other people were visible and no apparent damage in the Lounge's main room. We didn't go into the back to find Hart. He came out to meet us."

"Confirming his story," said Teeka.

"So what's this all about?" I asked. "Did you talk to Miseena?"

"Yes, madam detective, I did." Teeka grinned. He gestured at a server. He probably needed food also.

"Did she remember the actual words of the bomb threat? Are they recorded on the com system?" I asked.

"Both," responded Teeka, without elaborating.

Why did Irions love to tease me? Or maybe they weren't teasing. Maybe I didn't understand their comments in spite of the translator's attempts. "Are you able to tell me the words of the threat?"

"Yes." He looked at his com.

He tried to hide a smile, but I knew what'd just *literally* happened. Annoyed, I said, "So tell me."

"Yes, Syl. The caller said a bomb would go off. To tell the Martians to go home."

*Martians Go Home*! Sounded like an old movie. "What kind of bomb?" I asked.

"Nothing serious, a dust bomb. Protesters use them to spew dust to annoy everyone in the vicinity. Your back room needs quite a cleanup."

Interesting that Irion had protestors. What motivated their discontent I wondered?

"Area available for cleaning?" asked Dedare.

"No. You will be notified," said Teeka.

Hart and Sweety joined our lunch table. "Are you okay?" I asked Hart.

"I'm fine. Cleaning up solved everything; except for why this happened, of course." Sweety took his hand and held on tight. Speechless, they gazed at each other.

Teeka interrupted their moment. "Hart, order food. Then we can have our interview while we wait for our meals."

Hart and Teeka retired to another table and had a short conversation. I would've loved to hear the questions being asked. Sleuthing interested me, and I wanted to know how Irion detectives worked. How different were they from Martians?

Soon Teeka and Hart were back. Our food arrived a moment later, so we all dug in. Bombings, apparently, improved my appetite.

Sain joined us from the Lounge. I assumed he'd been checking on security. Did the hotel have cameras? To refocus our attention from the bomb, I mentioned, "Master Tyre wants me to take him on a tour tomorrow. Where should we go, and what should we see? He has his own vehicle and driver."

"Who is Master Tyre?" asked Teeka.

"Our first alien. I mean the first Skuttem alien to stay at this hotel. A bit strange, for example, he doesn't like my hair."

"No taste," said Teeka. "Your hair has a gorgeous hue."

I tried not to preen, while I sneaked a look at Teeka.

"Master Tyre is *black*," said Sain. "Are you going on this tour alone?"

A typical comment from our chief of security. "What do you mean by *black*?" I asked.

"His *tangle* is evil."

*Tangle* was another unknown word, according to my translator, but I guessed something similar to aura or image.

"Well, the Skuttem just asked me this morning for a tour, so I put him off until tomorrow. That's why I'm bringing it up now." Was Sain being protective because of his role as security chief?

"You should not go alone," he reiterated. "I am busy tomorrow. We should talk to Mama A when she is back this evening. She will have ideas on what to show Master Tyre," said Sain.

"Who is Mama A?" asked Teeka.

"She's my mother, but she likes to parent my acquaintances, so everyone calls her Mama A." I rubbed my forehead. "The letter A being the first letter of our mutual last name." I had to admit the name Mama A would sound strange to anyone, not just someone from an alien background.

"I would like to meet her; I hear respect whenever her name is mentioned," said Detective Cole.

"She's writing a book for Dedare about the history of Sath Enterprises, so she's around the hotel a lot and lives here, too."

Teeka smiled. "Manager Syl, I must leave. I have much work." He studied me. "I have many questions about Martians and their world. Dinner this evening? I know a lovely restaurant."

All conversation around the table suddenly stopped.

Before I had a chance to respond, Dedare said, "We have dinner together each evening."

For some reason, Dedare's statement annoyed me. "I think a change of pace would be nice, Teeka. I'd love to join you. Please make sure there's something I can eat at this establishment."

"Thank you for the reminder; I will inquire. Shall we meet in the lobby at seven?"

"Perfect. I'll join you then." I gave Teeka a big smile as he left.

I ignored all glances directed my way. "Time for work. I'll see everyone later, sometime, maybe tomorrow."

Walking out of the restaurant, with my back to everyone at our table, I tried to keep a smile off my face. So far, my day had been full of surprises.

My afternoon turned out somewhat duller. I did, however, make great progress on the procedures manuals. Having employees come into my office and discuss their jobs, gave them a feeling of importance— a win-win situation.

When my work day ended, I went up to my suite and changed. Not sure what to wear, I compromised. After all, what expectations would any Irion have about my clothing?

Teeka arrived at the appointed time. He found me standing by the front desk talking to Siska.

"You look lovely," said the detective. "Ready to see another part of town?"

"I'm looking forward to our evening." And I really was. I hadn't had much of a chance to get out of the hotel, and I liked Teeka.

Siska tried to hide her smirk, but had minimal success—at least, from my point of view. I was sure she'd teased me later regarding my dinner companion.

"My vehicle is outside." He gestured toward the lobby entrance. "The restaurant is located in an area you should like. On a hill overlooking Satre, you will get a great view of the city you live in."

The ride to the restaurant didn't take long, and I enjoyed our enroute conversation.

After we ordered dinner, I took a sip of my wine. Our evening had gotten off to a great start—Teeka had arranged to have a bottle of Martian wine available and he shared it with me. "Where do you work?" I asked, gazing over the expansive city capital.

"A couple of blocks from your hotel," he replied, pointing out the Sath-Satre Golden hotel and the police station.

Satre's city center didn't have much greenery, but the surrounding areas were covered in blue-tinged vegetation. In the distance, I saw the space port where we'd landed and I'd experienced my interrogation.

"What is wrong?" asked Teeka. My distress had broadcasted, obviously.

After I explained my introduction to Irion, he said, "I can arrange for an apology."

"No, no. I'm fine. The experience wasn't that bad, just a shock to not be welcomed." I pointed beyond the city. "Are those mountains?" My eyes had trouble deciphering the distance involved. I thought I saw a long dark ridge with a flattened top. Perhaps a plateau or a row of gigantic buildings?

"Those are reservoirs feeding Satre. The water is pumped from the ground, stored, and then sent to the city along *milts*, when water is required."

*Milts* turned out to be the equivalent of covered aqueducts.

"Only needed recently because of our current solar cycle," he explained.

I sent a questioning look his way. I knew so little about this planet.

"Irion is in a dry cycle. Scientists postulate within ten years we will begin to return to our normal watery planet. *Milts* allow us to cope with the dry spell."

"Satre must have mounted a huge effort to build those immense reservoirs." From my perspective, they looked as large as the pyramids.

"The storage ponds are ancient. We refurbished them and also rebuilt the aqueducts, which had fallen into disrepair."

"Impressive. Not only the original builders, but your preservation." For the rest of our meal, I peppered Teeka with questions about Irion society. I discovered his daughter and Reena were approximately the same age. And the currently unattached Teeka, found raising a teenage daughter, with his work schedule, a challenge.

A yawn escaped and embarrassed me.

"A long day?" my companion asked, with a smile on his face.

"All my days have been long, since I arrived." I put my hand on his. "This has been a great evening, and I've learned so much, but I think I should return. Tomorrow will be full of new challenges."

We drove back to the Sath-Satre Golden Hotel in a companionable silence.

"I will not come in," said Teeka. "You do not need to generate more gossip."

An extremely astute comment, I thought.

"I enjoyed our evening. Perhaps we can do it again." Teeka reached over and rubbed my cheek, which took me by surprise.

"Yes, yes, a lovely evening," I stammered. "Very nice to experience new parts of Satre, and I enjoyed our conversations. Take care, Teeka," I said, and unlatched my door. "Good bye and thank you." I got out of his vehicle and walked to the hotel entrance. I desperately needed oodles of reflection time.

Much to my surprise Sain leaned against the front desk. "How was your dinner?" he asked.

Why was Sain here?

"Good. Teeka is an interesting Irion. How was your evening?"

"Much better if you take a walk to the roof top with me," Sain said. "I have a bottle of wine." He hefted a bag dangling from his right hand. "I thought we would sit and relax. We have not had much time to converse recently, and today has challenged me. You could tell me about your day, so I can ignore mine."

Did I have the energy for another encounter? I studied Sain and decided I really did like him, so time together would be a positive step. "Sure. Sounds like a plan."

We took the elevator up to the rooftop, and then strolled out amongst the greenery. Finding the public center area empty, we sat on a bench and Sain poured me a glass of wine. He poured himself a different beverage.

"What's that?" I asked, pointing to the purple-hued fluid in his glass.

"This is *assinst*, a local brew I enjoy. I did ask about your tolerance but a chemical in the liquid came up on our warning list. You are stuck with Martian wine."

"Well, make sure Dedare keeps importing wine."

"Dedare tries to keep everyone happy." Sain studied my face, after he uttered his words.

We sipped for a few moments.

"Hart and Sweety are happy," Sain commented.

"Yes. I think they'll make a great couple, even though they haven't known each other long." Actually, a really short time, in my opinion. Of course, my sad track record with Martian males was nothing to write home about.

Sain gave me a glance. "How long is long enough?"

"Oh, I don't know. Hart now tells me he believes in love at first sight, contrary to his previous scientific ruminations. I'm a little skeptical, though. What's your opinion?"

"Not discussed." Sain put his arm around my shoulders. "Hart did mention this spot as being romantic."

Alarm bells rang. I studied Sain and tried to read his expression. Deciding he was an inscrutable Irion, I asked myself, what did I want? Romance? Yes.

With Sain? With Teeka? Then Dedare popped into my mind to confuse the issue.

A very perceptive Sain noticed my hesitation. "Tired?"

I nodded. More like emotionally exhausted, I thought, but I didn't say the words out loud.

"Time to leave," he said. He walked me to my door, and then without a word or gesture of any kind, he left.

Chapter Twenty

I noticed a relaxed group at the breakfast table the next day. Hart and Sweety couldn't take their eyes off each other, and my mother had a rosy glow.

"Mom, how was yesterday's sightseeing?"

"Wonderful! Charles and I found the greatest spots. You need to visit them on your next day off." Mom and Charles exchanged sweet grins.

"The locations and cultural buildings were amazing. They gave us lots of information about Irion's unusual history," said Charles. "Your mother is going to write up an account, a blog I guess you could call it, so we can be sure we don't forget anything we saw."

"Syl, I'll give you a copy at dinner tonight, and you can edit away to your heart's content. And I've gathered excellent information to add to my research."

From the Irions' faces, I understood their confusion. "Editing is studying a document and finding the errors in grammar, punctuation, logical order and such. It'll be interesting to see how the translator and your reading device for written words handle the translations into Irion, because I'm sure Mom will need an Irion to also edit the content. Content of her history I mean, not necessarily her blog."

Hart and Dedare exchanged glances. "I may have to work on software updates," responded Hart.

Sweety's squirming attracted my attention. "How

are you today, Sweety, oh engaged person?"

"Very, very happy." She beamed at Hart, but then turned back to me. "I have a question. How was your evening with Teeka?" A maniacal grin assaulted me. "Dish the gossip," she urged.

Again the Irions were confused, but this time I ignored everyone. "We had a lovely dinner at a restaurant with gorgeous view windows overlooking Satre. The Martian food was great. Teeka made the arrangements. We spent a good deal of time talking about the differences between Martians and Irions. I think, as a police officer, Teeka needs to understand our culture since he might be solving future problems involving Martians, given recent activities. Then he brought me back to the hotel."

Sweety started to ask another question, but Sain interrupted. "Syl and I went up to the roof top garden for a drink after she returned."

His comment silenced the table, and everyone glanced our way.

Uncomfortable, I shook my head at Sweety to stop her from asking more questions. "I'm taking Master Tyre on a tour today. Any suggestions? Mom, some of the areas you saw yesterday, perhaps?"

"A better idea would be you feign sickness, and postpone the tour until tomorrow. I am unavailable today, but I can accompany you the next day," said Sain.

Was Sain being protective, or just acting as the hotel's security chief?

"An excellent idea," said Dedare. "I have topics I need to discuss with you today, Syl. They cannot wait."

Was the urgency true, or did Dedare also hover?

My mother caught my eye. No matter. "I'll talk to Master Tyre, but I take no responsibility for any complaints the Skuttem may have. Now I need to work. I have a lot to accomplish today if I'm not going on a tour."

Miffed with the overprotectiveness displayed, I left the restaurant.

To compound my irritation, my conversation with Master Tyre didn't go well. "If that is the case, I expect a full day of touring tomorrow. You have upset my schedule."

Knowing no way to make him happy, I ignored the Skuttem's comments and went on with my day.

I met with numerous hotel employees to discuss my procedures manuals. Then I was introduced to Chef Lasto, the new chef chosen by Sweety and Dedare.

"Manager Syl, happy to meet. The kitchen staff, and my new favorite friend, Sweety, have talked much about you. If you have any ideas about the kitchen, let me know. This is a great opportunity, and I intend to make the best of it." Lasto clasped my hand and patted my forehead.

After he left my office, I thought, I really must get Reena to make up a list of Irion mannerisms. My brain seemed to think some of them meant more than one thing, but the differences still escaped my rudimentary understanding.

Then Dedare poked his head through my doorway. "Syl, lunch?"

"Yes, a welcome break. Giving employees procedures manuals, and then trying to understand their writing, has given me a massive headache. Your transcription software has helped a lot, but the whole operation's still confusing and time filling."

"I am not sure Hart and I can find an easier way." A concerned look grew on his face.

"Oh, I know. I'm just going to have to find an opportunity to learn the Irion spoken and written languages." Mountainous tasks, and I saw no window of opportunity in my near future.

Dedare smiled, pleased with my suggestions.

Our walk to the restaurant included no conversation. We were both immersed in our own thoughts.

After we settled at a table, Dedare said, "Syl, I have received a few complaints about your procedures manuals. However, I believe your idea to train everyone so they understand their duties, and prepare for emergencies, is excellent." We ordered food and discussed numerous topics related to the hotel. Then Dedare said, "Hart and I went to the Lounge. We had a further discussion regarding the renovations."

"Everything is approved and on schedule?" I asked. I looked forward to having a little bit of home on Irion.

"Yes. Your suggestions were innovative, although I needed further explanations."

I wondered what he'd been confused about, and I'd ask Hart later. One of my pet projects was proceeding! I'm sure a contented look appeared on my face. After our food arrived we discussed the procedures manuals, in depth.

"Syl, tell me about your dinner with Teeka," said Dedare, as we neared the end of our meal.

"What do you want to know?" Dedare's intrusion into my private life, for some reason, upset me. "I believe I explained my evening during breakfast this morning."

"Of course. I must return—endless meetings." Dedare stood, then patted my forehead. First Chef, now Dedare? More than one reason to talk to Reena.

Alone in my office the doorbell interrupted my continued tedious editing of procedures manuals. "Come in," I called out.

Branson entered. I stood and said, "Mr. Branson, how may I help you?" I pointed at the chair across from me.

After he settled, he asked, "I'm interested in many of the companies Sath Enterprises owns. Is it possible to take a tour?"

"What's your interest?" Obviously, Dedare would need to know more before he granted access.

"I may want to acquire one or two, to perhaps expand my operations to Irion. My ancestor was Richard Branson. Do you know of whom I speak?"

I smiled. "Yes, my science advisor explained your history." I had to laugh at the notion of having my own personal science advisor. "Mr. Branson, by the way, what is your full name?" I asked.

"Richard Branson, the fourth. You may call me Richard."

Not a surprising answer. "I'm giving a tour tomorrow which includes a couple of properties belonging to Sath Enterprises. Would you like to join us?"

He nodded, and then added, "A good start for my knowledge base."

We agreed upon a meeting time, and then he left. I made a note to mention the situation to Dedare and

Sain.

A little later in the afternoon, Reena appeared at my office door. Her hesitation and stuttering convinced me the two of us needed some personal time, so we travelled to the roof top garden—a favorite place for both of us. We started by having a long chat with Lain Tisis about hydroponics and gardening. Then Reena and I settled down on a bench in the public area, and she told me what occupied her mind.

"I want to tell you about my mother, since you are becoming friends with my father."

Whoa, what did she mean by *friends*? Was she upset about the situation? "I'd love to hear about your mother, Reena. I know little about Gyra Sath except everyone holds her in high regard."

Reena beamed.

A bit of an exaggeration, on my part, but I certainly hadn't heard any negative comments. "What are your earliest memories?" A safe topic, I hoped.

"We were at the Satre Zoo looking at a *leirie*, and the animal scared me. I think I was three."

"What's a *leirie*?" I asked. The translator had let me down again—not a commonly used word, I suspected.

"A very big animal, at least to a three-year-old, with a long snout and six legs. I was afraid his snout would come through the fence holes and touch me."

"Pretty freaky, I agree. What did your mother do?"

"She took me to the feeding stand, and purchased *leirie* food. Then she asked if I would like to feed my new friend." Reena smiled.

"Did you?" I pictured her looking up at her mother in horror.

"After she went first. I was not a brave child."

We laughed. "Do you still enjoy the zoo?"

"Yes. I got over my fears, and our whole family went lots of times. Shall we go to the zoo, Syl?"

"I'd like that very much. I have so much to learn about Irion." How could I refuse Reena? "What else can you tell me about your mother? One of your happy times? I know you have many, but perhaps a favorite?"

Reena gazed at the sky—the rooftop garden certainly gave plenty of opportunity. "My mother excelled in teaching me about science. My father is all about commerce, much like you, but Mom thought I needed variety in my experiences in order to choose my path. The two of us spent a lot of time at museums and historical sites."

"Was she correct? Does history appeal to you, in addition to science?" Reena's dilemma concerned me.

"Being with her made the past exciting, but entrepreneurship is my current career goal and you are helping me enjoy the field."

Such a sweet young woman. "We need to plan some outings, Reena, and I will look forward to them. However, I think it's time we went home and cleaned up for dinner. We've had a great chat. Perhaps you would tell Mama A and Sweety some of your stories. They'd love to hear about your mother."

Reena nodded, but sadness covered her face.

A thought popped into my scattered mind. "Reena, before we go home, I'd like to show you something in my office. Do you mind?"

"What is it?" A portion of her teenage energy returned, and she grinned at me.

"Let me surprise you," I said. I had no idea how to

introduce my subject.

After we got to my office, I pointed to the painting I'd done the other night. I'd stuck the canvas on my wall, so I could stare at it until the subject was revealed. So far, my understanding stood at zero.

"What?" asked Reena, after she glanced at my painting.

"I created this, Reena. Do Irions have paintings?"

"Yes," replied a hesitant Reena. "But usually the image is understandable."

I laughed. "I paint abstract art. I let my mind wander as I paint, and then I see what my fingers unveiled. Usually, the painting reveals an unknown issue troubling me."

"I understand," said Reena.

I didn't believe her statement, probably a bizarre concept for an Irion.

"This is the first painting I've done on Irion. I have no idea what it's trying to tell me. I'd hoped you'd be able to shed some light." I hoped any comments Reena had would expand my understanding of Irions—a long shot, I realized.

She studied my painting. After a few moments, Reena said, "The only thing I see is love."

"What do you mean?" Certainly not the answer I'd expected.

"A majority of reds and blues. These colors are associated with Irion romance."

"Really?" Dedare, Sain, and Teeka flashed into my mind.

Reena nodded.

I waited for her to comment, but she remained silent. "Would you take me to an art museum, sometime? Satre has one, I assume?" I asked.

"Yes. Our paintings and sculptures will astound you." She got a faraway look in her eyes, and a smile on her face.

I gave Reena a hug. "Thanks for today. Your insights have helped me a lot." I laughed. We travelled upstairs and retired to our suites. My encounter with Reena had touched me. Actually, my whole day had revealed numerous insights.

The three Saths arrived at my door before I had a chance to travel downstairs.

"Please enter," I said. Noticing Dedare and Sain carrying cases, I asked, "What do we have here?"

"Wine—in case your supply is low," said Dedare.

"Not allowed," said Sain.

The Sath boys were teasing me. "Well, thank you, everyone. Just put them anywhere. I really haven't yet had a chance to make my home my own." I gazed about. I'd done nothing and barely even any laundry. How had this come to be?

"Syl, Syl," admonished Sain. "Have you had the time?"

I took a deep breath. "You're right. Okay, first chance, I'm making this mine. And for that I need furnishings. Reena, will you take me to appropriate markets on my next day off?"

"Shopping is fun," replied Reena. We both grinned. Dedare and Sain ignored our female comments.

"Ladies, time for food," said Dedare.

In the restaurant, Mom handed me the account of her tour with Charles. Before I had a chance to read anything, Hart and Sweety joined us, and we settled down to order dinner.

A while later, our new chef came out of the kitchen and handed me my dinner. "I have been assured, Manager Syl, you will love the spices I used. Apparently, they are some of your favorites."

"Thank you, Chef Lasto. I'll let you know later."

He bowed and retreated to his kitchen.

"Okay, this I'm looking forward to," I said, gazing down at my plate of spaghetti.

"You're starting to get spoiled," said Sweety.

"Something I can handle." I grinned at her. I started on my food, and listened to the conversations.

"Sweety, please tell me about your wedding plans," said Reena. "I do not understand Martian ceremonies."

I focused on their words; I also wanted to know the plans. Then black spots began to appear in my eyes.

Chapter Twenty-One

A hand on my forehead surprised me. Was I dreaming or engaged in some sort of Irion ritual? No, the skin gave the impression of human origin, but I decided I might be dreaming since I had no desire to open my eyes. A peaceful state enveloped my being.

"Syl, wake up. You're okay now." A familiar voice, but who'd interrupted my slumber?

I opened my eyes. "Hart…hovering?" I tried to sit up, but my limbs had no strength.

"Yes, I'm hovering. Don't move," said Hart. "Not yet, anyway." Although my mind swirled in a fuzzy manner, I thought I detected concern.

"Where am I?" The ceiling I stared at needed paint, and I hadn't gazed at many recently to know where I lay. Was I in the hotel, or another facility off site?

"You're lying on a table in the restaurant. You had an adverse reaction to your food and passed out, so I gave you a general antidote. You've just regained consciousness. How do you feel?" Hart touched my wrist to take my pulse.

I mentally checked out my body. "Tired, but no real pain. Help me up," I demanded.

"Just rest for a bit. I guarantee your energy will start to return if you give your body a chance." Hart took my blood pressure. Evidently, he'd retrieved his medical bag.

While I waited, I tried to reconstruct what'd happened, but I couldn't even remember what I'd eaten for dinner. Wait, yes, a specially spiced dish. What was—

"Causing trouble again?" I looked up and saw Teeka .

"I think I got poisoned at dinner. There was a spice…"

"So I have been told. I am going to the kitchen to talk to your new chef. He has much to explain." He picked up my hand, and held it between both of his.

"Let me go with you. I want to know what happened." Again I struggled to sit up, but both Teeka and Hart gently held me down.

"No," said Teeka. "Dedare gathered the hotel stretcher and, from what I see, all your acquaintances will be escorting you back to your room."

I gazed about but lying down made viewing difficult.

"Syl, listen," said Hart. "Have a good long rest, and tomorrow you'll be back to your lovely self. You only received a mild poisoning. My magic injection cured all, but you need rest. Allergic reactions are exhausting."

I gave in. "Fine. I am feeling less than optimum, unfortunately, so I'll take your advice." I let Dedare and Sain lift me onto the wheeled stretcher and push me to my suite. They helped me off and bundled me inside. Mom and Sweety shooed everyone out, except for the three of us.

"Let's put you to bed," said Sweety.

I shook my head. "Actually, I want to sit on my couch and drink tea. I don't feel that bad. And with all that's been going on, I haven't had a chance to talk to Mom about Charles."

My mother blushed, and then disappeared into my tiny kitchen.

I whispered to Sweety, "Do you want to stay?"

"I do, but let me talk to Mama A." Sweety left my living room. The two of them came back carrying a teapot and cups.

After they served tea, I asked, "Mom, why didn't you tell me who my father was?" I needed to ask my real question. "Actually, what I really want to know is why you didn't stay together?"

Before Mom had a chance to reply, Sweety jumped in. "You really must learn some social graces, Syl. Let me handle this." Sweety turned to Mom. "When did you know you were pregnant with Syl?"

Social graces? Humph...

Mom laughed. "Charles and I were dating and getting serious, I have to admit. Then he received a huge promotion within the diplomatic corp. However, the job entailed relocation to Earth." Mom sighed. "We had lengthy discussions about what we should do. Unfortunately, this promotion was important to Charles, and my career fascinated me. Since our relationship was still in a somewhat early stage, we chickened out and promised to keep in touch. Well, you know how often long distance relationships last."

I gave Mom a hug, but I didn't know what to say.

"A couple of weeks after Charles left, I realized I was with child. I had a difficult decision to make—to tell or not to tell."

Sweety poured Mom more tea. We all sipped, for a moment.

"In the end, I decided to say nothing. I didn't want to force Charles back to Mars—especially since neither one of us had made any commitment to the other." Mom sighed. "And I didn't want to find out he'd perhaps already moved on from our relationship."

"However, when you realized he was on Irion, you wanted to let him know?" Sweety asked.

"Yes. I'd heard he was back on Mars, but neither one of us made any attempt at contact. However, when we all ended up on Irion, I knew he had the right to know about his daughter." Mom paused, and then said, "Maybe my decision was wrong or unfair, way back when, but what was done was done."

Mom had always been a little fatalistic.

Sweety asked, "So what happens now? Are you seeing Charles—in a romantic way, I mean?"

"We're exploring our past relationship. That's all I'll say."

Mom's last statement made me tongue-tied. I tried to read her facial expression, but she concentrated on drinking her tea.

Sweety glanced at both of us. "Time for us to leave, Mama A. Syl needs quiet time, for more than one reason."

Once they left I sat back and tried to quiet my mind. I had much to think about, especially my continued allergic responses. Of course, Charles figured prominently in my jumbled brain.

Then my doorbell chimed. Rousing myself, I answered the call.

"May I come in for a moment?" asked Dedare.

I wasn't sure I wanted more company tonight, but his concerned face convinced me otherwise. We sat side by side on my couch, and he clasped my right hand in one of his. We stared at each other.

"Your days are too exciting," Dedare murmured, while stroking my cheek with his other hand. "You must be tired. Let me take you to your bed."

Before I had a chance to reply, he'd picked me up and carried me into my bedroom.

"Okay?" he asked.

Startled, I looked at him and realized what he meant—no small talk from Dedare tonight. It didn't take me long to decide everything was very much *okay*.

\*\*\*\*

"How do you feel?" asked Mom, after I settled at the breakfast table. "Your color has certainly improved from last night."

"Actually, my lethargy has subsided and I'm quite hungry. I guess I didn't receive much nourishment from the poisoned food." Not about to discuss the real reason I felt energetic, I mentally searched for a discussion topic.

Teeka suddenly sat beside me. "Looking good, Sylvestine. Perhaps in a few days, we can have dinner again." He smiled. "I have news." The detective's remark got everyone's attention. "Someone named Tareera gave the culprit spice to your new chef. He knew Tareera, so didn't think anything about her action."

I fumed—more trouble from Dedare's sister-in-law.

"Perhaps she did not know the spice would upset Syl," said Dedare. "Have you spoken with her?"

Dedare's objectivity concerned me. Why would Tareera know anything about Martian tastes or sensitivities?

"I am trying to locate her, but she is not home this morning. Do you know where she works, Dedare?" asked Detective Cole.

"At my spaceship manufacturing plant. Let me give you the information." Dedare wrote on a piece of paper, but I couldn't read it, of course—without being too obvious and pulling out my special equipment. Even if I knew where she worked, what was I going to do? Confront her? I thought not. It might provoke her into escalating.

"Breakfast?" I asked Teeka, returning to the present.

"No, I must proceed with my duties. I will call later, Syl." He smiled and got up from the table. Out of the corner of my eye, I caught Sweety smirking.

I suspected she'd corral me later and want to gossip. After Teeka left, I asked, "So how're the wedding plans? Any details?"

"Dedare, our wonderful employer, has offered the roof top garden for our ceremony and reception," said Sweety. "That's our favorite romantic spot—so it's perfect. And I'm letting your mother do most of the planning."

Mom grinned. Planning Hart and Sweety's wedding gave her practice and a measure of hope regarding me, I suspected.

"Do you have a date picked out?" I asked.

"Actually, quite soon," said Hart. "In two days, if all goes well." A panicked look appeared on his face. I suspected the realization hadn't hit home before now.

Life moved quickly on Irion. "Hart, I do believe you're nervous," I said. "Don't worry. Your match was made in Heaven."

Of course, I then had to explain to the Irions what *match made in Heaven* meant. I'm not sure I succeeded.

"You have the rings?" I asked. "Actually, are you exchanging rings?"

"Ah, ah…" Hart's face paled.

"We discussed this yesterday, Hart. You and Dedare have this under control," said Mama A. My mother exchanged glances with Sweety, and tried not to laugh.

"Right, right—same place as before."

I hadn't envisioned Hart as a nervous groom. Actually, I hadn't thought of him as a groom, at all.

"We will purchase today what you require. An appointment this afternoon," commented Dedare.

I swore Dedare held back a smile. Such a good sport trying to keep his employees happy.

Sweety kissed Hart's hand. "Everything'll be fine. Our friends have taken control, since we're a couple of basket cases, my love." She beamed at the table, and Hart's shoulders relaxed.

Of course, Sweety had to explain *basket cases*.

Sain decided to change the subject. He put a fairly large box on our breakfast table. "I have the new pins for Sath Enterprises' employees. You each need one." As he distributed them, he wrote on his com. "Mama A, would you arrange for all hotel staff to receive one of these? Syl is busy today with our tour, and I wish everyone to have the pins as soon as possible."

Mom nodded. "Of course. The project will give me a chance to meet more Irions."

"Record the serial number and name, as you give them out." Sain gave Mom a smile.

I took the pin he offered, and attached it to my top. A classy deep blue pin with a silver design matched the outfit I wore today. "Is this your company logo?" I asked Dedare.

"Yes. Like?" Dedare reached out and touched the pin on my chest.

My heart fluttered. "I love it. It embodies all your enterprises—at least, the ones I know about." I gave him a huge smile—we both had much to consider regarding our personal lives. I reminded myself to talk to Dedare about adding the logo to the room bibles and the procedures manuals, and... Later, Syl, later.

"Sain, tour time. I'll go to Reception and give the Skuttem a call. Join me shortly, please." I got up and gave a short wave around the table before I left.

Master Tyre answered his com, and said he would be down in thirty minutes. While I waited I chatted with Miseena and Siska about scheduling and procedures manuals. They grabbed the manuals I'd made and promised to get back to me with their suggestions and corrections.

Branson arrived and while we waited we discussed what he'd seen so far on Irion.

When Master Tyre appeared, much to my surprise, Coline, Simon, and Dial Deen accompanied him. More than glad Sain had decided to go along on the tour, I didn't make a fuss. Although, I did wonder how the Skuttem had met the other three.

However, Master Tyre did make an issue about Branson. "This is my tour, why do you invite others?"

"Probably for the same reason you invited others without my knowledge." A somewhat nonsensical statement, but the Skuttem didn't pursue his objection.

We gathered outside the hotel, and then Master Tyre produced a strange vehicle.

"Is this one of ours?" I whispered to Sain, although I suspected what his answer would be. He made a left to right motion with his head. I knew this meant no.

"Master Tyre, where did you acquire this vehicle?" I asked. Covered with check marks and other strange symbols, I'd never seen an Irion vehicle decorated quite this way.

"This is a planet-side conveyance we carry on my spaceship. Suitable on strange worlds because of its own power supply."

Of course, he had his own spaceship and planetary vehicle. That's why no one had known he'd arrived.

"Itinerary?" asked the Skuttem, interrupting my thoughts.

"Depending on time, I thought we'd visit the zoo, a couple of Sath Industries buildings, the bell tower, and perhaps the market."

"Coordinates to the first location," demanded Master Tyre.

I let Master Tyre look at my com, and then we were off. The time to the first location would be about an hour, so I expected conversation amongst the group, but I was mistaken. Sain and I sat next to each other and relaxed without speaking. We both needed quiet time after the past few days. The others ignored each other and the two of us.

Finally we arrived at the Satre Zoo, which located amongst the outlying farms.

We split into two groups. Master Tyre and myself, were group one, and Branson, Coline, Simon, Dial Deen, and Sain made up the other group. I knew Sain wasn't happy, but he voiced no objection.

The five of them took off to a grove of large trees where, according to our guide books, *tritle* were housed. Master Tyre and I wandered off, in the opposite direction, to view the *dyllene*. After a few moments, the Skuttem said, "I am unwell. I need to go to my vehicle and rest."

Alarmed, I helped him back, and then inside. He slumped into a seat. "Can I get you anything?" I asked.

"No. I will be better soon."

I sat on a long bench inside the vehicle and studied him. He didn't appear to suffer any respiratory distress, and his color seemed normal. I decided he'd probably had an allergic reaction to an animal in the zoo. Our metabolisms and body chemistries were all so different.

Coline, Dial, and Simon returned without Sain or Branson. Simon came over and sat on the bench beside me.

"Where's Sain?" I asked. I had a bad feeling about this.

"Master Tyre summoned us with his alarm. We'd previously set that up in case of an emergency. We told Sain we were going back to the car, and he said he'd be along shortly. He wanted to purchase a present for you."

I turned away and thought, "Sain is so sweet."

Then I felt a prick on my neck.

## Chapter Twenty-Two

The light made my head hurt so I closed my eyes. Wait a minute, where am I? My mushy brain had no information.

"I know you are awake. Respond," said a deep voice.

My heart stuttered after hearing those words, so I opened my eyes again only to recognize Master Tyre leering over me. Then Simon and Tareera grabbed my arms and pulled me to a sitting position. Thankfully the dizziness quickly cleared, but my heart continued to beat irregularly. The trio walked away and conferred, so I studied my surroundings. I kept an eye on them while doing so. The room included rough gray stone walls, black shuttered windows, a single bed, and not much else.

"Why am I here? Why did you abduct me?" I asked, but no one responded.

I needed information. "Why are you here, Tareera? Why did you poison me at the hotel?" Not particularly appropriate, but the words spilled out. My brain had yet to catch up with my surroundings.

"No questions. You will remain," said the Skuttem.

"Where is Sain? Did you hurt him?" I started to shake thinking about what they could have done to him and Branson.

"Master Tyre said no questions. If necessary, we'll

tie you up and cover your mouth," said Simon. The Skuttem and Tareera walked to the door—Simon did so backward, keeping an eye on me.

Should I jump up and attack? Then I got a grip on reality—three to one weren't great odds.

After they left, I waited a minute, and then tried the door and window. No luck in either case. Then I noticed another door hidden in a corner. I tried the handle. Not a getaway portal, but I had washroom facilities. A few moments in the restroom refreshed me, and then I went back to the bed. I had no other place to sit. Still affected by whatever I'd been injected with, I lay down on the bed to rest and promptly fell asleep.

I woke and sat up after I heard the door open. Dial Deen entered with a tray.

"Your lunch." She put the food beside me. "Eat up, or Master Tyre will be upset." Dial backed away.

"Why are you with the Skuttem?" I hadn't known Dial Deen long enough to understand her personal motivations.

"I believe in his ideals." One of her hands rubbed the back of her neck, and I couldn't catch her eye.

"What ideals are those?" Maybe I'd learn something new about the Skuttem, or even Dial, with my questions.

She walked toward me. "You are a criminal, and the situation must be resolved," said Dial, with the Irion equivalent of a smirk.

"Criminal, really? More likely you don't like me working with Dedare."

Much to my surprise, she smacked my face. I raised my hand to retaliate, but thought better of doing so. Instead, I rubbed my cheek, and asked, "Why did you hit me?"

"Dedare is too good for you," she said. Her blue-tinged skin paled.

Her reaction made sense with her being Dedare's ex-girlfriend. No matter what planet you lived on jealously reared its ugly head.

"Perhaps you should let Dedare make his own decisions. After all, he did so regarding you." I could be as snide as the next.

I watched her hands in case she decided to strike me again, but nothing happened except her face flickered with emotions, not all of which I understood.

Eventually she said, "Eat," then marched out the door, locking me in from the outside.

Since my stomach growled, I ate the lunch Dial had provided. I hoped I wouldn't be poisoned again. Since they'd included Martian food my abduction must've been planned.

An anxious couple of hours passed, and then I heard the door open again. Master Tyre stepped into my prison, along with Coline, Dial, Tareera, and Simon.

Dial picked up my food tray and left—the remaining four studied me.

"I understand," said Tareera. "Her hair matches the pictures you showed us. Irions do not have that hair color."

Actually, the females didn't have much hair at all, but for once, I kept my mouth shut.

No one spoke, so after a couple of minutes of silence I asked, "Where are we? Why am I here?" Vague questions but I needed any tidbits of information I could dig out.

Master Tyre picked at his skin. "We are at the Bell

Tower where you were going to take us today."

"You mean the bell tower where Tareera and Simon tried to push me off the top?" I needed confirmation we hadn't been paranoid in blaming them for the incident.

"You deserved an accident," said Tareera. "Dedare needed to pay for the death of my sister."

From the calculating glance Master Tyre gave Simon and Tareera he hadn't known about their antics.

"What exactly did I have to do with the death of Gyra Sath—I wasn't even on Irion." I shook my head violently, and a headache popped out. "Better yet, what did Dedare do to kill his wife?" Her Irion logic escaped me.

"You made me lose my job at the hotel," replied Tareera, ignoring my questions.

I didn't agree with her assessment, and I noticed she didn't answer my question about Dedare and his wife. Labelling Tareera psychotic seemed a logical option.

To someone I'd never liked, I asked, "Coline, why have you joined Master Tyre?"

"You are a criminal," said Dedare's assistant.

For the first time, I experienced Coline's smile—not a pretty sight. "Maybe to a Skuttem I am, but I've broken no laws on Irion."

"You have stolen Dedare's attention." Coline twitched and wouldn't look at me.

Stolen his attention from what or whom, I wondered? Then I realized jealousy had reared its ugly head again. Not a situation I'd expected from Coline.

Last, but not least, I asked, "Simon, why are you here? A fellow Martian, why would you want to hurt me?"

"I don't need to answer." Simon stared over my shoulder.

"Answer," demanded Master Tyre. Apparently the Skuttem wanted or needed additional information on his cohorts.

"I wasn't happy with your abrupt termination. Your disappearance left the hotel shorthanded." Simon stood straighter and put his hands behind his back.

"I thought you came here to look for opportunities for advancement of the Mars Best chain." I wasn't buying his statement. His body language indicated deceit.

"Yes, I did. The owner of Mars Best wants to expand."

I studied Simon. "I don't think my leaving the employ of Mars Best was the only reason you decided to hook up with Master Tyre and abduct me."

Simon stomped his foot. "Your mother spurned my advances—she had no right."

My dig had found its mark. Thank goodness, Mom had confessed, so I understood his utterances. "She had every right. It's her decision with whom to be involved."

Master Tyre interrupted. "I do not understand these issues, but you will not be able to talk to your mother. Criminals are thrown off a high place at dawn. Tomorrow morning is your time."

"What are you talking about?"

"Your hair indicates a criminal. So you will die tomorrow morning, and I will gain status in the eyes of my God," the Skuttem said.

"If I'm about to die, you'd better give me a better

explanation." My mind refused to accept his words. Always my hair? I'd forgotten about the Skuttem's fit, and my reason for wearing berets.

Master Tyre turned his back to me, and then gestured to the others. Everyone left my holding cell. The door locked behind them.

What could I do? I needed to extricate myself from this situation. I paced and paced, but my mental processes had frozen with the specter of death.

A few hours later, Dial showed up with another tray of food.

"Food for the condemned person? My last meal?" I asked. My ruminations hadn't cheered me up.

Dial plunked the tray on my bed, and left without uttering a word.

The tasteless food exacerbated my worrying.

An hour later, all five of my captors returned. "You are on the news," said Master Tyre. "Popular with everyone, except the *Martians Go Home* protestors."

"So a lot of people will be looking for me. Perhaps the monks will tell the authorities where I am." That thought brought a smile to my face.

"No. I rented this tower for two days, and made the monks go away. No one knows where you are."

"Someone is going to find me." I crossed my fingers.

"Not before I throw you off the roof at dawn," said the Skuttem. "I must follow the rules for criminals."

"Come on you guys," I said to the others. "This isn't right. Stop Master Tyre," I pleaded.

No one spoke. Now what was I supposed to do? "Have you spoken to Detective Cole or Dedare or Sain?" I asked.

"Why would I?" Confused, the Skuttem stared at me.

"Perhaps you can make a deal for my release, and then they'll let you leave without any penalty."

"What do you mean? Why would I have a penalty?"

"Do you really think the authorities are going to let you leave Irion if you throw me off the bell tower?"

"Why would they not? I will have done nothing wrong."

"Killing is wrong—whether a criminal or not." I hoped he understood my argument. His Skuttem way of thinking eluded me.

Master Tyre looked at the Irions. Then Tareera said, "Yes, killing is wrong. Consequences."

"They will not catch me," said the Skuttem.

Everyone, including me, stared in disbelief. Master Tyre got the message. I continued to be unsure why the others were going along with his antics. They must've known there'd be repercussions for them too.

Then I glanced at Simon. His physical reaction was a little frantic, I realized. He really hadn't thought the situation through. And the Irions were exchanging numerous glances, and looking at the door. What a bunch of idiots, they're going to run away, *now*?

How could I turn this situation to my advantage?

"Master Tyre, your buddies here," I said, pointing to the four, "want to let me go and save themselves. How're you going to deal with this?" I asked.

The quartet remained silent while Master Tyre studied their faces. "I believe you are correct." He waved his hands. "Go away, get out of my sight. Leave this building. I do not want you near me."

Moving faster than I could've imagined, they vacated my jail cell.

One left. Could I be as successful with Master Tyre?

Chapter Twenty-Three

What to do, what to do? I tried to calm my ragged breathing, but I couldn't stop sweating. This reminded me of a scene from one of my graphic novels.

"Master Tyre, please call Detective Cole. He's an Irion policeman and will help you leave this planet." I crossed my fingers and hoped the Skuttem would take my bait.

"Do Irions treat criminals the same way my world does?" he asked, picking at his clothes.

"I don't know. I'm not an Irion and don't know all their laws." Of course, something I should've looked into before my spontaneous decision to travel to Irion. "Detective Cole will be able to answer your questions." I watched for any response. None appeared, at least, any I could interpret. "Maybe you could release me to Detective Cole so I could explain your problem. Then he can take care of your situation in his own Irion way." I crossed my toes this time.

"No, you will stay. Punishment must be done the proper way, but I will call Detective Cole to gather further information."

For a brief second, I'd experienced hope, but his statement regarding punishment erased any positive thoughts.

The Skuttem studied me. "I do not trust you—you must be disabled." He exited my holding cell and soon returned. He grabbed items, similar to twist ties, from the large bag draped over his shoulder, and bound my hands and feet.

"That's too much," I complained. Master Tyre had pulled the ties so tight my skin had squished up.

He ignored me and walked out of my cell.

I fussed about, unsuccessfully, and eventually my hands and feet began to lose feeling. Thankfully, the Skuttem returned after a short time.

"Please release me. Look, my hands are turning red. The ties are way too tight." I had a headache, and the bindings were only one reason.

Out of his voluminous shoulder bag, he retrieved an instrument similar to a pair of scissors, and snipped the ties binding my hands and feet.

"Thank you," I said, rubbing my wrists. My feet weren't quite so stressed. "What did Teeka, I mean Detective Cole, have to say?"

"We did not come to any agreement. Irions do not treat criminals in the proper way and, in addition, you are not considered a criminal." Master Tyre's face exhibited surprise.

"Did you talk to Dedare or Sain?" I needed hope from one, any one, of my Irion friends.

"Yes," he answered.

I waited for further information. When none was forthcoming, I asked, "What did they say?" I crossed my fingers Dedare, the businessman, would've been persuasive.

"Dedare made offers but I declined all. You are business I need to take care of. Criminals need to be brought to justice."

With desperation, I said, "Well, I bet they know

where we are. They probably tracked you when you used your com—with the GPS, I mean."

"Explain GPS," he demanded.

"It's a location tracker all coms have. Electronics find your location using your com's signal."

"This is my com, and we do not have this GPS. Although, I must mention the concept to the authorities when I return home."

I started to shake. "So that's it. You're going to murder me tomorrow morning?" I had no idea what to do next.

"Justice not murder. Lie down." He waved one of his hands.

"Why?" My heart pounded. I didn't like the sound of this.

"You need to be restrained for the remainder of the evening." The Skuttem pulled out more ties.

"Why?" I hated being unable to move.

"This is the way." Master Tyre continued digging in his bag.

"At least let me use the washroom before you confine me. You don't want a mess to clean up, do you?" Did he care?

He took what looked like a gun from under his clothing, and waved it at the small corner room.

Any ideas I might've had about overpowering Master Tyre and escaping disappeared. After I returned, he tied me to the bed, but more comfortably this time. When the Skuttem touched my cheek, I tried not to recoil.

"Why did you do that?" I asked. Not sure I actually wanted to hear his answer, I kept very still—perhaps he'd go away.

"I desired to know how your skin compared to a Skuttem female. Is your skin the same everywhere?" His hand reached out and tugged at my pant leg.

"Stop!" I yelled. My skin crawled.

Master Tyre's hand jerked back. "Why? What is wrong?"

"You can't do that. You can't touch me anywhere else." I had no idea what he wanted from me, but he was too close already. What Skuttem ritual occupied his mind?

"Why not?" He sounded and looked genuinely confused.

"All other areas are private." And I wanted them to remain so.

My answer apparently satisfied him. He left and locked the door from the outside. Hopefully, he'd keep his distance until he threw me off the tower tomorrow morning.

Oh crap. Reality plummeted into my senses. What was I going to do?

I tried to free my hands, but to no avail. Although Master Tyre had not made the bonds as tight as before, they were still effective. I couldn't even roll off the bed to try to find something to cut the bindings.

Despite being uncomfortable, because I couldn't turn over, or move very much, I fell asleep. Then the dreams came—bad, bad dreams. Dreams that included suicide jumpers, vats of molten magma, and my mother ascending into the sun.

Chapter Twenty-Four

I woke up because a hand affected my breathing—apparently, I'd been breathing through my mouth, also known as snoring.

"Syl, do not say anything. Be very quiet," someone whispered.

I opened my eyes. Teeka removed his hand a bit to let me breathe, but only a bit. He was leery of my response, I imagined.

"You are safe. Sain is going to break your shackles, so remain still." He put his hand on my cheek. "Master Tyre does not know we are here."

My eyes filled. Much to my delight, last night's dreams weren't coming true, but I had so many questions.

After my ties had been cut, I sat up and gazed upon my heroes. Dedare and Branson were there also. I started to thank all of them, but Teeka shushed me. "Stay here with Dedare and Branson. Sain and I are going to give Master Tyre a little surprise, and then your adventure will be over. Do not talk," Teeka whispered. He gestured to Sain, and the two of them left my cell.

Dedare sat on the bed next to me, and held me close. Branson stood a short distance away, and gave us a bit of privacy. The time stretched and stretched, almost to my screaming point.

Suddenly and definitely startling us, Sain and Teeka returned dragging a tied up Skuttem. Master Tyre didn't lift his head.

I jumped off the bed. My energy renewed. "You guys are my heroes," I said. "Now, can we throw Master Tyre off the roof since he broke Irion law?" My sense of humor had returned—which astounded me.

My rescuers smothered their laughter.

Finally looking up, the Skuttem said, "I am no criminal. I wish to return to my spaceship."

"Abduction is a crime," responded Detective Cole. "Planning to throw someone off the bell tower is also a punishable offense." Teeka looked at me. "Should we wait for dawn to go to the roof and give the Skuttem his punishment?"

Before I had a chance to reply, Master Tyre said, "You cannot. I demand to speak with the Skuttem ambassador."

They had an ambassador on Irion? When had this happened? From the looks running around the room, no one had heard of this new ambassador.

"I shall investigate," said Teeka. "In the meantime, Sain, would you help me take Master Tyre down to the police station?"

"Delighted." Sain grabbed one of the Skuttem's arms, and Teeka the other. They hustled him out of my sight.

"Would you really have thrown him off the roof?" asked Dedare.

"No, but I wanted to scare him. Give him a taste of what I've been going through." Then I began to shake.

"You have had a bad time." Dedare pulled me into a hug. "Let us go home and have a glass of wine.

Perhaps a couple."

**\*\*\*\***

While I was in the shower, Dedare gathered everyone and ensconced them in my suite. And then the party began. I was greeted warmly by all, and I settled down on my couch. I didn't know how long I'd last—my recent experiences had been both emotionally and physically exhausting.

While I was still awake, I asked, "Charles, is there really a Skuttem ambassador?"

"After Dedare brought the topic up, I did find another Skuttem on Irion. Apparently, visiting ambassadors are housed in different buildings to avoid conflict. That concept is contradictory, in my experience. Ambassadors should meet and understand one another's worlds."

A pale, trembling Charles continued. "Sylvestine, I've been upset by your situation. Your mother and I have comforted each other, as best we could, but your abduction stressed us, as I'm sure you can imagine. Our biggest concern was our lack of control—we had no way to help our daughter."

What should I say? "Charles, you were out of my life for so many years. Actually, I didn't know you existed. Well, I knew I had a biological father, but I didn't know who."

I glanced at Mom and noticed she'd grabbed Charles' hand. "I've been stand-offish but I needed to get to know you a bit first. I want you to understand I'm glad you're now in my life."

I gazed at him, and then noticed the tears in my mother's eyes. "May I call you Dad?"

Charles looked at Mom and then jumped up and

walked over to me. He pulled me to my feet, and gave me a long hug. A profound silence enveloped my living room.

I sat down, and Charles returned to sit by Mom. Reena's wide-eyed look summarized the situation. I knew Dedare and Sain would be peppered with questions.

"Are there more ambassadors on Irion?" I asked, trying to divert everyone's attention.

"I don't know. I'm going to pursue that tomorrow," said my father.

"If you find any more, let me know. If I have a heads up, I might be able to anticipate future hotel needs. And a heads up about whether any of them dislike my hair, or any other part of me, would be appreciated." Laughter rang around my living room. I didn't want any more surprises, especially of a criminal nature.

"I'm still a little confused about how your distressing situation came to be," continued Charles. "And how all participants are connected."

"As I think we all know, Master Tyre decided I was a criminal based on my hair color. What a bizarre concept for a species to have." I shook my head.

"Actually, not so far out," said Hart. "We make our criminals wear the same clothes, and after they're released from prison they have a tracker device inserted. Well, at least those convicted of violent crimes. Not so different."

Hart did have a valid point. I noticed Teeka and Sain had entered my living room. They found seats on the floor.

"Speaking of which, how did you guys track me?

I'm ever so grateful, by the way."

"Sain is the clever one," replied Teeka. He pointed at my top. "Your new pin emits a signal. Sain gave me the frequency."

I studied my personal GPS. "No wonder you wanted Mom to record the serial numbers; each one has a unique frequency, I imagine."

Hart got a far off look on his face. "How did—"

"Not now, Hart. Let Syl relax," said my mother.

"Sorry, sorry." Hart's scientific curiosity had gotten the better of him again.

"Mr. Branson helped refine our search," said Teeka. He pointed at a corner of my living room. I hadn't noticed Branson quietly standing against the wall.

"Your pin indicates a fairly broad area. We knew you were somewhere close to the area you'd visited on the tour, but Branson overheard a couple of your captors discussing the bell tower, so we started at that spot," said Sain.

I looked over. "Thank you, Richard." I gave him a big smile. "Have a drink and sit down somewhere." After my glance, Sweety jumped up and got Branson settled—always the hostess.

Mom asked, "How did all these others—Simon, Coline, Tareera, and Dial Deen—became involved with Master Tyre?"

"Tareera is easy. I kind of got her fired," I said. "She didn't like the changes I started to implement, and she also blamed Dedare for his wife's death. Totally irrational from what I've been able to gather. So Master Tyre and Tareera had negative feelings about me, but I have no idea how they met."

We all looked at Dedare.

"Tareera did blame me for letting Gyra go to work alone."

"That makes no sense," said Sweety. "How could you protect her? Weren't others at her workplace? Maybe you would've caught the infection, too."

Dedare made a movement with his head indicating agreement.

Such a sad state of affairs, I thought.

Dedare raised his hand. "Tareera also locked Syl in the Bone Room."

Of course I had to explain the Bone Room incident to those who didn't know about my experience—which weren't very many as most of the Martians had seen my frigid self, after Hart and Dedare's release.

"How did you know it was her?" I asked.

"Tareera will no longer bother anyone," said Dedare, without answering my question.

"What do you mean?" I asked.

"Tareera is banished from Satre," he replied.

Apparently, Dedare had god-like powers on Irion—at least, in the capital city.

"And Dial Deen? What about her?" asked Hart. "I haven't seen her around the hotel much."

"She is one of Dedare's old girlfriends," said Sain. "You know how they are."

We all laughed after Dedare scowled at Sain.

"Then there's Simon," I said. "He didn't like my abrupt departure from the Mars Best and, sometime in the past on Mars, Mom had spurned him. For some reason, that turned out to be my fault."

For several moments, everyone pursued their own thoughts about the various participants. Then Teeka said, "I have an update on Chef's death."

The detective caught our attention, *big time*.

"After extensive analysis, Simon Worth has been determined to be Chef's murderer. Simon is now in custody."

Everyone started to talk at once. "Quiet," I said, in a loud voice. After the voices subsided, I asked, "Do you know why Simon killed Chef?"

"I am sorry, Syl, but he confessed to trying to make your life miserable. He said if you didn't have a decent chef, then perhaps Dedare would send you away."

So Chef's death was my fault. My tears started to fall.

"And we found bombs from Dedare's factory in Simon's room. He has not yet confessed as to why he had them, but I will find out," said Teeka.

And I knew he would.

Silence gripped my living room.

To distract me and everyone else, Mom asked, "There's one person we haven't discussed. How's Coline involved?"

I had the answer but I needed to be very, very careful. "Coline decided, after our first meeting on Mars, I diverted too much of Dedare's attention. Jealousy was his key." As bland as I could manage.

We all noticed Dedare's face pale.

"So you were the catalyst bringing them all together," said Sweety, trying to defuse my last statement. "How romantic!"

Laughter rang around the room.

The spotlight needed to turn away from Dedare and me. "Speaking of romantic, how're the wedding plans?"

Sweety grinned, and Mom said, "Everything's under control. The wedding is tomorrow afternoon in the roof top garden, and after the ceremony we'll have dinner there too. It's such a lovely area. We'll make many memories."

"Tomorrow's still on? Wow, you guys are amazing. Good thing my heroes rescued me." I grinned and smiled at everyone.

"We would've postponed, don't you worry. We're just happy you're back," said Sweety, "but we do need to have a talk, you and me. So, making an executive decision, as the bride-to-be, this party is now declared over. We'll have another party tomorrow, of course. What are weddings for, anyway? Everyone go home, get some sleep, and wake up ready to party."

Laughter erupted and my suite emptied. Accompanied by a glass of wine, Sweety and I had an informative talk regarding romance.

She grilled me about Dedare, Sain, and Teeka until my head—and heart—spun out of control.

Chapter Twenty-Five

Late the next morning—Wedding Day—Sweety showed up with my dress, accompanied by Mom and Reena. They'd let me sleep in, thank goodness. Yesterday had sapped my emotions and energy.

Sweety had decreed Mom and I'd be her wedding attendants. The two of them, with Reena's help, had created four dresses.

"Where did you get these gowns? I don't think I've seen a single dress on Irion, other than Martian ones, I mean."

Sweety grinned. "Reena found a seamstress—a seamstress with a huge collection of fabrics. Drawing and explaining the designs I wanted took the most time."

"Bima was amazing! She took only one evening to produce our garments," said Mom. "Reena knows the best people." Mom gave the teenager a hug.

I tried on my dress, and the fit was perfect. Twirling in front of my full-length mirror, I said, "Beautiful! You guys astound me."

Reena sported a wide grin.

"Syl, take off your dress, and we'll have a quick lunch here in your suite. Okay, maybe not so quick," said Sweety. "I've arranged for the kitchen to send up a bridal luncheon. Then we'll get the flowers from Hydroponics, and decorate the roof top." Four females had a giggly time, and the food was delicious.

After we arrived at Hydroponics, we discovered Lain had already taken the wedding flowers upstairs. We found her and her assistant setting the stage for the ceremony.

"Wonderful, Lain!" gushed Sweety. "Your flowers outdid my expectations. Please stay for our nuptials." She gave Lain a hug.

"I would love to. In the meantime, I must return to Hydroponics. I will be back for your wedding." She studied the rooftop, for a moment. "May I speak with you, Mama A?"

Mom's nickname had spread. They wandered away while Sweety and I admired the setting.

"Where's Hart?" I asked Sweety, while we waited for my mother to return.

"I don't know. Dedare promised he'd keep him occupied until *the time*."

"Who's going to perform—"

Mom returned and interrupted our conversation. "Let's have a glass of wine. We have about an hour until we need to be back for the festivities."

So the three of us drank and relaxed in my suite. During the whole time, Sweety kept saying, "I'm getting married. I'm really getting married."

Reena had joined us, but she stared at Sweety and her antics. "Why is she saying that? Why does she keep repeating that phrase? Is that not why we are gathered today?"

"Yes, dear," said Mom. "Sweety's extremely happy so she's babbling a bit, humor her."

Reena appeared to understand Mom's comment and said nothing else.

Then Mom caught our attention. "Ladies, let's get dressed—the time has arrived."

Mom and I shimmered in shiny blue, while Sweety glowed in an off-white floor-length beaded dress with a short train. Reena's dress exhibited a strange almost-orange glow magnifying her coloring.

While we were giving each other a last perusal before going upstairs to the roof, a knock sounded. I opened my door, and there stood Charles.

"Dad, how nice. We were about to leave."

"I'm here to escort you lovely ladies. You may not know, Syl, but since I'm an officer of the law, Sweety and Hart asked me to officiate at their ceremony. However, the wedding party needs a little discussion about the arrangements since we haven't had time for a rehearsal. It's time for a meeting."

After we arrived at the rooftop, we heard joyous music filling the air, and many people were arriving for the ceremony. I noticed almost the entire hotel staff in attendance.

"Ah, Lain spread the word," said my mother, noticing my astonishment. "And she put out more chairs."

"Is that what the two of you talked about?" Sweety asked, having overheard our conversation.

"Yes, indeed. Apparently everyone loves you, and wants to experience a human commitment ceremony. Since the wedding party encompasses just about every Martian on Irion, I made the decision to open the ceremony to the staff, and anyone else who wanted to attend."

Sweety beamed. She'd made quite an impression during her short stay, and the crowd exuded a happy vibe.

After a short discussion with Charles, the time to begin had arrived.

Charles walked down the aisle, and stood on the slightly raised platform. Mauve and yellow flowers with gorgeous large spreading blooms surrounded the dais.

Then Hart's attendants, Dedare and Sain—looking handsome in their Irion shiny blue coverings, with pinned on mauve flowers—walked down the passageway.

Next up were Mom and me, and I think we made quite an impression. Our bouquets of yellow flowers complemented our dresses, judging by the crowd's reaction.

From the side, Hart quietly joined Charles on the platform.

Then the music changed and Reena, with her basket of flowers, started down the aisle.

She tossed flowers to each side of the glowing blue carpet and, as the audience noticed her actions, the Irions stood and put their hands on their heads.

After Reena stood beside me, I whispered, "Why did the Irions stand and make that motion?"

"The Irion commitment ceremony, like a wedding, involves spreading flowers."

I had no idea the significance of her statement.

"Sweety asked me to be her flower girl. So, after she explained what she wanted, I told her Irions would understand the symbol," said Reena. "We are much alike."

I gave her a hug.

"Hands on the head indicates approval. I would

also like to think they like my garment," commented Reena.

"Of course they do. You're gorgeous." Such a teenager!

The music changed, and then the radiant bride started down the aisle.

The Irions stood again, clasped their hands together, and held them out toward Sweety as she smiled at everyone.

Reena whispered, "They are wishing both of them a joyous, beautiful life. Their energy is flowing to her through their hands. We must do the same after Sweety and Hart are joined."

A perfect idea from a perfect kid.

After Sweety reached the platform, she gave me her bouquet, and then joined hands with Hart.

From my proximity, which was very close, I detected moisture in their eyes.

Charles said a few words—actually more than a few, because he wanted the Irions to understand our rituals. The wedding ceremony had an attentive audience.

"The bride and groom have written their own marriage vows. Sweety?" asked Charles.

Mom passed Sweety a piece of paper. With a luminous smile, Sweety began:

*"Hart,*

*I promise to encourage your unique and wonderful compassion,*

*I promise to nurture your dreams where your soul shines,*

*I promise to help shoulder our challenges,*

*For there is nothing we cannot face if we stand*

*together.*

*I promise to be your partner in all things, working with you as part of our whole.*

*Lastly, I promise to give you love and trust.*

*For one lifetime with you will never be enough.*

*This is my sacred vow to you, my equal in all things."*

After Sweety finished, I noticed a few weepy people—particularly the Martians, and especially the bride.

I handed Reena a cloth I'd been smart enough to tuck into my dress, and asked her to pass it to Sweety.

Sweety gave Reena a hug, and then wiped her eyes.

Tactfully, Charles gave Sweety a moment to regain her composure, and then indicated Hart should proceed.

Hart fished a piece of paper out of his suit pocket, and cleared his throat. After taking a deep breath, he began:

*"Sweety, on this day,*
*I give you my heart,*
*And my promise,*
*I will walk with you,*
*Hand in hand,*
*Wherever our journey leads us,*
*Living, learning, loving,*
*Together,*
*Forever."*

After Hart finished, the Irions stomped their feet.

"All is well," said Reena, interpreting my glance. "An Irion sign of joy."

Charles held up a hand, and the stomping stopped. "A human custom is to exchange rings as a further sign of commitment." He added a few words of explanation for the Irions' benefit.

Dedare passed the rings to Charles, and he gave the appropriate rings to Sweety and Hart. "Please put these on your partner's hand, and then hold hands and repeat after me."

A little fumbling ensued, but eventually Charles continued,

*"You are my partner, and you have my heart,*
*Our journey begins today and continues forever.*
*And with this ring, I thee wed."*

Sweety first spoke the words, followed by Hart.

Charles smiled at them. And turning to the gathering, he said, "Please stand." He waited for a moment for everyone to do so, then he put his hands on top of Sweety's and Hart's still joined ones. "By the powers vested in me, I declare this ceremony complete. Your journey begins today." He beamed at the two of them. "Now show the Irions what kissing's all about."

The Martians laughed, and Sweety and Hart complied. The Irions followed our lead, after we started clapping.

Charles turned Hart and Sweety around to face the audience. "I would like to introduce Mr. and Mrs. Finn-Adair."

Sounds of joy filled the rooftop, and Hart and Sweety proceeded down the aisle. Reena skipped ahead spewing petals, and the Martians and Irions made world-appropriate noises.

Charles followed Hart and Sweety, and Mom and I joined up with Dedare and Sain to do the same.

The five of us stood with Hart and Sweety to receive wedding congratulations, and then we all settled down for an intimate wedding celebration.

Mom's arrangements were wonderful—she'd even talked Chef Lasto into making a wedding cake.

After our dinner and copious drinks, we watched Hart and Sweety dance. Then my parents joined them. Still freaking out a little whenever I said *my parents,* I knew I needed more time to adjust.

Reena got up to dance with Hart and Sweety. They made a cute trio, and I'd never seen an Irion dance before.

I waited for either Dedare or Sain to ask me to dance, but my dinner companions were silent.

My mind wandered, and then Mom flopped beside me. "I really must get more exercise." She puffed a bit. "Syl, how about taking a walk with Charles and me?"

Dedare raised a hand—to make a comment, I supposed—but Mom interrupted, "Charles and I have something we need to discuss with Syl."

Getting the message, Dedare didn't comment. My curiosity aroused, I followed my mother and Charles to a corner of the rooftop.

Noticing Mom's unease, I gave her time to regain her composure by studying the vegetables growing in my vicinity.

"Syl?" asked Mom, to get my attention.

I turned around, and noticed she and Charles held hands. "Yes?"

"Charles and I have an announcement."

She'd definitely caught my attention, and not only because I noticed her shaking voice. "Are you leaving Irion?" I asked.

"No, no. Nothing like that." She gazed at the ambassador. "Charles has asked me to marry him, and I've accepted."

Speechless, I tried to breathe. Mom asked, "A little surprised?"

More than a little, but I didn't utter that comment out loud. "I hadn't really thought about you two getting together." I sighed. "Okay, my statement came out all wrong. Just knowing who my father is, has kept my mind spinning quite enough." Then I recognized my babbling for what it was—nervousness. "Forgive me. I see how happy you both are, and I think this's wonderful!" I held my arms out, and the three of us embraced.

"When's the wedding?" I asked. Another Martian wedding on Irion?

"Not for a while," said Charles. "We don't want to overshadow this one."

"Good plan. Now go and dance with the newly married couple. And, Mom and Dad, you have my blessings, for what they're worth."

Mom laughed and kissed my cheek. After a moment's hesitation, Charles did too.

They walked away, hand in hand, gazing at each other. Mom and Charles made a great couple and, I giggled, they'd also made a wonderful offspring.

Wandering back to the dinner tables, I sat beside Teeka. I was glad he'd been invited. I knew Hart and Sweety recognized he'd been part of our lives and had treated Martians fairly.

"How did you like the wedding ceremony?" I asked.

"I now understand Martians better. You are not that different from Irions in your need for attachments and offspring," replied an analytical Teeka.

"Well, I'm not sure what Hart and Sweety have

decided about offspring, but eventually they'll let us know."

Teeka clasped my right hand. "Syl, I would like another dinner with you."

I looked down at our joined hands, and then glanced over at another dinner table. Dedare and Sain stared at Teeka and me.

Crunch time. Who did I want in my life, in a personal way?

Although flattered by Teeka's attention, I recognized an imminent decision. I pulled my hand back. "Teeka, I like you. You have a great sense of humor—at least the bits I understand—but, at the moment, I like you as a friend. I'd like to get together, occasionally, to discuss our lives, of course. And perhaps some of your cases—criminology is fascinating. I think we're good friends, but not in a romantic way."

I couldn't decipher the emotions on Teeka's face. Had I misinterpreted his gesture? Perhaps dinner was all he'd wanted.

He grabbed my hand again. "Syl, I like you a lot. Where your emotions lie is clear to me. Although I would like to have a physical relationship, I know where the *frindes* are merged."

*Frindes?* Come on, translator, help me out!

I started to speak, but Teeka interrupted, "Syl, I understand. Call me in a couple of eight-days, and then we can get together. We will have much to discuss, as friends. You have such a fascinating life."

Teeka stood, and then reached out a hand and rubbed my cheek. "Do not speak," he said. "I will talk to you soon." He walked away, while I tried to de-cloud my mind.

Speaking seemed impossible, so I worked on breathing.

Before I had a chance to understand my recent emotions, Dedare and Sain transferred to my table. Flanking me, Sain handed me a glass. "Wine, Syl. You seem stressed."

"Why would I be stressed?" I asked. "My best friends just got married." I took a big sip. "My parents are getting married; why would I be stressed?" I babbled. My parents are getting married? My brain refused to parse my thought.

"The air is in love," said Sain.

"A very human sentiment, Sain. Are you sure you're not part Martian?" I asked. I didn't have the heart to tell him I thought he had his words in the wrong order—love is in the air. Oh, well, his emotions were appropriate.

I sighed. I'd hated to disappoint Teeka but, other than that, the day had turned out well—likely thanks to Mom's organization.

"Syl," said Dedare, interrupting my thoughts, "I would like a discussion. Let us find a quiet corner of the rooftop." Dedare and Sain exchanged glances, and then Sain got up and walked away. I followed Dedare to a secluded spot, away from the party.

I refocused my attention. "What do you want to talk about?" Serious was the only word I found for Dedare's demeanor.

"Why were you talking to Teeka?" asked Dedare.

None of his business, really. "Well, I do like Teeka. He's been good to us Martians. However, I will tell you what we talked about, since you are my friend."

I sighed. "We had a short discussion about having ah, ah, a relationship but, in the end, Teeka told me he knew it wasn't possible. He said, *he knew where the frindes were merged.* Of course, I have no idea what he meant, and my translator proved useless again."

Dedare studied me.

"*Merging frindes* means having a romantic relationship," said Dedare, finally.

"So what did Teeka mean?" If my favorite Irion wanted to be obtuse, I'd match him.

"Teeka decided I wanted a relationship with you," said Dedare. He grabbed one of my hands.

"Was he incorrect?"

"No. Teeka was correct. I wanted to wait until after today, but the proper time appears to have arrived. The romantic moment, as Hart would say," said Dedare.

"Say yes, say yes!" said Reena, after popping out from behind a tree. "I want you to be my new mother!"

A deep breath appeared required, so I hyperventilated. "Reena, come here." I gestured to her. She ran over, and I gave her a hug.

"Reena, Dedare and I have much to discuss." How should I handle this? "May I call you my best-best friend?"

"Great!" she said, bouncing in front of us. "You do know your painting foretold this?" asked Reena.

I'd forgotten about her interpretation of my painting; something to discuss with Dedare, at a later time. "Okay, best-best friend, I need time with this scoundrel." I pointed at her father. "Can you go and talk to Mama A and Charles? They might have news to impart."

"Syl, you are my best-best friend, too." Reena

waved as she turned away.

I said, "Don't nag."

"I am subtle, do not worry," Reena replied, grinning at us over her shoulder.

I wouldn't argue with my new best-best friend, but I didn't necessarily agree—a teenager, after all. Dedare and I smiled and watched her leave our vicinity.

"Okay, now that we're alone again, what do you really want?"

Dedare rubbed my cheek. "Syl, you enamor me. You are intelligent, well-organized, business-like, full of creative ideas, smell nice, and pay attention to Reena."

"Not difficult, she's an exceptional young woman."

Dedare held up his hand. "You stir emotions in me, ones I had never expected to feel again." He rubbed my cheek again.

I assumed Dedare meant, after Gyra's death.

I caught my breath. Dedare wasn't the only one exploding with feelings. "I must admit I long for you when we're apart."

Arms surrounded me, and I was more than comforted. Our recent physical encounters had satisfied me in more ways than I'd ever imagined.

"So what now?" Not sure what happened next, especially on Irion, I made my statement as generic as possible.

"I want to live with you, and merge our *frindes* on a permanent basis," said Dedare.

Unsure as to his meaning, I asked, "You want to live in my suite?"

"Yes. I think that arrangement would be appropriate. We would have privacy from Sain and

Reena," said Dedare. "However, more importantly, I want a permanent relationship. I want you to be my wife." Dedare smiled, grabbed both of my hands, and waited for my response.

*Permanent* was perfectly clear. "You make me happy. Very, very happy. Let's not talk about our living arrangements until tomorrow. Hart and Sweety need their special day." I paused. "Dedare, I do want to spend the rest of my life with you."

My emotions gushed. We hugged each other and I proceeded to kiss him thoroughly. I took in his aromas and touches with my awakened senses.

Dedare broke our emotional huddle. "Syl, a Martian custom I have learned about, and I am happy to embrace."

I had no idea what Dedare meant. Custom?

Dedare plunged a hand into one of his pockets. "I want to show you my desire to merge *frindes* by giving you an engagement ring." He put a ring on my fourth finger. The ring had blue stones and a silvery base—the colors I associated with Irion.

"Yes, yes," I muttered and gazed into his eyes, while he held both of my hands.

"Hey, sorry to interrupt your conference," said Sweety, "but it's time to cut the cake. Follow me."

We followed the bride to another table set up amongst flowering shrubs. I desperately needed alone time with Dedare, but I told myself to focus on Hart and Sweety.

We all got a glass of bubbly, and watched Hart and Sweety gobble cake.

"To the bride and groom," said Dedare. "May they have a long and happy life together." We drank, and then Dedare went up and hugged the happy couple.

After a moment of imbibing, Dedare got everyone's attention. "I have been pleased with how well the Martians have adapted to Irion life and helped me run my businesses."

He lifted his glass and took a sip. We reciprocated, of course.

"A toast to my innovative science advisor, Hart, and to the exceptional person he calls his wife. Sweety can calm and instruct any temperamental chef, and I know Sweety has many more talents."

We laughed and sipped.

"And, of course, my historian, Mama A. She, in only a short time, has discovered many hidden layers I had forgotten about, and some I never knew existed."

Dedare waited while Charles gave Mom a hug, and I gave her a kiss on her cheek. We all took another sip or two. Dedare really knew how to make speeches.

"Ambassador Charles. Thank you for easing the way with some of our issues." My father appeared pleased to be recognized by Dedare.

The servers circulated and refilled our glasses.

"And last, but not least, Sylvestine," Dedare said, as he raised his glass. "I knew when I first met you, you were the consummate hotelier. You are making my flagship hotel the very best."

"You ain't seen nothing yet," I replied.

The Martians laughed, but I wasn't sure the Irions grasped my quip.

"Before I give one more toast to the happy couple, and we continue the wedding party, I have an announcement to make."

Dedare's dramatic pause captured everyone's

attention.

"Irion has recently discovered a new world called Particle."

He waited for the whispering to die down. "The Particlans are humanoid, and have a technological development similar to Irions and Martians."

Where was Dedare going with this? I glanced at Sain, but he seemed as confused as I.

"After negotiations with various governments, I have agreed to open—actually renovate—a hotel on Particle. And I would like everyone to help with the implementation. A new adventure awaits us."

In so many ways, my world—and life—had changed today.

~*~

Continue to enjoy the life and antics of the Martians and Irions in the next book of this series: *Innkeeper on Particle*.

~*~

## A word about the author...

After accumulating books on writing for many years, Roxanne kicked thirty years of procrastination out the door in 2011, and started writing.

*ALIEN INNKEEPER* is the first in a series of novels investigating hotels around our galaxy.

Roxanne can be reached at
hyperlight@hyperwarp.com.